Concrete Jungle
By: Darrell Bracey, Jr.

Bout Dat Lyfe Publications, LLC Washington, D.C.

To Order Books Contact:

Bout Dat Lyfe Publications, LLC
Bloc Extension Publishing, LLC
Attn: Ordering Processing
C/O Darrell Bracey, Jr. or Byron R. Dorsey
P.O. Box 457
Riverdale, MD 20738
Web: www.blocextension.com
Email: BoutDatLyfe70@gmail.com
Email: info@blocextension.com
Facebook: blocextension

First Trade Paperback Printed Edition 2016
ISBN-13-digit: 13: 978-1534754744 (Trade Pbk.) ISBN-10-digit: 1534754741

Library of Congress Cataloging-in-Publication Data

1. Darrell Bracey, Jr., African American, Contemporary, Urban Crime, Washington, D.C. - Fiction

Credits
Revised by: Darrell Bracey, Jr. and Byron R. Dorsey
Published by: Bout Dat Lyfe Publications in conjunction with Bloc Extension Publishing
Cover Design: Crystell Publications
Book Productions: Crystell Publications

Printed in the U.S.A.

Acknowledgements

First, I would like to thank my higher power for giving me the gift of painting pictures through the expression of words. It's been a tumultuous ride, but I made it, accomplishing yet another goal that I had set for myself.

With the deepest gratitude I wish to thank all the individuals who came into my life and inspired, touched and illuminated me with their presence. I would also like to recognize and express gratefulness for their limitless support of my debut novel. I am speaking of those who lent me their ear, read my vision, offered their assistance, and conveyed to me their honest opinion. Your contributions are greatly appreciated. They say God gives his hardest battles to his strongest soldiers, so to all the people that stood with me through my battles, here's your purple heart shoutout; Bobby "Scrap" Johnson, Antwan "Boogie" Delaney, Tyzer "Tyson" Muse, Ronald "Block' Toms, Frank "Nitty" Canady, Dwayne "We.ezy" Shorter, Eric "E" Harris, Anthony "Andy" Pixley, Donte "Fat Tay" Faulkner, Samuel "lOO" Oatis, Percy "P" Peacock, Sean "Dread" Gayle, Warren "Rico" Glasco, Kavon "Dizzle" Copeland, Leroy "Biggs" Coley, Zachary Hunter, Derrick "Gordo" Boyd, and Nardo "Marvado" Landy, Donnell "Blac" Johnson, Francisco "Chico" Kelly, Shareef Atkins, Courtney Bailey, Ode Hawkins, Mark "Wop" Buie, Steven Edwards, Andre "Dre" Reid, Robert "Bobby Diesel" Dickerson, Nicole "Nikki" Cavins, Kijana "KK" Glispery, Tasha George, Latisha Wadlington, Markeith "Homie Loc" Perine, Carmen Price, Barry "Big B" Taylor, Darryl "Lil Dee" Blackwell, Michael "BJ," Dat Contraband Mob: Delonte "Mayo" Fortune, Adrian "Nut" Scott, Thomas "TJ" Boykin, and William "B.D.R." Harrison in connection with Boobie and that ONE WAY CREW. Shout out to the YOUNG FARM ERS as well.

Continue to give them that official real live D.C. rap, OY. Shoutout to the good men Oliver "O" Hancock and Ronald "Ron Ron" Harrison.

Special shoutout to my child's mother, Christine Johnson for giving me the greatest gift the world has to offer, my son.

Also, to Marcus, Diamond, Tara, and Ketoria Johnson; I will forever love and cherish you all's existence.

A very special shoutout goes out to my family, my most valuable asset and foundational support system. Words can't express how much I am grateful for the life lessons, whether directly or indirectly, that was handed down to me by y'all. It's my pleasure to give thanks to my mother, who's been my biggest supporter my entire life, and is the true definition of a ride or die. Ladies, take notes from my mother on how to hold a nigga down. :) Special shoutout to my father and stand up man, Darrell Bracey, Sr. Likewise, to my uncle Linwood Grey and my cousins Kevin Grey and Kenneth "Bink" Grey. Y'all's legacy is signed and sealed in the streets. The love is there as it should be for family. Keep ya boxing gloves on, 'cause we all in the same fight tryin' to give this time back. Much love go out to the rest of my family members Keisha Bracey, James "Jimmy" Nowlin, James "Tank" Hargraves, Lanell "Really Doe" Cooper, Sabrina Simms, Kennisha Shade, Keyonna Laws, and John "TY" Washington. To my brothers, Durell Pollard, Welford "Bear" Pollard, Rashawn Pollard, Charles "Shay" Williams, and Vincent "King LV" Young. I would like to give praise to all my family and friends that are no longer here physically, but spiritually looking down, resting in peace and to never be forgotten as follow: My grandmother, Mary Alice Bracey, my aunt, Felicia "Peanut" Bracey, Olla Jean Grey, Richard "June" Grey, Aunt Ree-Ree, cousin Curtis Oliver, my aunt Wanda Motley Edwards, Shirletta Motley Brewster, my first cousins Derrick Delonte Rogers, Mark Twain, Vincent "Big Vee" Young, Dewayne Womack, and to my close friends, Shawn "Whodi" Dixon, M.T.A.Z. Muhammad, T-Bone, Donnell, Davon Weems, Lil' Kurt, Super Dave,

Nee-Cee, and Mike Jefferson. Love and miss you all, and just know that as long as I'm breathing you all will live through me.

Another important acknowledgement goes out to one of my closest comrades, Jason "J-Rock" Poole, author of the best-selling classics *Larceny, Convict's Candy, Victoria's Secret,* and the most recent, *Prince of the City.* Also, be on the lookout for Jason's T.V. original drama series "Torch" and other Street Literature to follow under his Gangster Chronicles Books Imprint. Slim, you truly inspired me to pursue my own writing career when we was in FCI Butner II together. To that I give thanks and honor. By the way, I'm glad to see that you made it home to see your goals through. Hopefully, we'll be able to do some business together in the future. Stay real, my nigga.

Special shoutout to my homie and fellow author, Eyone Williams, who authored the popular titles, *Hell Razor Honeys* series, *Fast Lane,* and the more recent, *Lorton Legendz.* I respect and honor your grind, slim. Continue to strive towards building your legacy. It's worth being documented and memorialized. I'm proud to see good men out of Washington such as yourself, represent the city the right way.

I want to now take the time to honor some of the other D.C. authors who graced the Urban Book Industry with their true-to-life street tales: Anthony "Bucky" Fields, author of the smash hits, *Angel, The Ultimate Sacrifice* pts. 1-4, and *Ghostface Killa*; Nathan Uelch, author of A Killerz Ambition; Danette Majette, author of *Deep, Bitter,* and Good *Girls Gone Bad*; Miss KP, author of the *Dirty Divorce* series; Zane, publisher and author of the *Sex Chronicles, Purple Panties, The Hot Box* and numerous other steamy reads. T. Styles, publisher of Cartel Publications and author of *the Black and Ugly* series, the *Hustler's Son* series, *Face that Launched a Thousand Bullets,* and the *Raunchy* series. I'm glad to see that you offered two of my homies, Eyone and Jason, an opportunity for their work to be published through your company. You're one of the good ones. I wish you nothing but success. Make sure you visit T. Styles' Urban Bookstore The Cartel Books & Cafe in the Washing ton, D.C. area.

Special shoutout to Tristina O. Gilchrist, author of *Dirty Roses.* Keep penning them hits. I love to see women from D.C. do their thing.

Keep ya head up. Shoutout to the urban crime authors who pioneered this lane for us. You know who you are. I appreciate your vital contributions.

Shoutout to some of the staples in the game namely: Dutch (Kwame Teague), K 'wan, Nikki Turner, KiKi Swinson, Deja King, Ashley & JaQuavis, K. Elliot, Shannon Holmes, Jimmy DaSaint and Seth "Soul Man" Ferranti.

Special shoutout to Tiah Short, publisher of DC BookDiva. I admire your business acumen, hustle and body of work published under your brand such as, *Dutch's Dynasty* series, which was first brought to my attention by my business partner and co-publisher of this book. Stay positive and inspiring.

Special shoutout to Wahida Clark publisher of W*Clark Publishing and author of the *Thug* series, *The Golden Hustla*, the *Payback* series and a plethora of other titles. Sista, I've followed your work since you were incarcerated. It's amazing how you rose to stardom from where I stand today in a prison cell. You got a hell of a backstory. You're deservant of recognition on any page of any urban book. You've set the bar quite high for those of us in the industry, and you are the blueprint of how to succeed on a major level in it. Stay real & humble and continue to represent black culture in its true form.

Shoutout to some of the homies making noise in the music industry: Wale, Shy Glizzy, Fat Trel, Boobie and One Way Records, and

Lola Monroe –aka- Angel. Also, shoutout to my man Bolo from the go-go band TCB. Keep ya head up out there, slim.

Special acknowledgement go out to my business partner's comrade and author Gregory A. McRae, author of the riveting and compelling classic *Corruption* pt. 1 & 2, *Cross Addiction, What Goes Around Comes Around,* along with a string of other hits published under his Gregory McRae Publishing Imprint. For more information on how to purchase some of the above titles or in general, log onto: www.gregory mcraepublishing.com. Gee, your pen game is on one thousand and your imagination is extraodinary and pretty much on mass market status. I don't know much about you, but judging by what my partner give me is that you're a real, stand-up, official man. I look forward to meeting you. Until then, stay on your grind. Oh, by the way, I like the story lines to the books you sent B-Bo. They were well written.

Shout.out to my beautiful D.C. homegirl Taraji P. Henson for adding a lot of spice to television's #1 rated show, Empire. Keep givin' them that D.C. sass and class played out in your character. I love it.

Without further ado, I would like to especially thank Crystal Perkins-Carter, C.E.O. of Crystell Publications, and staff for playing such a pivotal role in the production process of my debut novel. I must say that you and your team did an exceptional job of turning my vision into a tangible product. I appreciate y'all's contributions and patience. Crystal, thanks for your consultation throughout the procedure. I really like how you conduct business. Your IQ is to be respected. Shoutout to Crystal's partner Flex, publisher of Big Flex Publications and author of *Detroit: City Limits* and *Designated Hitters* in conjunction with Crystal Perkins-Carter. Also, check out some of Crystal's self-published titles, *Hood Rich,* and *Life After Cash Money.* I encourage all to subscribe to her Mink Magazine as well. For more info log on to her website:

www.crystalstell.com. Again, thank you Crystal. Keep motivatin' and providing your services to those of us who want to see our work in print.

Last but not least, I would now like to exalt my brother, homie and business partner, Byron "B. Bo" Dorsey, co-founder, along with myself, of Bloc Extension Publishing. What can I say? It's been a long journey, but we managed to make our vision a reality. I appreciate your vital contributions to this project and sound business advice. I'm looking forward to climbing the ladder of success wit' you. Now, it's time for us to launch your book and get it in the public's eye. It's definitely an action- packed, powerful read. Be on the lookout for my partner's upcoming urban crime novel, *Eyes of Betrayal: Divided Loyalties* along with Gregory A. McRae. Slim, there's honor amongst men and as men and visionaries we shall continue to propel ourselves to a path fit for a king by using the gift that God has given us to positively achieve our goals and water the seeds we've planted, so that they can become productive beneficiaries of our legacies. No matter what life throw our way, we always seem to rise like the Phoenix from its ashes. This is our calling, now let's seize the opportunity and make the best of it. 4ever bonded by loyalty, blood, sweat, tears and the code. Much love.

Whoever I missed, charge it to my head, not my heart. Enjoy!

Dedications

First, I would like to dedicate this masterpiece to my lifeline, the motor that keeps me running, my son Darrell Bracey III. This is from me to you; pops materialized a platform for you to build upon. Cherish the opportunity.

Second, I would like to dedicate this classic to my mother, Robin M. Motley, who has been my rock since my inception. Love you, Ma.

Third and finally, I dedicate this original tale to all my readers, who made my book the choice from many. I'm humbly grateful and appreciate the support, and promise to deliver the best I have to offer each and every time. Stay Tuned.

Chapter 1

It was the middle of June; the sun was out. The wind was circulating just enough, and people were all over. Since the weather was so enjoyable, Lynwood a.k.a., Big Lyn decided to pull the cover off of his old school, mint condition, black on black, 67 *Lincoln Continental* with suicide doors. As he continued to drive, he glanced over and noticed that his passenger, Shawn Dixon a.k.a., Scrap had his eyes closed. He was bobbing his head to, *The World is a Ghetto* by the group *War*.

"What you know about this? This way before your time." Big Lyn smiled as he questioning Scrap.

"It might be before my time, but I can most definitely relate to it, cause the world is a ghetto," he continued, stressing his point.

Big Lyn was whom Scrap looked up to as a father figure, mentor, and advisor. He was always trying to feed Scrap's mental with useful information. Scrap reminded Big Lyn of himself because they were both omnipotent. He knew if he could persuade Scrap to first think things over before reacting, he would make it a long way. This skill would not only help him in the streets, but in the corporate world or anywhere else he chooses to put in work. Big Lyn's reasoning for having Scrap with him in this moment was not to just cruise the streets with no direction, but to merely give Scrap some since of direction. He figured the moment was right to give Scrap his views on endurance; abiding in a world full of animosity, and envy. When Big Lyn spoke people were very attentive, because not only was he massive in size, he was the O.G of the game. Big Lyn was the spitting image of the actor, Michael Clark Dunken. Scrap on the other hand stood 5'9 and only weighed 160 pounds. His complexion was light brown with a medium afro he normally kept in cornrows. Big Lyn was a firm believer in not judging a book by its cover. Although Scrap was small in stature, his heart was as solid as the concrete ground he walked on.

He immediately reached up and hit the off button on his radio, though Scrap still had his eyes closed and kept bobbing his head to the music.

"Why you do dat?" Inquired Scrap after being brought out of his melodious moment.

"Cause I wanted to talk to you." Big Lyn replied.

"About?"

"About doing well in this heartless game." He emphasized.

"I'm listening." Scrap retorted

"You can't avoid the inevitable, but you can make better decisions that'll hinder your chances of being victimized, or hoodwinked. You gotta be willing to sacrifice for the better. You gotta change certain ways in order to last. Change requires that action be taken. People can talk about change, promise to change, but until one is actually committed to change, nothing will ever change," he illustrated, glancing over at Scrap. Big Lyn caught him gawking at a group of young females walking along the sidewalk as they drove by.

"See, that is what I am talking about!" he exclaimed in a matter of fact way.

"What...What I do?" questioned Scrap, directing his attention back towards Big Lyn. "I heard everything you said loud and clear," he assured him while taking in the food for thought.

As Big Lyn continued driving eastbound on Florida Avenue, he continued with his idle talk.

"You know one of the main reasons I lasted this long in this concrete jungle wasn't just because I had the heart, but because I always used my mind first. Conclusions always seems to come out better whether the choices you made was good or bad. I want you to always keep the concept in mind before making a pivotal decision. Always know what you want, expand your possibilities, and then evaluate it and decide from those choices. Most importantly, always know the consequences before you act," he stated firmly. "Trust me it works!"

"I'll keep that in mind," replied Scrap before looking back out the passenger side window to collect his thoughts. As he was digesting the game that was just disclosed to him, the vibration of his cell phone snapped him out of his mental lapse.

"J.R. wassup?" he answered.

"Slim! How soon can you meet me on 1st and O Street?" J.R. inquired. He was speaking in code referable to one ounce of crack.

"It depends on where you at?" Scrap pried basically asking him how much money he had.

"I'm around da way on 12th street," he responded, letting him know that he was around his neighborhood with twelve hundred dollars.

"Bet! I'll meet you on 1st and O in about twenty minutes," Scraf assured him.

"See ya in twenty," J.R. said before hanging up.

Scrap looked at Big Lyn and asked him to drop him off at his vehicle to go handle his business.

"No problem, Sir," Big Lyn countered, fooling around. "On a more serious note, if you want to escape an easy indictment, never say nothing incriminating on them phones. You gotta always talk like the feds are listening."

"Dat goes without sayin so da bar understood on dat aspect, plus I learned from da best," Scrap enunciated candidly, giving his big homie his signature smile along with a compliment.

Big Lyn reciprocated with a signature smile of his own, while thinking how much Scrap embodied his same characteristics. Fifteen minutes later they pulled up alongside Scrap's newer model Buick Lucerne CXL, courtesy of Big Lyn. He was the owner of a chain of car dealerships throughout the metropolitan area. Big Lyn thought the Buick was the perfect vehicle for Scrap because it was elegant, but also inconspicuous. He didn't want Scrap driving around in something that would draw too much attention to himself. As Scrap was about to get out, he turned towards Big Lyn.

"I understood your point about giving thought to my actions in the streets, but there's going to come a time where I 'm not going to have the time to think before I make a move," Scrap expresses.

"What you just said is true. In some cases, your hand will be forces, but it's best that you play the prevention game and avoid all situations that may force you to opposite in a reckless manner," replied Big Lyn.

"I feel you on dat. "Preciate the advice, Big Homie. I 'll holla at you later, "Scrap assured as he pulled the door handle and exited Big Lyn's vehicle.

Chapter 2

Scrap finally made it around his neighborhood on Georgia-and Rittenhouse Street. The first thing he noticed was his right-hand man Worl, sitting on the hood of his 2015 Chrysler 300M, talking to four nice looking females.

This nigga keeps some action, Scrap thought to himself parking. Once he exited his car he walked towards the group. Worl was a brown skin dude, stood about two inches taller than Scrap, a few pounds heavier, with short wavy hair, and a goatee. He also looked a bit older than your average 17-year-old with his facial hair. He was considered to be the smooth laid back type that enjoyed the company of multiple women. Scrap crept up on him, and then placed his finger on the back of his head, as if he had a gun.

"Damn Slim! These broads got you slippin' like dat!"

"Nigga I thought you knew me better than dat," countered Worl with a grin on his face.

"Why you smilin' Nig…" he tumbled off his words after feeling a piece of steel press against his lower back. He slowly turned around and locked eyes with a vanilla complexioned female, holding a 63 Llama switch blade. She had a sweet grin on her face.

"Do you know how to use dat lil knife you holdin?" Scrap inquired.

"Maybe… Maybe not, but I rather it be bigger," she responded with a wink and a flirtatious smile.

He examined her from top to bottom and marveled at what he saw. He noticed her full juicy lips and slanted eyes that gave her a mixed look. She had a set of B-cups that were nicely placed on her petite frame, but he could tell by the thickness of her thighs that her rear end was also nicely proportioned. He also took a liking to her short Halle Berry hairstyle. Once he finished his brief inspection, he slowly introduced himself.

"Hi, my name's Scrap and what's yours, Shawty?"

"My name's China, not Shawty," she shot back.

"Well Ms. China, you gon put dat away, or you plan on using it?"

"I'll put it away, besides you don't pose no threat," she replied, concealing her blade back in her handbag. Afterwards, she brushed past him, which gave him a full view of her curvy figure.

Damn she got it goin on, he lustfully thought, as the other three females melted into giggles from the way he was eyeballing her. He had to smile to himself after noticing he got caught thirsting so hard.

Damn Slim, it's like dat?" Scrap turned towards his partner to ask, "I see they on point."

"I thought dat was a good thing replied Worl."

"Dat's wassup," Scrap said, acknowledging his partner's viewpoint.

"Have you seen J.R., cause he was just out here waitin on you?" asked Worl.

"I'm lookin fo' em now. You know where he went?" Scrap asked.

"I think he walked over towards Sam's liquor store not too long ago."

"Let me go holla at this fool right quick, I'll be back."

"Don't take too long, cause I gotta holla at you bout somthin dats jive important."

"Aight, I'll be right back," countered Scrap, walking off thinking about what his partner wanted to speak to him about.

Chapter 3

The moment the sun begun to descend, the more alive the neighborhood became. Over in Riggs Park on the northeast side, a crap game came into existence. A group of about ten individuals were grouped up on the side of Lasalle Elementary school gambling. Some tension started to build after a short period of time, because the individual that was rolling the dice was accumulating all of the money. To make matters worse, he was a stranger to the neighborhood. The person who was betting against the stranger didn't seem to care that he was losing small lump sums at a time, but a few of the small time hustlers who was side betting felt otherwise. One of the small timers that was side betting whispered something to the individual that was fading the stranger, and that is when the crap game took unexpected turn. The stranger shot the dice three more times before one landed on his number.

"There she go!" shouted the animated stranger about to gather up the pile of money.

"Point no good! I gated those!" countered the fader.

"O.T. you ain't gate them dice," the shooter replied.

"Like I said youngin' I gated those!" he shot back.

"How you gate da dice without sayin nothing?!" he challenged in an agressive tone.

"By sticking my foot out."

"By sticking ya foot out," he repeated irritable, "O.T you neva moved ya foot when I rolled them dice!" he barked while gesturing as if he was getting impatient with the constant back and forth.

"You heard what I said young nigga, and that's that!" the fader scolded sarcastically.

"You just going to carry it like dat, huh?" the stranger stated calmly. He stood up, leaving the pile of money on the ground, "I can tell when I wore my welcome out. I thought y'all was some get-money niggas, but I guess I was wrong. Y'all can keep dat. Ode, let's get outta here," he told his partner that he tagged along with to the neighborhood. Ode was disturbed about the situation, but kept his thoughts to himself because they were outnumbered. As the two marched off, the stranger continued to reflect about the incident and quickly decided he didn't want to leave without some form of retribution.

"Fuck dat!" the stranger hissed, pulling out his P90 Ruger and headed back toward the group.

"Hold fast slim, they too deep," Ode bellowed, grabbing his homie by the arm, but the stranger snatched away and kept moving.

"Damn!"

Ode cursed to himself cause he knew that he had no choice, but to roll with his partner. Ode immediately pulled out his own pistol and followed suit.

The group was so egotistic that once the two walked off, they instantly went back to congregating amongst each other without contemplating the after effect. One of the small timers was gathering the money from off the ground, when the outsider rushed up showcasing his pistol, followed by Ode.

"You might as well leave dat bread on da ground and stand ya bitch ass up!" the outsider barked with malice in his eyes, catching the group off-guard.

The small timer that was picking up the money immediately threw it back on the ground before raising his hands in the air cautiously.

"Nigga put ya hands back down and stop tryin to draw a tip before I demonstrate on ya sucker ass!" the stranger barked, causing the small timer to put his hands back down.

"All that ain't necessary," stated the fader who went by the name Maurice. He was also the main supplier of that neighborhood and quite a few others throughout the city. Maurice was respected by some, feared by many, money was stable, and had plenty of pawns that were willing to sacrifice themselves to protect their "so called king."

"Oh it's definitely necessary, since you decided you wanted to get over on a nigga," countered the stranger.

"Ode, this ain't for us," stated one of the onlookers that knew Ode on a more personal level from school.

"Y'all made it this way when y'all carried my man, and I'm ridin wit'em regardless," replied Ode.

"You taking this situation a lil too serious by pullin that hamma out. If it's 'bout that money, go ahead and take it," Maurice told the stranger nonchalantly.

"If it was 'bout the money we'd be digging in y'all fools' pockets! This got nuthin to do with da money. It's da point of respect!" the ousidered hashed out.

"Point taken," retorted Maurice.

"Yeah just like my point was taken when you claimed you gated my dice," the shooter shot back to Maurice who just stood there with a blank look on his face. "Matter of fact, why don't you show me what foot you used to gate da dice wit again," he said, taunting Maurice who never shifted from the stance that he was already in. "What you waitin fo'? Stick it out!" he barked, aiming the gun directly at him.

"I'm not stickin my foot out. Don't do anything that you might regret later on," Maurice replied calmly.

"Oh yeah! What's dat – some kind of threat, cause if it was you should've thought about dat earlier!" the stranger shot back, and then pulled the trigger, shooting Maurice in his left foot. Maurice immediately fell to the ground, grabbing his foot as he yelped from the pain that accelerated through him. The stranger quickly scooped the pile of money off the ground and began to walk off. Suddenly, he stopped, thought about things for a quick second, turned around, and threw the stack of money in Maurice's face.

"I almost fo'got, my point wasn't good!" the stranger exclaimed then trotted off with Ode trailing close behind.

Chapter 4

Ring…Ring…Ring…Ring.

"Boy turn that music down and answer the phone. You know it's for you!" shouted the woman's voice from upstairs.

"Who dis?" Block sizzled into the receiver.

"Dis Ode nigga! You would've known who it was if you answered ya cell phone!" he blasted back.

"Why you talking to me like I'm ya bitch or something? I was in da basement workin outthat's why I didn't hear my phone. Anyway wassup?

"Maaaan ya boy Ty just tripped out and done some wild shit!"

"What he do?" Block inquired.

"We ran into dis crap game over in Riggs Park… As a matter of fact, let me get off dis phone. We'll holla at you when we get there cause we on our way after we switch cars," assured Ode.

"I'll see y'all when y'all get here then."

"Dats a bet. Aye did you talk to Scrap or Worl?" Ode asked.

"Not since earlier."

"Try to get in contact wit dem and let dem know to meet us over there, so we can holla at all y'all at da same time."

"I got ya. I'ma hit 'em' now. Look I'ma leave da basement door open just in case I don't hear my phone ringin again. Just come in.?

"Aight. See you in a minute," Ode responded before hanging up.

Chapter 5

"You jive been quiet since we got in da car. What you over there beatin ya brain about?" Worl asked Scrap, who was sitting on the passenger side in a daze.

"Just thinkin" 'bout da conversation I had with Big Lyn earlier."

"What was he talkin about?"

"You know how he is, always tryin to feed ya mind and give you some insight as far as the game go."

"Yeah, dats him, so whatever he said, you might need to take into consideration 'cause Big Boy neva steered you wrong."

"I know and dats why I was over here zoned out, replaying our conversation in my head."

"It's good to have someone like Big Lyn in ya corner," Worl stated.

"No question Slim do a lot for me. Look not to shy away from what we talkin' about, but what was it you wanted to holla at me about?" Scrap asked.

"Oh yeah! Do you remember me sayin' somethin' to you 'bout a broad I was fuckin whose people got some work in New York?"

"Yeah, I remember you mentionin' it, but you neva went in depth about it. Plus, dat was a while ago."

"Well dat was Ra-Ra, da Dominican girl dat was standin' next to me, around the way earlier," Worl enlightened.

"So why you just now bringin' it back up?"

"Cause she had went back up top to stay wit her father for a minute 'cause he had gotten sick, but he must be doin' better cause she's back for good."

"Dat's wassup, so when you tryin to put that thing back in motion?"

"Soon... Real soon, just need to check into a few things first before I go up there."

"Aight, do what ya have to do, and let me know what ya need on my end."

"Dat's a bet," Worl replied.

"Let me ask you somethin?" said Scrap.

"What's dat?"

"How do you know dat her folks can be trusted?"

"I don't, but I trust her, and I doubt her peoples would put her in harms way," Worl answered, glancing over towards Scrap with a look that signified you should know better.

"Say no more, cause I trust ya judgement," said Scrap as his cellphone began to light up, interrupting their conversation. "Aye, it's Block callin," he stated before answering."

"Wussup Big Boy!"

"Where you at?" asked Block.

"Ridin' wit Worl. Why, what's good 'cause you soundin' like somethin' wrong!"

"I need y'all to slide past my jo'nt 'cause I got a call from Ode sayin Ty done some wildshit around Riggs Park!"

"What happened!" he hissed, sitting straight up in the passenger seat.

"He said somethin' bout a crap game."

"Where they at?"

"On their way over here. Ode want y'all to come through, too, so they can give us the run down."

"Aight, cause we on our way too!" assured Scrap.

"See y'all when ya get here," replied Block.

"Bet!" replied Scrap before hanging up and relaying the conversation to Worl.

Chapter 6

As Ra-Ra was riding with her sidekick China and their other two buddies, Sky and Toya, they were joking about how Scrap was staring at China so hard.

"Girl! Worl's friend was lookin at you like he wanted to suck the secretion out ya pussy!" Sky blurted out, causing the others to burst with laughter.

"You ain't lying!" Toya agreed in a ghetto tone, sounding as if she was Laquisha from the Martin Lawrence show.

"I am a sight for sore eyes," countered China conceitedly. "Plus, he is kinda cute and it looked like he was workin with a lil something-something," she stated flirtatiously.

"Bitch, you crazy!" said Ra-Ra.

"I'm crazy! You saw that print! It looked like he was packing for vacation and you talkin about I'm crazy. Bitch you crazy!" China shot back humorously. "What was his name again?"

"I think I heard em' say Scrap," answered Sky.

"Yeah that was it," confirmed Ra-Ra.

"Well let me know when you goin back around there to see Worl so I can see Jake," China cooed.

"Jake! Bitch how did you get Scrap confused with Jake that quick?" Ra-Ra jokingly questioned.

"Like I said Jake, as in Jake the snake. I'm trying to see that snake in his pants, cause I already know how Scrap look," China replied amusingly.

"Girl, you need help," said Toya.

"If you say so, but hopefully I'ma need some help walking after I introduce Jake to Ricki Lake. If y'all know what I mean."

"Girl! You a supa freak," said Sky, laughing at China's graphic remarks.

"You need to stop it with ya silly self," replied Ra-Ra, giggling at China's comment.

"Stop what! The only thing I'm stopping is traffic when I hop my sexy ass out this car."

"And where do you think that is, cause I'm taking you home," Ra-Ra responded.

"Not just yet cause I'm so hungry. "Stop pass Ruff-n-Ready before you take me home. I'm hungry," China said.

"I can use something to eat myself," agreed Toya.

"Me too," Sky followed.

"Ruff-n-Ready it is," replied Ra-Ra. As she drove to the seafood spot, the four of them continued to joke and gossip until they reached their destination.

Chapter 7

After Big Lyn dropped Scrap off at his vehicle, he decided to spend some quality time with his significant other. He was out having dinner with his wife at Hop's restaurant in Crystal City, Virginia when he received an unexpected phone call.

"Baby, are you going to answer your phone?" asked his better half.

"I didn't plan to," he replied sourly.

"Well turn it off, 'cause it's rude."

"I'm sorry, Baby. You're right. I should've known better," Big Lyn replied with a smile. He glanced at the number before turning it off and figured he should take the call. But before doing so he paused. "Imma take this call before I turn it off if you don't mind."

"Hurry, 'cause I like it when I have all of your attention," she whined.

"I know, and I wouldn't have it any other way," he retarted sincerely before answering his phone. "Hello!"

"We have a problem!" said the caller on the other end.

"What kind of problem? Wait a minute. Hold that thought for a second," Big Lyn stated, turning his attention back to his wife. "Baby excuse me for a moment while I take this call, it's kinda urgent," he said before excusing himself from their table. He went outside to finish the conversation. He separated himself from his wife, because he never spoke of or conducted any illegal business in front of his better half. "I'm back," he spoke into his cellphone.

"I heard some chatter about a crap game over in Lasalle schoolyard that ended with Maurice catchin one in the foot," the caller informed.

"Well I'm pretty sure a man of his caliber is on top of the situation," Big Lyn replied, unconcerned.

"He is and that's where the problem comes in."

"And how's that?" questioned Big Lyn.

"It was one of Scrap's lil partners who's responsible," assured the caller.

"Damn! That's not good! How long ago was this?"

"I'm not sure, but Maurice is still in the hospital as we speak."

"Good lookin on the Intel, but let me get back with you at a better time. I'm out with the Mrs., plus Imma try to contact Scrap to make sure he's on point."

"Aight I'll get wit' cha later and give the wifey my luv."

"Will do!" Big Lyn replied, ending the call and quickly dialing Scrap's number.

Chapter 8

The whole crew Scrap, Worl, Ode, and Ty finally met up in Block's basement to converse about the recent incident. Ode who was the youngest, smallest, and the most talkative of the group was the reason why they were in that neighborhood in the first place. Ode wanted to breeze through to holler at one of the neighborhood dudes that went to high school with him. That is when the two stumbled across the crap game that concluded with Ty shooting the neighborhood's top dog in the foot. Ty on the other hand was more of a comedian, but seemed to always find himself in some form of trouble. He was like the hard-headed brat that is always touching something he is not supposed to after you tell him not to a hundred times. Block wasn't just the oldest, but he was the biggest and most muscular individual of the group. He wore his six foot two inch, 208-pound frame well, and he had a low-tolerance for bullshit. All five of them grew up from the sandbox together and their bond was an armor that has yet to be tarnished. Ode and Ty launched into their reason for the cause of their current situation. After it was all said and done, the others kind of understood why Ty reacted with vengeance.

"What I don't understand is why you would shoot a nigga in da foot! If you gonna shoot somebody, finish it. You already know you can't just shoot a street nigga and not expect some form of retaliation! So basically, it's only one thing left for us to do!" exclaimed Scrap.

"What's dat?" inquired Ode.

"Strike first! Suffocate dem niggas and let em' know they ain't fuckin wit no youngins dats goin' sit back and wait for somethin' to happen," scolded Scrap in a belligerent tone.

"Dats what da fuck I'm talkin' bout," hissed Block as he stood up and flexed his muscles.

"Let me say somethin cause we all in this together. No matter what, we all at fault from one's mistakes, and we also come together to correct those mistakes. From this point on we all need to be conscious of what we're doin'," Worl cut in to say.

"Hold on for a minute, cause this Big Lyn callin' me," Scrap interrupted before answering his cellphone.

"Scrap listen closely. Im'ma keep this brief 'cause I'm kind of pressed for time, but I just received a call about one of your partners. Supposedly he got into something around Riggs Park that's more than likely out his reach," explained Big Lyn.

"Yeah, I know all about it. Matter of fact, me and my men are together now discussin it," assured Scrap.

"Good! Y'all stay put cause more than likely he got some foot soldiers lookin' for your partner as we speak. So stay out the way for tonight and meet up with me by noon tomorrow."

"Meet up where?"

"Come to the spot on 14th street."

"Gotcha."

"And remember what I said about using your head."

"I know," said Scrap before ending the call.

"What he say?" asked Worl.

"He heard about what happened and said for us to stay out da way for tonight 'cause slim probably got some of his men out on the hunt. Plus, he wants us to meet up wit him tomorrow," explained Scrap.

"I wonder how he found out," Worl questioned.

"Don't know, but he's talkin' like slim must be somebody."

"So what y'all wanna do in da meantime?" asked Ty.

"Hook da Madden Football up, roll some of dat loud up up dat Block got in his stash, and fall back til tomorrow," Scrap insisted. And that's exactly what they all agreed upon for the remainder of the night.

Chapter 9

The following morning, Maurice was lying in his den with his wounded foot propped up. He was watching television when his pitbull sounded off; alerting him that someone was at the front door.

"Charity!" Maurice called out to his niece.

"Yes!" She yelled back from upstairs in her bedroom.

"Get the door, please!" he politely asked.

"And grab my pain pills from off my dresser, 'cause my foot's starting to throb again!"

"K!" she answered, quickly grabing his pain pills. After she marched down the steps, she tossed her uncle his pills, and went to open the door. "It's Blac and Reggie!" Charity said after looking through the peephole.

"Send them back here."

"I can't open the door until you call Remy first!"

"Remy!" Maurice called out to his well-trained dog.

"Y'all can go in the back. Would y'all like something to drink?" Charity asked, closing the door.

"Where that mean ass dog at?" inquired Blac.

"Maurice got em in the back wit him," she answered.

"Good I'll take something to drink. What y'all got?"

"A lil bit of everything. We have Kool-Aid, orange juice, Ginger Ale, cranberry juice, and of course bottles of spring water."

"I'll take some orange juice," answered Blac.

"Give me a Ginger Ale," added Reggie.

"Y'all can go in the back, I'll bring the drinks back there."

Blac and Reggie were Maurice's enforcers. They were the only two that he trusted around his family to some degree. Normally one of the two would be in sight of Maurice. At the time of the incident, the two were sent to handle a situation of high importance. If the two were around when the episode had taken place, there would have been a high chance that the encounter would have taken a different course. Meaning the outcome would have been very tragic, because of their willingness to protect the hand that fed them was seriously punitive.

Maurice was swallowing the pain pills when the two reached the back den.

"What's up wit y'all?" he asked, placing his glass on the table and looking towards his men with a distressing look on his face.

"Slim, you look like shit!" stated Blac.

"I don't know 'bout all that, but I know my foot's hurtin' like shit! What y'all find out?"

"Not too much, but after Dave told us he knew them youngins be around Rittenhouse, we immediately took 'em wit us and rode through a few times. That jo'nt was like a ghost town. There was no one out there except for a few stragglers," replied Blac.

"Them youngins' probably duckin' that work that's 'bout to be brought to 'em. We should give it a few days to let things cool off a lil bit," suggested Reggie.

"A few days!" Maurice blurted out, "Nigga I'm missing one and a half toes. Them lil niggas had the nerve to throw some money in my fuckin face like I was some type of nothing ass nigga, and you talkin bout a few days. Shid! If anything, them youngins only got a few days to live!" Maurice barked as his niece was walking into the den to hand Blac and Reggie their beverages. As she proceeded to walk out, she overheard her uncle mention something about finding someone named Ode. Once she got into her room, she decided to call her close friend to gossip about the latest news pertaining to her uncle's injuries.

She quickly dialed the numbers and instantly got an answer.

"Ay girl!" spoke Charity.

"Why you sound so wide awake this early?" asked her friend.

"Because I am. I been ripping and runnin for my uncle all morning."

"For what?"

"Girl you not goin to believe what happen last night!"

"What?" she inquired anxiously.

"He got shot in his foot around Lasalle," she exclaimed.

"Bitch you lyin! Not Mr. I think I'm untouchable!" hissed the friend.

"Mmh huh, and that's why I'm up. He been runnin me ragged all morning, talkin' about answer the phone, go to the store, hand him his pills, get the door and shit like I'm his maid! If he ask me to do something else, I might shoot off another fraction of his toes myself!" she joked.

"Fraction of his toes?" her friend questioned confusingly.

"Yeah… Fraction, cause he's missing one and a half toes on his left foot," Charity stated, making some humor out of the situation, but actually relieved that nothing tragic happened to her uncle. He has been sheltering her ever since both of her parents died in a car accident caused by a drunk driver.

"You serious!" she bellowed, giggling at Charity's last remark, "I'm sorry for laughin, but I can't believe someone was stupid enough to do that around that school where all those people be hangin out at."

"That's what I said, but he must know who it was, cause I overheard em' tell his two buddies to find someone name Ode," she explained.

"Ode," her friend repeated, thinking about where she heard that name at before.

"Mmh huh," confirmed Charity.

"That name sounds kind of familiar."

"Well whomever it is better be careful, 'cause I know this ain't the end of it," Charity said, confidently knowing that her uncle wasn't going to sit back and let the situation slide.

"I know that's right girl."

"Let me get off this phone. I hope you got some lawyer money for me," Charity stated.

"For what?"

"For assault, cause Mr. Superior is calling for me again. I told you what was going to happen if he called my name one more time," Charity quipped.

"Bye silly! Go tend to your uncle's needs and I'll talk to you later."

"Bye," Charity responded, ending their conversation.

Chapter 10

Around noon, Big Lyn received a phone call from Scrap. He'd called to inform him that he was pulling up at the house. He peeped out the front window and noticed Scrap and his four partners stepping out of a white diamond Cadillac DTS. Not wanting to make them wait, he went to open the door.

"Wassup fellas," greeted Big Lyn as they walked up.

"Wussup Big Lyn!" They spoke back in unison as they walked past, entering the house.

"That's a nice ride out there," he complimented. "Who's is it?"

"It's mine," Block spoke up.

"It definitely fits you. Big car for a big guy."

"Thanks!" Block replied, laughing it off.

"Well, let's go in the basement so we can talk," said Big Lyn, leading the way to the rear of the house where the basement was located.

"Have a seat," directed Big Lyn after reaching the basement. He allowed them to take a seat, and then he immediately took the center of the floor straight to the point.

"First of all, I wanna say that a lot of people love the game, but can't handle the pressure that comes with it. This dude Maurice is a distinct individual that has the sources to apply pressure on all ends of the city, 'cause his hand call for something," he illustrated trying not to intimidate them, but to merely warn them of what was at stake.

"We understand where you're comin from, but we can't take back what's already been done. So from this point on, how do you suggest we go about da situation?" Scrap questioned.

"If it's one thing I digested not only from experience, but from gangsta movies was that the goal of war is to overpower the enemy. We have to have enough potency that they would either surrender or be killed. And we all know these days no one surrenders," Big Lyn explained, allowing his words to permeate, before continuing. "So my suggestion to ya'll is simple... Show no mercy, 'cause he's not gonna have any for ya'll!" he concluded, emphasizing his point.

All five friends simply looked at one another fully aware that the stakes were high.

"Big Lyn, do you mind if I ask you somethin?" asked Ty.

"Say what's on your mind," he replied.

"How did you find out about da incident so fast?"

"Let's just say, I have associates everywhere," he slyly responded, cracking a smile. Then he reached into his pocket and tossed Scrap a set of car keys.

"What's these for?" questioned Scrap about the car keys.

"For assistance and for personal reasons I won't physically get involved, but I still feel as though I have to at least aid ya'll in some kind of way."

"Where's the car?"

"It's parked on 14th and Somerset. When you leave from here, look for an all-black, Ford Crown Victoria. Make sure you move it to a more stable location," Big Lyn suggested.

"No problem," replied Scrap.

"Not to be disrespectful or anything, but uhh... Can we smoke in here?" asked Ode.

Big Lyn just gave him an expressionless stare for a few seconds before finally giving him the okay to do so.

"Thanks!" he responded uncertain after being stared down for a few second. He still reached into his cargo pants pockets to retrieve the small sandwich bag containing marijuana. He immediately began to break the buds down when Big Lyn surprisingly inquired to see what grade of marijuana they had. Ode unhesitately handed the sandwich bag over while continuing to break the buds down that he had already taken out.

"Not bad, but hold on to that 'cause my nephew Elmo left something behind the other day that's a few grades up from that," he stated, turning to leave the room. He came back moments later and tossed Ode a Ziploc bag full of the high-grade marijuana.

"Man what da…What kind of loud is this?" Ode questioned after observing its content. The smell was escaping through the Ziploc bag and was as rank as the scent of a skunk's spray. Most impressively, its scent could be smelled from a distance.

"I'll ask'em when I see'em, but ya'll can split dat up, cause he knows better than to leave that mess in here," replied Big Lyn.

"Good lookin out" stated Ode, pulling out a pack of Backwoods and started to roll some of it up.

Big Lyn sat back smiling at their reaction once he witnessed their demeanor regarding the potency of the high-grade marijuana. He was more amused at the thought of how eager they were to pollute their lungs. Ode immediately lit it up. He deeply inhaled as the others waited for a turn.

"Damn she hit good!" he blurted out, inhaling it twice more before passing it over to Ty.

Ty's anxiousness caused him to inhale too much at once and he instantly started choking to the point of tears spilling from his eyes. Block immediately began to laugh at him before taking the Backwood out of his hand.

"Let me get this, amateur!" he teased. Block took in a mouth full of smoke, and then blew it directly into Ty's face, causing him to choke even harder.

"Da fuck!" hissed Ty, fanning the cloud of smoke out his face. "You see I'm already chokin!"

"You'll be aight," countered Block, lifting the jo'nt to take another puff. Afterwards, he passed the Backwood over to Scrap.

"I'm cool. Y'all do y'all, and I'll do da drivin. That way when we roll, one of us will be on point while we go pick this car up," he declared, placing a grin upon Big Lyn's face.

Big Lyn instantly thought that his detailed speech had begun to soak in.

"Speaking of the car, make sure that you put that situation up before y'all pick that car up," instructed Big Lyn.

"No problem," replied Scrap.

As the others continued their smoke session, Big Lyn's mind wondered off visualizing hopeless circumstances amongst Scrap and his crew. He loved Scrap like a son, but he also loved the realm that he built from the ground up. Getting entangled in the current situation could eradicate everything he worked so hard to build. He wanted badly to extinguish the situation for the sake of all parties, but once gunfire was exchanged, the only conclusion is retribution. Big Lyn was a well-calculated thinker and was formulating different ideas in his mind. Suddenly, his train of thought rode off the tracks due to a loud noise that filled the room.

"Ay Block, on everything you over there lookin just like dat strong ass gump dat played in dat movie Holiday Heart!" Ty joked, causing everybody to laugh.

"Oh yeah! I know your lil ass ain't over there talkin lookin like Sha-Wanda!" countered Block.

"Who da fuck is Sha-Wanda!" Ty questioned.

"Nigga it's Shanay-Nay and Wanda! You look like a combination of both them ugly bitches!" Block spat back as everybody burst out laughing even harder.

"Ya fake ass Swartza-nigga lookin' ass would say some dumb shit like dat!"

The roast session went on for a little while longer even causing Big Lyn to share a few laughs himself. He finally decided to bring everyone back into reality and the reasoning behind their meet-up.

"Listen up! I hate to mess up this brotherhood convention, but I have someplace to be in a few. You all need to get to handling business," he stated before getting up and gathering his belongings to leave. "I want y'all to always remember something... Blood makes y'all related, but loyalty makes ya family," Big Lyn concluded, ascending up the basement steps. He exited out the front door and was followed by Scrap and his men. They had the quote that Big Lyn recited stuck in their heads.

Chapter 11

Around two o'clock in the afternoon Blac and Reggie were navigating through their adversary's neighborhood with hopes of stumbling across one of the two, if not both. They were on the hunt ever since leaving from Maurice's spot an hour ago.

"Where in da fuck these bitch ass niggas at?" hissed Reggie.

"Them youngins probably know they fucked up and too noid to show their faces" replied Blac as he drove.

"Scared or not, Imma empty this choppa in their ass as soon as we see'em!" scolded Reggie eagerly."

"You don't have to convince me, I already know what it is, but you know what?"

"Wassup?"

"I think I got an idea. You still got that block of yay on you that you was goin' give to Tumor for detailin' the cars?"

"Yeah, but why?"

"Give it to me and watch this!" Blac instructed.

They pulled up alongside a woman on the corner of 7th and Tuckerman Street, who he assumed was a drug addict. Blac stuck his head out of the window to say something while she walked slowly with her head tilted towards the ground. It was as if she was searching for something.

"Excuse me Ms. Lady, did you lose something?" he inquired, initiating small talk.

"Who wants to know?" she countered nonchalantly.

"A concerned citizen," he replied.

"Yeah right! What - you the police?"

"Neva dat, Ms. Lady."

"Then why you so damn nosey! See the first business in this line of business is to mind your business! So I suggest you go find some business and stay outta mine!" she responded defensively.

"Damn, she's feisty," whispered Reggie.

"I got her," Blac murmured back with confidence. He directed his attention back towards the woman. "I'm not tryin' to be nosey, but I thought that maybe we could help one another."

"How's that? Ooohh I get it! You two see something y'all like on the old lady, huh?" she smiled with excitement, strutting closer to their vehicle.

"I'm a devoted man, so it ain't nothing like that," Blac lied.

"Then what is it, 'cause y'all holding me up?" she inquired now standing just above the driver side window.

"I was hopin' you could assist us with findin some old friends of ours."

"Who."

"We're lookin' for the homies Ode and Ty. And if you can help, I promise to make it worth ya while," Blac added to lure her in.

She thought about it for a minute before telling them that she haven't seen them around lately.

"You haven't seen 'em', huh?" he reiterated, placing the block of crack on his lap. He pretended to reach for something in his backseat to give her a clear view of the enticing coco. She immediately began to act different after observing the small block posted on his lap. The sight of it made her start stuttering instantly.

"Wha... Wha... Wha... What's that on your la...lap?" she stuttered, smacking her lips and pointing at the addictive drug.

"What... Ohh this?" he asked, referring to the drug.

"Mmm hmm," she desperately replied, nodding her head in agreement.

"See there you go. What you tell me? The first business in this line of business is to mind ya business. I suggest you play a position, or pay this no attention," Blac shot back, giving her a taste of her own medicine.

"And what position is that?" she inquired, catching on quickly.

"It's nothin serious; just give me a call when you run into Ode or Ty."

"And what's in it for me?" she questioned, eyeballing the drugs.

"Depends on what you want."

"How about some of that."

"I tell you what... How about I give you the rest of this, plus extra when I get that call," he assured her.

"So let me get this straight. You gonna give me all of that, plus extra after I call you."

"Yep."

"And just to be clear, all I gotta do is tell you when I see Ode or Ty?"

"That's it and that's all, but keep this between us, 'cause we want it to be a surprise," Blac confirmed.

"No problem! You have a contact number?" she eagerly asked, anxiously wanting to get the drugs in her possession.

"My partner writing it down as we speak. By the way, what's ya name?"

"Patricia, but everyone calls me Pat."

"Aight Pat. I hope you don't disappoint me, 'cause I hate to just give my stuff away," Blac emphasized, handing over his contact number along with the block of crack.

"I won't! Is this shit any good? 'Cause I would hate to render my services for some garbage," Pat stated, referring to the grade of the product.

"I don't deal with nothing but the best!" Blac responded with confidence.

"That's what they all say, but I'll make sure to call when I run into either one," Pat stated, rushing off to go take a hit of the substance.

"That shit just might work," stated Reggie.

"Only time will tell," responded Blac, pulling off.

Chapter 12

Shortly after parting ways with Big Lyn, the five cronies were on their way to get the vehicle, and then relocate it to a better spot. As they were nearing their destination, Block glanced over towards Ty. He was resting his head on Block's shoulder and a moist and warm spot was on his shirt about a centimeter away from Ty's mouth.

"Ty! Nigga, wake your ass up! You slobbin and shit!" barked Block.

"Mmh-mmh," replied Ty, shifting in his sleep.

"Mmh-mmh shit! Get up!" Block shouted for the second time, shrugging his shoulder to wake Ty completely up.

"Man what!" hissed Ty, hopping up.

"What nothing! Get off my shoulder wit your wet ass mouth!" Block hissed, wishing he would've driven instead of allowing Scrap to.

"My bad, Slim! I was high as shit!" he replied apologetically. He then fired Ode,"fuck you laughing at, nigga?"

"I'm laughing at your water park mouth havin ass!" Ode joked, "You always hoggin' all da loud then be da first to pass out," he verbalized.

"Yeah whatever, nigga!" Ty answered with slight saltiness in his voice. Then he leaned over in Ode's face and dryly stated, "Fuck you!"

Ode jumped back, and put his hands up to his nose. "Slim on everything your breath smells like dumpsta juice! Turn back dat way!" he commented, pointing towards Block.

"Oh yeah! You tryin to be funny, huh?"

"Nah, but you know what's funny? All dat white shit caked up around ya mouth. This what I wanna know, how in da fuck are you droolin' when ya mouth look like cement. You need to wipe dat shit!"

"Y'all niggas silly as shit. Straighten up though, 'cause we 'bout to pull up to da street," Scrap said in an assertive tone.

"Dat's it right there," stated Worl, pointing in the direction of the vehicle that Big Lyn described.

"Ty we need you to drive da Crown Vic up to Donnie's spot. We gon' park it in his driveway until we make use of it," directed Scrap. He pulled up adjacent to the vehicle so Ty could hop out.

"Get ya cotton mouth ass out," teased Ode, getting out first to allow Ty to hop out, since he was sitting in the middle. Ty hopped in the Crown Vic and with a light turn of the wrist, the 5.7-liter came to life with a loud roar.

Damn I know she's fast, Ty thought after hearing the power in the engine of the V8. He looked over and gave the thumbs up, indicating that he was ready to go.

Scrap signaled back to him, letting him know to pull off and they were going to follow behind. Ty was so eager to test the power of the V8 that once he put the car in drive, he instantaneously stomped down on the gas pedal. This caused the tires to skid and a cloud of smoke to unfold. By the time he let off the gas, the Crown Vic was at the end of the block. After his brief experiment, he quickly straightened up and drove normal until they reached their destination.

Chapter 13

Ra-Ra had just stepped out of the tub when she started thinking about Worl. She had not heard from him and he usually called to check on her. Dripping wet with just a towel wrapped around her, she picked up her cell phone to give him a call.

"Hola," he answered after about the fifth ring.

"Como esta Papi?"

"Muy bien Mami."

"Why haven't you called to check on me like you usually do?"

"I've been jive busy tryin to take care of a few things."

"Too busy to at least pick up the phone to see how I was doing, huh?" she inquired with a hint of boldness.

"I wouldn't necessarily say dat, but somethin unexpected came up dat couldn't be avoided."

"Mmh mmh, you bet not be lyin to me. You know how I get worked up when I don't hear from you."

"I wouldn't lie to you, but I would lie for you if I had to, cause I fucks with you like dat. And I definitely wouldn't want you to get worked up unless I'm da one putting dat work in," he stated smoothly.

"It's funny you say that, 'cause not only am I dripping wet from getting out of the shower, but my woo-ha is soaking wet just thinking about you," she said seductively.

"They say da body says what words cannot, so what she sayin' now?" he said in a soft soothing voice.

"She saying how much she's missing you," she countered in a sweet provocative manner.

"She has a mouth of her own, so if dats da case put her on da phone and allow her to speak for herself."

"Anything for you, Papi," she said softly, placing her phone on speaker. She spread her legs wide, and then rested the phone next to her clitoris, "Ooh Worl!" Ra-Ra purred, as the thought of him inside of her gave her the motivation to please herself further.

She closed her eyes and started licking her lips as she persistently rotated her fingers over her clean shaved vagina. Worl was immediately sucked in after hearing that familiar popping sound seeping through his receiver, which caused him to unintentionally squeeze his manhood through his G-star jeans. *Damn she's got to be soaking wet,* he thought as the enticing intonation of her moans and the constant smacking sounds were serenading his ears.

"Papi, ooh Papi! She misses you so much!" Ra-Ra uttered almost at the point of ecstasy.

"I miss her, Mami," he whispered, trying to keep his homies from hearing him. Nonetheless, they were in the background conversing amongst each other and were not paying him any attention.

"She's so creamy, Papi. She... She... Cum... Cummin, Papi. She ahhh!" she yelled, climaxing all over her fingers.

"Damn Mami. You sure know how to get a nigga's attention," Worl proclaimed, wishing that he were there with her sharing the moment.

"That's because the thought of you inside of me gets me to that point," Ra-Ra teased.

"I see Worl has your head spinning, huh?"

"That's because it's my Worl until somebody proves me wrong."

"So now I'm yours, huh? Well answer this for me, do you think you could handle all the responsibilities that comes wit me?" Worl inquired.

"So far have I not taken care of my responsibilities?" Ra-Ra countered.

"You have so far."

"See, you just answered your own question. So when am I going to see you?"

"I tell you what; get us a room tonight so we can work on some more of those responsibilities."

"A room where?"

"You pick and choose, and then call me wit da info. I'll meet you there by ten wit' da extra necessities. I'll reimburse you on da room when I get there," Worl assured her.

"Reimburse me! Don't insult me, you just make sure you be there."

"Oh I'll be there," he promised.

"Sounds like a date... Oh, I almost forgot, see if Scrap's busy tonight 'cause China asked about em' and I know she would like to cum, too," Ra-Ra metaphorically implied.

"I like how dat rolled off ya tongue. Well get two room's 'cause I'm pretty sure I could make dat happen," Worl assured her.

"Guess I'll see you tonight, Papi. Muah!" she concluded with a juicy kiss before hanging up so she could go free herself from her love juices.

Chapter 14

"Worl, what da fuck are you doin' over there!" hissed Scrap as they were about to pull into Donnie's driveway to park the vehicle that Big Lyn gave to them.

"I ain't doin nuthin'. Why you say dat?" countered Worl after just hanging up with Ra-Ra.

"'Cause it looks like you over there on some wild freak shit, grabbing on ya self and shit!"

"What!" he blurted out before acknowledging that he was unconsciously doing what he was accused of doing. "My bad Slim," Worl said with a smile on his face, "But Ra-Ra just mentally fucked da shit out of me! Plus, her and China tryin' to hook up later on."

"Dats what's up! Around what time?" Scrap inquired.

"Probably around 10 o'clock. I told her to hit me after they got da rooms."

"Bet!" Scrap consented, pulling into the driveway behind Ty. He then parked, and got out.

As they were walking towards the vehicle Ty was in, he stepped out with a huge grin on his face until Scrap approached him with a frown on his. Scrap questioned him about pulling off the way he did.

"I just wanted to see how much power she had," Ty answered.

"I feel ya, but it's a time and a place for dat 'cause we don't need to be drawin' no attention to a vehicle dat we more than likely goin' to be makin' a move in," he explained.

Ty thought about what Scrap said for a split second before agreeing with him, "You're right about dat, dat's my bad. I wasn't tryin' to draw any attention, I was just testin' her out, dats all," he replied apologetically.

"What's done is done, just think next time," countered Scrap.

"Dat's a bet."

"Enough about dat. Did you check da inside?" Worl questioned, walking towards the passenger side of the Crown Victoria.

"Naw. I never got da chance to, 'cause as soon as I got in I pulled off."

"Always check da car first," insisted Worl. He opened the passenger side door to do a brief scan, only to come out empty handed. "Nuthin!" Worl announced after getting back out.

"Before we roll out, check da trunk right quick," Scrap said to Ty since he still had the keys in his possession. When Ty finally opened the trunk, their jaws dropped.

"Damn that's wassup!" Ty exclaimed, pertaining to the contents found.

"Big Boy always find a way to come through," said Worl.

"No bullshit!" countered Block.

"I think it's bout time we let our presence be felt," Scrap declared, looking to the others for confirmation.

"I think so, too," agreed Worl along with the others.

"Dat's what it is den. Let's lock up and get outta here until later on," Scrap insisted, closing the trunk and locking the Crown Victoria. They began piling back into Block's Cadillac and once everyone was in, they pulled off.

Chapter 15

Later on that evening Maurice received a call for him to drop off a package to one of his dealers. As he was getting in the passenger side of his newer model Mercedes Benz CL 63 AMG Coupe, he noticed his two trustees riding down the street towards him.

"What's up Boss Man?" asked Reggie, pulling along side of him.

"The same shit. What's up with y'all? I haven't heard from you two since y'all left me earlier. Did y'all find out anything?"

"Nuthin," replied Blac.

"Ghost town," added Reggie.

"They can't hide forever. Even a whale has to come up for air every now and then," stated Maurice.

"We'll be there to snatch em when they surface, 'cause we got some eyes on their block that'll hopefully call us when they run into 'em."

"That's what's up, but if you don't get no call soon, we goin' to find a way to make them come out," assured Maurice.

"However you wanna do it," said Blac.

"So what y'all doin in the meantime?" Maurice inquired.

"Nuthin particular. Why you need us to do somthin'?" said Blac.

"Yeah I do. Since y'all ain't doin' nothin', go past Marcell's spot and pick that bread up. While y'all do that, Im'ma go and drop these couple of joints off to Black Moe uptown right quick. "Aight," answered Blac.

"Call Slim and let em' know we on our way,"

"I'm 'bout to do that now," replied Maurice, instructing the driver to pull off.

Chapter 16

As the nightfall came, the streetlights illuminated all stragglers that roamed throughout the neighborhood. Over the years, Riggs Park had quietly become an industrious spot and nighttime is where most of the activities took place. Everybody from users, dealers, drinkers, smokers, gamblers, strippers, and so called pimps would make pit stops in the neighborhood throughout the course of the night. Although there were illegal activities being conducted in the observation of law-abiding citizens, no one ever called the police to discontinue what was considered to many as the number one cause of community decimation.

Maurice used his profits as his power to affect people's decisions. He knew how money won friends and more importantly the influence it had over people, even the righteous. He made sure to give back to the neighborhood by throwing free for all cook outs on holidays such as Memorial Day and Labor Day, and then he also passed out free food on Thanksgiving, and free gifts for Christmas. That stood for something in the eyes of the less fortunate. He had things under control, plus he was well organized when it came to the drug trade. He dealt with his immediate circle and allowed his inner circle to deal with the outsiders. He credited a lot of his longevity in the community to his service to the residence in his neighborhood. He wanted to keep the violence down in the area, because he believed that violence was for petty people and he had too much on the line to lower himself to their standard. He wanted the neighbors to feel at ease when walking in the streets without the worries of being victimized. In return, complaints were at a minimum and that kept him off the radar or from being under the surveillance of law enforcement. He also didn't tolerate disrespect. By allowing an outsider to come into his neighborhood, shoot him in his foot, and walk away unharmed was unacceptable. He had to send a clear message to all the people who might get any bright ideas. That is why he wanted to handle the situation as soon as possible. What he didn't anticipate was that the same people he was looking for were also searching for him. Both parties had the same agenda, which was to murder the problem.

Chapter 17

"*Look, if you ain't know ask somebody they'll tell you 'bout me nothin' fake, nothin' fraud, nothin' bitch about me I'm a G. I been runnin' these streets since a youngin', since I was fourteen, I been buckin, slangin heat, ain't nothing you want beef, say somethin' - you can get it. I ain't trippin' once it's on just know you better not let me catch you slippin'.*" The sounds of B.G. Kill or be Killed blared through the speakers of the Crown Victoria that Ode and Ty were riding in.

The pair were driving through Riggs Park to scope-out the scenery to relay to the others what they saw before they all met up. Scrap, Worl, and Block rode in a separate vehicle to avoid drawing attention to themselves. They were about five minutes away from meeting up with the others. They were driving down Eastern Avenue, passed Lamont Ridge Recreation Center, when Scrap received a call from Ode. He was basically conveying to Scrap what they observed.

"Any familiar faces?" questioned Scrap after answering.

"Can't really tell from our angle, but it's quite a few people in front of da schoolyard over on da steps," Ode replied.

"Aight, we on Eastern Avenue comin' across New Hampshire Avenue; we'll be there in a minute," stated Scrap.

"Aight. We parkin' on da side street until y'all get here."

"Bet, and stay out of sight 'cause dem bammas know y'all faces," Scrap countered.

"You already know," responded Ode before disconnecting the line.

Chapter 18

Ra-Ra was simultaneously calling China's phone and pulling up to her home to let her know she was out front. The time was nearing and she still had to get those rooms. Plus, she'd need to call Worl with the location.

"Girl, where you at?" answered China.

"I'm out front," Ra-Ra replied, looking through her sun visor to gloss her lips.

"That was a lot quicker than thirty minutes! Where the hell were you? Next door!" China jokingly stated.

"Girl, you silly! Are you ready yet?" asked a laughing Ra-Ra.

"Almost! Just come inside, 'cause I need about ten more minutes."

"Open the door!" Ra-Ra hissed, smacking her lips.

"What's that for," China asked, regarding the smacking of her lips.

"'Cause I told you to be ready when I got here."

"I am. I just have to throw my clothes on. The front door is already unlocked," she voiced, disconnecting the line to finish getting dressed.

Ra-Ra found a parking space and got out wearing a two-tone grey and silver mini body skirt. She knew she was sexy because her outfit showed off every curve of her slender voluptuous frame. Her well-built legs had a glow tint that could be seen for miles. An older gentleman that was a member of the neighborhood had to stop and stare after seeing the young lady who could clearly ruin his home if given the opportunity. The neighbor lustfully watched as she ascended the porch steps, leaving him in his own thoughts.

"China!" Ra-Ra yelled after entering.
"Come upstairs!" China shot back from her bedroom.

As Ra-Ra proceeded through the house, she found herself once again admiring the inside of the home that was beautifully furnished. China and her relative resided in an average detached, two-leveled, single-family home that had a refurbished interior. The kitchen was recently modernized with all stainless steel appliances cherry wood cabinets and a Café French door refrigerator. The hallway that led from the kitchen to the living room had huge framed pictures of well-known actors, celebrities, and historians that were thought to be inspirational. The living room that no one ever sat in was decked out in all Ralph Lauren, including the huge floor rug that covered the floor. Company was welcome to lounge in the extended den that was furnished with all black leather furniture, glass tables, and a fifty-seven inch plasma on the wall. All in all, the interior was upgraded so that the wealthy could even appreciate it.

As Ra-Ra moved about to China's room, she thought to herself that hopefully one day she would be able to afford a similar home.

"Bitch, where you going!" China inquired.
"Why you ask me that?" countered Ra-Ra.
"Because it looks as if you goin' to a Musiq Soulchild Concert rather than a hotel," she jokingly stated.

"That's because I'm giving my man something to look forward to at the end of the night."

"Well in that case I should wear my trench coat with just some lingerie under it, like Robin Givens in that movie *Boomerang,* huh?"

"Maybe you should, but whatever you decide I wish you'd hurry up!"

"Why you rushing like we have a deadline?"

"That's because I still have to get the rooms and call them with the location by ten. And it's almost nine o' clock."

"Well I'm ready anyway. While I squeeze my ass into these jeans, hand me those shoes in the corner."

"Why it look like your butt got bigger?" asked Ra-Ra, handing China her shoes.

"That's what somebody else said, but I can't tell," she replied as she slipped on her shoes and grabbed her keys. She gave herself one last look in her floor model mirror, before the pair made their way out of China's room.

Chapter 19

Scrap was just turning onto Riggs Road when he wrapped up abrief conversation with Ode. Ode had informed him that a few individuals had recently stepped off, but neither Ty nor himself were able to zoom in on who they were. Scrap suddenly decided to take a ddifferent approach to his destinantion point from where they would attack by turning onto a street that sat on the opposite side from where the school was located. Scrap thought that it was best if Block, Worl, and himself come from across Riggs Road and catchtheir adversaries off guard. From the top of the school's steps while Ode and Ty hit from the opposite side to ensure that no one elude their attacks. As they turned on the opposite street, Worl looked over and caught a glimpse of what he questioned to be Ra-Ra's vehicle. However, he didn't get a good look because of the expeditious passing of the vehicle. Scrap found a parking spot on the next streetover. He quickly placed another call to Ode and explain to him the change of plan. After hanging up, Scrap, Worl and Black proceeded to grab their wigs, weapons and scraves before exiting the vehicle.

"Everybody needs to be on point and be each other eyes. That way shit doesn't get out of hand," said Scrap, who was thee first to step out of the car.

"Dat goes without sayin," countered Block.

"Aight, let's go!" concluded Scrap, placing his wig and scraf on, followed by Worl and Block.

"Hold up, let me lace these boots up right quick," stated Worl before they continued.

Chapter 20

China finally turned off some of the lights and exited the house. Ra-Ra was already waiting on her inside the car. When China got in the car, she was welcomed by the serenading sounds of *Seduction* by Usher. She looked at her best friend who was singing the words with a seductive facial expression.

"Girl! Look at you! Singing and blushing! Somebody feeling sexy tonight," stated China.

"I always get like this when I'm about to see my boo," Ra-Ra replied before pulling off.

"I thought Usher was your boo?" questioned China.

"He still is, but what he doesn't know won't hurt 'em" she countered, bending the corner so she could get back onto the main road.

"I know that's right. Your secret is safe with me," proclaimed China as the two shared a laugh.

As Ra-Ra made one last turn heading toward Riggs Road, she peeped to her left and grimaced after thinking she saw what happened to be Scrap placing on a wig. She started to ask China did she see the same, but noticed she had her eyes closed as she swayed to the music. So without giving it a second thought, she quickly disregarded the matter and turned onto Riggs Road on a quest to get the rooms.

Chapter 21

When Worl rose from tightening the laces on his boots, he thought he saw Ra-Ra's vehicle again, but the car was turning onto the main road before he was able to determine if it actually was or not. He made sure to keep a mental note before focusing back on the situation at hand.

"Aight, y'all ready?" he asked.

"You already know," Block impatiently countered.

"Let's rock and roll," Worl replied as the trio began stepping towards their mission.

They all halted a few feet away from Riggs Road to make sure that it was safe for them to cross over without being described by people driving past or pedestrians roaming around. Once it was clear, they quickly sped across the intersection with their guns in hand and minds full of malice. When they reached the stairs, they leaped the flight of steps nearly colliding into one of the males that was kneeling down rolling dice. Startled, the teenager hopped up and tried to run, but was quickly apprehended by Ode and Ty who was approaching from their blindside.

"Where the fuck do you think you going?" Ty gruffed with venom in his tone, aiming a mini 14 at his chest.

"Get da fuck back over there wit ya associates!" Ode added, causing the young man to throw his hands up in defeat and stroll back over next to the others.

Scrap, Worl, and Block had the remaining group held up while waiting for Ode and Ty to confirm whoever it was that they were hunting for. They didn't want to single anyone out, so they allowed Ode and Ty to direct the situation.

"Errbody get over there in the corner!" Ode commanded, aiming his weapon in the direction he was referring to.

"Fuck y'all! I ain't goin nowhere! Y'all must be lost 'cause y'all definitely in the wrong neighborhood to be tryin' this bullshit! Y'all must don't know who the fu..." was the last word he said before his sentence get cut short from Block smacking the cold steel across the young man's face with ruthless force.

The impact caused blood to instantly shoot from his mouth. As the male fell to the ground in pain, Block's fury from the teenager's outburst caused him to bestow a more brutal beating on the young man to make a statement. He began kicking the boy in the ribs and striking him in his face with the butt of his gun repeatedly until Scrap stopped him.

"That's enough Big Boy! Calm down!" he stated, and then focused his attention to the other members who showed signs of fear and rage. "Now do anybody else wanna get slick out da mouth?" Scrap asked. Afraid to speak, no feedback occurred, which indicated that they didn't want any additional problems. "Now dat we have everyone's attention, place ya hands where we can see 'em. I'm definitely da nervous type, so dis for ya own safety!" he instructed, watching them do as they were told. Then Scrap gestured for Ode to lead the way.

"Da head nigga not here," confirmed Ode, noticing the individual whom he believed initiated the whole incident.

"So what you wanna do?" questioned Scrap.

"Since they chose to get disrespectful over some chump change, I figure we return da favor," Ode uttered with a devious grin.

"What you up to, 'cause I know dat look?"Scrap inquired.

Ode immediately singled out the same individual whom he believed instigated the ordeal and demanded for him to strip ass naked while pointing his gun at him.

"Huh!" the instigator blurted out nervously.

"I'm not asking twice! You heard me da first time!" barked Ode, racking a bullet into the chamber. Seeing the seriousness in Ode's eyes, the young man peeled off his clothes as if he were a male stripper preparing to hit the stage.

"Da rest of y'all empty dem pockets, and if I come around and find out you holdin back, you gon' end up like ya man over there," stated Ode, lacing his tone with venom. Then he ordered the male standing awkwardly in his birthday suit to place everbody's contents inside the two females' handbags that stood next to him. The young man was past degradation from walking around and placing the group's items into the bags before forking everything over to Ode and Scrap. When he turned to walk off, out of nowhere Ode smacked the man on his backside, causing him to instantly turn around with a look that paralleled disgust. "You did a good job Mr. Stripper man, so here's a tip. Next time yo sucka ass try to jump out there make sure you bring a parachute," Ode laughed.

The young male was so furious that tears were starting to leak from his eyes like a dripping faucet. Knowing he was in a no win situation, he just sucked it up, lowered his head and walked off.

Darrell Bracey Jr.   Concrete Jungle

"What made you smack dat bamma on his ass?" asked Scrap.

"Fuck dat clown, he lucky I didn't put a bullet in his ass, plus I'm more than sure he's da one who initiated da whole thing in da first place," Ode explained.

"Fuck em! What's done is done. Let's get da fuck out of here before we get caught up," Scrap suggested.

"Trust and believe me when I tell you all dat dis episode could've ended much worst. Luckily none of dis was meant for y'all. My future advice to all of y'all is…" He paused for a brief moment, "Stay da fuck from out here, 'cause the next time you just might be guilty by affiliation!" Ode warned before stepping off with his accomplices in tow.

Chapter 22

Ra-Ra and China purchased two rooms at the Double Tree Hotel in Silver Spring, Maryland. Shortly after doing so, Ra-Ra texted the room numbers and address of the hotel to Worl. She couldn't help but think about what she'd seen earlier. *I wonder was that him*, Ra-Ra questioned herself about seeing Scrap, putting a wig on his head. As the elevator door opened to their floor, her thoughts were disturbed.

"What you over there thinking about?" China pried.

"Oh nothing," Ra-Ra dissimulated, keeping her thoughts to herself as they exited and headed towards Ra-Ra's room.

At first the two were unsure if they should get one or two rooms, but Ra-Ra quickly assured her bestie that she needed alone time with her man. China didn't dispute, because she liked what she saw in Scrap; and if his personality or character matched his outward appearance, then she was going to make good use of the second room. One-night stands were not the norm for her, but she had done it before without a tinge of regret.

"These are some nice rooms!" China admired, as the duo entered the suite.

"It's real comfy and spacious," Ra-Ra agreed, hopping onto the bed.

"I know, right? Call them and tell them to bring some drinks," China suggested.

"I got you. Girl, you might as well get comfortable 'cause it's going to be a long erotic night," Ra-Ra smiled.

"Especially when a bitch get them drinks up in her," China retorted, referring too herself in third person. The pair shared a laugh at China's remark and began preparing for their rendezvous.

Chapter 23

"Maurice! You need to get back around the way ASAP! Five dudes just slid through and robbed everybody, plus put Lil Man in da hospital!" noticed the caller on the other end of Maurice's phone.

"How y'all allow that to happen!? I know niggas was strapped, right?" Maurice asked with a furious tone.

"Yeah niggas had hammas stashed out there, but them bammas just popped up and caught a nigga slippin' like they came from out da ground or something!"

"Man y'all niggas... Mmh... Mmh... Mmh... Y'all need to tighten the fuck up! What happened to Lil Man?"

"They jive pistol whipped and stomped slim out, plus they made Bo strip butt ass naked and had him collect everybody's bread."

"Dat's crazy," Maurice responded calmly even though he was very heated from the information he'd just received. "I'll be there as soon as I handle this quick business," he assured.

"Aight," said the caller.

Maurice immediately ended the call, then dialed up Blac's phone. It quickly went to voicemail. His next notion was to call Reggie, but decided to leave a quick message with Blac instead. Infuriated, while remaining composed, he then placed his phone into the car's seat and gathered the materials needed to handle his business. Right before exiting the vehicle he turned towards his driver and said, "Keep the car runnin', I'ma be in and out."

"You sure you don't need me to come with you? You know 'cause your foot and all," inquired the driver, referring to Maurice'sinjury and the fact that he was moving around with a walking boot that was used to protect his foot.

"I'm straight," he replied, stepping out the car.

Once Maurice vanished into the building, the driver grabbed his cell phone and placed a call. It only took a few seconds for the individual he was contacting to pick up. The driver spoke briefly and ended the call a hair of a minute before Maurice returned.

"That was quick," stated the driver.

"I told you I would be in and out" Maurice reiterated unintentionally sitting on his own cell phone that he had left behind in the car's passanger seat. He quickly grabbed it from underneath him and pressed the end button after realizing that he had forgotten to do so earlier on. "Head around the way," he instructed, placing the money he'd just received under his seat.

Chapter 24

"Slim, you disrespectful as shit! What da fuck made you smack dat bamma on his bare ass like dat?" Scrap questioned. "I wanted to laugh like shit, but it wasn't the right time," he concluded as all five cohorts strolled into Block's basement.

"Fuck dat clown, plus I know he's da one who initiated everything, but da scared nigga was shakin' like it was freezing and its fuckin' summer time," explained Ode.

"Yeah, slim was terrified," added Worl.

"Dat's an under statement. You see his eyes? They say da eyes neva lie and his most definitely told da truth," proclaimed Ode.

"No bullshit, but like you said - fuck 'em! Plus, I'm trying to see what we stumbled across while bracing these fools." Scrap asserted as Ode, Block and himself emptied the bags full of contents onto the floor.

As they sorted through everything, Ty sat down and started rolling up some of the exotic weed they'd received from Big Lyn. Worl checked his missed calls and messages, and once they finished summing up everything, the group wasn't disappointed about their decision to rob the group, even though that wasn't their primary mission.

"Ay Scrap!" Worl called. "We got action!" he said, referring to Ra-Ra and China. "Ra-Ra left a message with the hotel's info, so we need to hurry up and be on our way. I ain't tryin' to keep them waitin' too long. Plus, we need to go change clothes and stop by da liquor store."

"We almost finish splittin up this bread, anyway," replied Scrap. As they continued to divide the money five ways, a sudden thought popped into Worl's mind. "Know what, we might need to keep dat bread together. We can use it to make the move up New York."

"Why you wait for us to split da money to say dat?" questioned Scrap.

"Cause I didn't think about it until now."

"What move ya'll talkin' 'bout?" Ty inquired, exhaling a cloud of smoke.

"Im'ma fill y'all in tomorrow, 'cause me and Scrap need to roll out. But trust me, it's a power move if everything goes right," Worl assured him.

"Dat's good enough for me. See y'all tomorrow den," Ty replied.

"Ya'll cool wit dat?" asked Scrap.

Everybody agreed, so he gave all the money to Block to put up until they were ready.

"Grab them two purses," Worl told Scrap, before they got up to leave.

"Fo' what?" asked Scrap.

"Nigga just bring da purses, and stop askin' all them damn questions!" hissed Worl.

"Drop me off at my car. I think Im'ma stay over Tyshelle house for tonight, since it ain't shit else to do," Ode annoounced.

"Be careful if you goin up there, 'cause them niggas might be ridin' around, especially after dat move we just pulled," said Block.

"I'm straight! Plus, them niggas don't know my car."

"Just be careful, and stay outta low key," suggested Worl. "Wassup wit y'all two? Y'all chillin' for tonight?" he questioned Block and Ty.

"I'm stayin in," Block replied.

"I'm gon' chill for a minute, den I'm goin' in," Ty added, feeling the effects of the high-grade marijuana.

"Dat's a bet; we goin' catch up wit y'all tomorrow," Worl concluded, as all five dapped each other up and proceeded to finalize their evenings.

Chapter 25

Shortly after Maurice got dropped off, he waited for his two trustees to show up at his home. Hearing a knock at the door, he got up to open the door, but quickly remembered that his over protective pit bull was wandering around, so he went to secure her in the kennel before doing so.

"Where's Remy?" asked Blac before entering.

"Bring y'all scared asses in. She's put-up," joked Maurice, walking back towards his den.

"Whatever! That dog don't fuck wit nobody but you and Charity," Blac countered, stepping in with Reggie trailing behind.

"I take it that y'all got my message?" Maurice inquired after having a seat.

"Yeah, but that's not that only message we received," Blac replied.

"What do you mean?" Maurice questioned with a puzzled look on his face.

Blac simply pulled out his cellphone, dialed his voicemail and passed it to Maurice so he could listen. After keying in on the conversation, one could see his jaws tightening and his body becoming rigid. To say that he was beyond pissed was an understatement, because in his mind betrayal was worse than murder. He immediately knew who it was and when the unloyal conversation took place. Who would have known by him unintentionally not ending his call and tossing his cell phone in the seat that it would unveil a snake in his immediate circle? Now the question was obvious, finding out who he was talking to, and then eliminating them both.

"I see why we can't never catch up with them youngins 'cause this fool keep putting them on point," said Blac.

"You want us to go handle it?" asked Reggie.

"Fall back 'cause we can use this to our advantage. Since he wants to run his mouth, we're going to bait his dumb ass in," said Maurice, ending the conversation on that note.

Chapter 26

Worl and Scrap pulled into the hotel parking lot where the females were located. Once they found a parking spot, they quickly grabbed the two bottles of liquor they'd purchased from the liquor store, the exotic weed that they'd received from Big Lyn, and the two handbags they took from the robbery. Once they had everything they needed, they headed up to the room. As the pair stepped off the elevator, Scrap started to second guess giving someone he'd just met an expensive purse.

"I don't know 'bout giving shorty this bag."

"Why you say dat?" Worl questioned.

"'Cause fo' one, I barely know her. Two, it makes me look like I'm on some trickin' shit, and three, I think we should've threw this shit away," Scrap explained.

"Throw them away fo what! You actin like they gon' know how we got'em."

"I mean it's cool fo'you 'cause dats ya folks, but it ain't a good look fo'me," Scrap countered.

"Go head wit' dat bullshit like you ain't never bought somethin' for a broad you barely knew. Don't forget who you talkin' to 'cause I know you remember da time you brought… Umh… what's shorty's name you met at the Peterson fight down at the convention center?"

"Imani," answered Scrap.

"Yeah, dats her name. You remember buyin' her dat Hermes bag on her B-day and dat was three days after y'all met. Oh, and don't forget about dat stripper broad, Stella, wit' them juicey azz lips. You brought her dat lingerie set for…"

"Stop right there," Scrap said, cutting Worl off. "Shorty from da fight was a twelve, and dat stripper broad not only had a body out this world, but her head game was a torch, so both gifts were well worth it," he explained, defending his actions.

"So what's the difference? 'Cause China is a bad jo'nt, and if Ra-Ra wasn't my folks, I'd be knockin her down. Believe dat!" Worl assured him.

"Yeah she jive official," admitted Scrap.

"Aight then nigga, stop actin' like dat and give her dat bag."

"Aight I got you, but you know how them broads think."

"How?"

"They always assume a nigga wants somethin' in return when we give them shit."

"So what! Either way, it's a good start," Worl stated before reaching for the door. "You straight?"

"I'm good."

After seeing that he convinced his partner, he knocked on the door. Seconds later, the door opened up with Ra-Ra standing behind it. Looking just as beautiful as ever, she had a huge smile on her face.

"What took y'all so long?" she inquired, giving her man a big hug and a kiss before allowing them in.

"Damn you lookin good! Here, this is for you," Worl said, handing her the bag.

"Ra-Ra wassup?" Scrap greeted casually.

She politely returned the greeting before complimenting on the bag she'd just received.

"Roberto Cavalli! Baby this bag is real nice! I've never seen one quite like this one before," Ra-Ra proclaimed.

"Dat should be a good thing," Worl countered.

"It is," she replied, sounding upbeat.

Scrap walked up to China in a smooth thuggish manner, greeted her, then passed her the handbag with the two bottles sticking out of the brim.

"I got you somethin' I thought you may like."

"Jimmy Choo! You know these are very expensive bags. I haven't even done anything to deserve this…" she replied suprised.

"Why should you, it's a gift. You like it?" Scrap asked.

"How could I not," China answered, taking the bag to pull the two bottles out. "These for me, too?" she questioned.

"Nah dat's fo all of us," he smiled, causing her to do the same.

The two seem to have gotten well acquainted as the night went on. The conversations were flowing just like the liquor and the champagne. The more alcohol they absorbed, the deeper the discussion became. Wanting to know more about her, Scrap found himself asking her personal questions. Inquiring about a female's personal situation was something he rarely did, and answering inquiries was one thing she barely did. The chemistry was definitely there between the two, and it was quite obvious. Ra-Ra and Worl noticed that China seemed to be blushing and laughing at every word Scrap said, and Ra-Ra enjoyed the fact that her bestie seemed to be having a good time. Before they knew it, two hours had flown past and the liquor had taken its effects. Ra-Ra wanted some alone time with her man. She unhesitantly spoke up after that warm sensational feeling assumed control. She was in the mood for some sexual healing.

"Sorry y'all two. It's getting late, and I need some quality time with my man. If y'all would excuse us, I'd sure appreciate it."

"Oh, so Ra, it's like that?" China teased.

"Yep, GET OUT!" Worl, jokingly interjected.

Everybody laughed it off. Scrap subsequently gave China that drunken craving facial expression that instantly triggered her wetness. In support of her friend's request, China grabbed Scrap's hand and led the way to the separate room she purchased..

Chapter 27

"You sure do know how to keep a nigga comin back for more," Ode huffed after pulling out from penetrating Tyshelle missionary style. He had it wide open. He couldn't get enough. Their friendship had started off platonic, but as time went on, feelings grew. The two never conversed about becoming equal, but as of lately, they had been spending a lot more time together. Ode was young in the streets and had quite a few lady friends, but out of them all, he found himself closer to Tyshelle. He truly admired the fact that she was not only sexy and built like a stallion, but she was well educated in more ways than you could imagine. The thought of her impeccable oral game aroused him once again and within seconds, he was ready for round two.

"You know you got me spoiled, right?" Ode stated flirtatiously.

"How could I not pamper someone as sweet and kind as you," Tyshelle replied, gently massaging his erection once again.

"I'm glad you feel dat way 'cause daddy needs some more special attention."

Without responding, she slowly began kissing on his neck, then went lower and lower, until she had covered every inch of his torso, which led to finding her final destination.

"Who would've thought someone so innocent and lady like would be so freaky behind closed doors?" Ode thought, lying back to relish in the moment.

Tyshelle had really fallen for Ode and was willing to do whatever it took to keep him happy. Tyshelle was one of the few females that lived in the 'hood that chose not to indulge in the negativities that surrounded her. She had a younger brother that she was overprotective of, because their father had died in their house from a drug overdose. That alone led her to have an adverse attitude towards underhanded activities. Ode understood Tyshelle's mental uneasiness, concerning the streets and vowed to never bring his street dealings around her or her family. While getting sucked up, Ode thought about solidifying their relationship and the had plans to do so the following morning. He really cared for her and wanted that foundation. Tyshelle's skilled fellatio quickly shifted Ode's thoiughts back to that moment as he floated in euphoria.

Chapter 28

Worl was in another world as he was laid back with one arm folded behind his head, digesting and enjoying Ra-Ra's sexiness. She strip teased for him while Beyoncé's, *Dance For You* softly played in the background. Her captivating moves had him craving for some of her love, but he managed to remain calm and allowed her to entertain him. Her moves were perfectly synchronized almost as if two masters were playing chess. She professionally moved her hips like Shakira, matching the rhythm of a beat. The more in tune she became, the more layers of clothing she shed, until she was standing there in her birthday suit. He eagerly sat up, but she delicately pushed him back flat on the bed. Ready to please her man, she climbed on top of him then sang the words to the song.

"I can't help but to think about it day and night. I want to make that body rock, sit back and watch - cause tonight, "I'm Gonna Dance for You," she intoned, kissing on his neck, and nhelping him out of his top. After freeing him from his shirt, she went to sucking on his neck then slowly used her tongue to trace the line down the center of his chest that led to his navel. Her scent and her foreplay had him more excited sexually than an inmate after getting released from a twenty-year bid. Knowing that she had his full attention had her even more excited. Things quickly heated up, and she wanted to please him more. She

gradually unbuckled his jeans, and then removed them before deciding to welcome his love muscle into her warm mouth.

"Damn, Mami!" he voiced in an ecstasy driven tone after he felt his body tensing up, which compelled her to absorb him even more. He eventually calmed down and relaxed himself to keep from cumming so fast.

It was somewhat difficult to sustain himself, cause she was putting her best work down. Her Dominican side must have assumed control from the way she was working her tongue while keeping his shaft well moistened. Moments later, he felt that swelling feeling increasing when he decided to stop her before he exploded. He pulled her closer towards him, touching the spots that she only thought she knew would send shivers down her spine. On Cue *Naked* by Marques Houston smoothly blended in the background intensifying the mood. He wanted her to feel the same pleasurable feeling as he did. He not only kissed, rubbed, and licked all over her body, but he also quenched his thirst by tasting her cum. Soft moans escaped her breath as he played a tune with her entire body. She loved the way he had her body feeling. It was almost as if she was in Paradise. Worl had her mind on another planet, and she wasn't in any rush to shatter her passionate chimera. Worl delectable and meticulous ways allowed her to cream twice back to back before he decided that it was time to enter her wet canal. She was yearning to finally feel him inside of her, but requested for him to be gentle. He honored her requisition as he entered her.

"Damn, you feel good," he whispered, caressing her breast and guiding himself further and further into her honey jar. Her eyes rolled as he began to speed up his pace. Her moans turned into light screams, which turned him on even more, so much so he commenced to long-stroking her harder and harder. He thought her screams of agony were cries of pleasure. Once the pain became too much to bear, she ended-up pushing him off of her, until she regained her resolve. She decided to get on top, so she could control the amount of pounding. Once the throbbing between her legs subsided, she went into over drive. She got into a squatting position, placed her hands on his chest, put her mind on cruise control, and rode his shift until she climaxed for the third time.

"Ahh yes, Papi! I... I'm cum... cumin again!" she bellowed, as she bit down on her bottom lip and threw her head back as if she was working a hula-hoop. She finally loosened up, and Worl was enjoying her every microsecond of her whimsical ways.

"Ride dat thing, Baby Girl!" Worl inspired, smacking her on her ass.

"Yes Papi! I miss you so much!"

Worl had enough of being manhandled, so he pushed her off of him, placed a pillow underneath her, laid her on her stomach, and then entered her from behind. He started off giving her slow, long, deep strokes, but sped-up once she used both of her hands to spread her cheeks apart, which gave him freer access. He began to pound her like a jack rabbit and that all too familiar swelling feeling returned.

"Damn Baby, I'm... I'm cumin," he struggled to say clearly. "Awwww! Shit! Damn, Baby Girl!" shouted Worl, after emptying his unborn children all over her plump ass.

The two momentarily collapsed on the bed immediately after their intense episode. Shortly after the pair settled down, they went into the bathroom to clean up before relaxing on the fresh bed. The music continued to softly serenade in the background as they both fell asleep.

Chapter 29

After a long night of being sexually gratified, Ode woke up to a nice warm smile and breakfast in bed. The rib-eyed steak and eggs with a glass of orange juice were just what he needed after a restless night. The pampering only intensified his emotions towards Tyshelle. After he ate and thanked her for everything she had done for him, he sat up and grabbed her hands. Wanting to connect with her, he looked directly into her eyes and told her that he would like to upgrade their friendship. The biggest smile spread across her face. She couldn't stop blushing because her feelings for Ode were heavy. Once they solidified their relationship, he went into the bathroom to freshen up. Then he went into the bedroom to converse with her little brother who was engrossed in a game of Madden Football.

"Let me see dat other controller," said Ode as he sat down and commenced to play Lil Kent in a head to head game. While they were playing, Ode asked questions pertaining to his grades in school, who his favorite athlete was, and what he wanted to do when he got older. Little Kent responded with being an honor roll student, LeBron James being his favorite athlete, he wanted to be a lawyer when he got older, and he planned to continue to beat up on Ode in Madden Football.

"Touchdown!" shouted Lil Kent for the second time. "Told you I was going to beat you," he confidently stated.

"I didn't know you was dat good," Ode replied. Ode put the controller down, and told Lil Kent he wanted to finish their conversation. He wanted to know what made him say that he wanted to become a lawyer, because not many black 13-year-old kids that resided in the inner-city neighborhoods wanted to become lawyers.

He told Ode, he wanted to keep his brother and sisters from going to prison. Ode was a bit surprised, but didn't find it hard to believe, because Lil Kent was a smart and brilliant kid with a bright future ahead of him.

"Dat's a good profession. You know dat requires a lot of studyin, so you make sure you stay in them books and learn ya craft. You never know who might need ya," Ode explained. He thought to himself that he might need him one day.

"Okay," answered Lil Kent.

"What about sports? I see you play da video games real good, but can you play in real life?"

"Yeah, I can," he replied, cracking a smile.

"You sure?"

"Yeah, I'm sure," he said with confidence.

"Da reason I asked is because you're big for your age. You're damn near my size. I'm just a lil bit taller. You still have a lot more grownin' to do, and I know a team would love to pick you up; especially if you got skills. What position do you play?" Ode asked.

"Linebacker and tight end."

"Which one are you better at?"

"Both," replied Lil Kent.

"Well whatever you choose to do, just know dat I have ya back." Ode spoke from the heart as he glanced up and noticed Tyshelle standing in the doorway with a grin on her face." How long you been standing there ear hustling?" questioned Ode.

"Long enough," she replied.

Ode told Lil Kent that he had a surprise for him out in the car. Shortly after, he got up and walked over to Tyshelle, giving her a hug and a kiss on the cheek.

"What I tell you about trying to spoil him," Tyshelle expressed.

"Dat's my lil man… So as long as he continues to do the right thing, I got 'em." Ode vowed.

Tyshelle never responded. She knew Ode wouldn't stop buying Lil Kent things, so she gave in because no matter how many times she told him to stop, he just continued. He told her he'd be right back, then he headed outside to get Lil Kent's surprise. As he opened the trunk of his car, he felt a tap on his shoulder. "Don't walk up on me like dat! Fuck wrong wit you!" Ode huffed. He was livid and more upset with himself for allowing someone to get that close without him noticing.

"I'm sorry if I startled you. I didn't mean to," a crackhead shot back; a little jittery after he screamed on her.

"Don't worry 'bout it," Ode stated calmly. "My bad for screamin' on you. Wassup wit you?"

"I just wanted to ask you did you have something on you."

"How much you got?"

"Twenty-five."

"Yeah, I got you. Put da money right there," Ode instructed, not wanting to past anything to her out in the open. He unnoticeably retrieved three dimes of crack, and then placed them in the trunk while he simultaneously pulled Lil Kent's surprise out, and grabbed the money.

"It's right there," he directed, allowing her to pick up the product before closing the trunk, "You straight?"

"Yeah I'm good," she replied before whisking away, and placing her purchase in her jacket pocket. She felt a piece of paper in her pocket, pulled it out, and then quickly realized that she could have gotten some for free by making one simple phone call.

Chapter 30

"Good morning Butcher," stated Ra-Ra jokingly.

"Butcher?" repeated Worl, frowning. "Where did dat name come from?"

"The way you tried to cut into my womb last night. I thought the neighbors were gon call the law and have you arrested for A.T.M.P?" she joked

"What's A.T.M.P?" he asked, looking towards her strangely.

"Attempted Murder on the Pussy," she replied.

"Oh yeah! You got jokes this mornin', huh! The way you threw it back at me, I'm sure I would've gotten off on self-defense," Worl countered.

"D.C. doesn't have a self-defense law."

"Yeah you're right, but don't fo'get dat D.C. is about five minutes away. We are officially in Montgomery County, Md. and you could bet they have one," he corrected her.

"We are in Maryland, aren't we? How did that slip my mind? Dang, and I'm the one who purchased the rooms. Speaking on rooms. Have you heard from our besties in the other suite?"

"Nah, but I'm sure they good."

"Hearing nothing, might be a good thing," Ra-Ra responded, getting up from underneath the covers and sashaying into the bathroom.

She put an extra switch in her walk, knowing that Worl was gazing at her nakedness.

Worl watched the way her ass jiggled as she walked to the bathroom, and instantly got an early morning erection. His mind quickly went from him watching a music video with Keyshia Cole singing a high note to thinking about following Ra-Ra into the bathroom. All he wanted to do was employ his sturdy instrument so a tune could be played on it by her southern lips. Without a second thought, he hopped off the bed and headed towards the bathroom just as the shower was turning on. He waited for a brief moment, and then tapped on the door just to make sure he didn't actually walk-in on her while using the toilet. He knew some women took offense to it.

"It's open," Ra-Ra replied, after hearing the tap on the door.
Worl walked in like a drill sergent, standing at full attention. He immediately stepped over to the shower, and then pulled the curtains back.
"Boy!" she blurted out with a smile on her face after seeing him standing there lustfully in his birthday suit.
"Boy?" Worl repeated, stepping into the shower. "Dis is all man right here," he stated, before commencing to sucking on her neck as if he was sucking nectar from a piece of fruit. Ra-Ra's breathing quickened as she tilted her head back to welcome his soft lips.

The friction from their naked bodies caused her to become hotter than an erupted volcano. Her love juices seeped down her inner thighs. All in one swift motion he spun her around, bending her over to enter his secret key, which unlocked her floodgates. As the water from the shower ricocheted off their backs, she turned her head halfway, raising her eyes to match his intense stare. Worl wasn't speaking, but his facial expression spoke volumes.

Damn, this pussy good, he thought as he elevated her left leg to dig deep into her love tunnel. Worl was so rock solid that Ra-Ra could feel the veins pulsating through her honey slit with each thrust. The sex was painful, but pleasurable. She tried to throw it back as much as she could while Worl was hitting spots that she never knew existed. The water mixed with their nakedness caused a continuing rhythmic slapping. Worl was in full throttle, almost as if he was in fifth gear, pushing it to the limit.

"Right there, Papi... Right there... Oooh.... She's cummin for you, Papi!" she blurted out, feeling that familiar tingle.

"Den let her cum! Let... Her... Cum... Ahh... Uuumm!" he shot back, pumping harder and faster. A few more srokes invited their climax simultaneously, which almost caused their legs to give out momentary.

After regaining their composure, Ra-Ra and Worl began to eachother, taking full advantage of their qualify time together.

Chapter 31

Blac and Reggie were just exiting from picking up an obligation when they received an anticipated phone call. After having a brief conversation, they avidly went to switch vehicles trying not to miss out on their opportunity of reprisal. The two quickly transformed into two wolves, eager to hunt their prey. The time wasn't of the essence, because they didn't know if and when they arrived if their target would actually be there. Unbeknownst, they still managed to make it to their destination in a timely manner. After picking up their informant, they headed to their location with vengeful thoughts. Reggie hopped in the back seat, allowing their stool pigeon to ride shotgun while she gave directions to their adversary's whereabouts. Patricia unaware of their perilous intentions, willingly pointed out Ode's whereabouts.

"That's the car he's driving right there," she announced.

"Are you sure it's dat blue Monte Carlo with da tints on it?" questioned Blac.

"Positive. He was getting something out of the trunk when I stopped to talk with em," she assured, "Now can I have what was promised to me?" she inquired, eager to get her hands on her drug of choice.

"Oh yeah, of course. Go ahead and give it to her Reggie," Blac asserted, giving Reggie the head nod through the rearview mirror.

"There's only one thing promised to us all and that's death," Reggie stated with Malice laced in his tone wrapped his forearm around her neck.

"No... Please no," Pat pleaded as she tried to loosen his grip, but her frail body wasn't no match for his strength.

Her body jerked violently as her lungs begged for air. The tighter he squeezed, the more her body rebelled. In a matter of seconds, her resistance became inferior, and she began to fade to black.

Chapter 32

The group coupled up in separate rooms where each was trying to get the particulars from the prior night. Worl was grilling Scrap, as if he were a detective interrogating a suspect.

"So wassup wit ol' girl?" questioned Worl, with a huge grin on his face.

"Ain't too much. Shorty cool as shit though, plus, she don't act all stuck-up and shit, feel me."

"Yeah, I feel ya slim, but fuck all dat! Nigga what's really up? Did you hit or what?" Worl impatiently asked, leaning towards Scrap.

"On some real shit, slim... I ain't even hit, but you know da crazy part about it, I didn't even try."

"What?" asked Worl indisbelief.

"Yeah, I ain't even try, slim," he confirmed. "But dat's not all." After about thirty minutes of getting more acquainted, she got real comfy and came up out her clothes, and got in the bed!

"Naked?" Questioned Worl.

"Not naked... She was in her bra and panties," Scrap cleared up.

"You mean to tell me you didn't try nothin'?" Worl queried in shock."

"Dat's what I said, nigga! Are you deaf?" Scrap asked, raising a brow.

"Nah, I'm not deaf, and you ain't blind or slow! So, she probably think you gay!" Worl quipped.

"Yeah whatever!" Scrap countered.

"Fuck is wrong wit' you. You trippin'.Shorty like dat."

"Yeah I might've been trippin," Scrap agreed, thinking back. "It probably was da drinks," Scrap stated, trying to justify his actions or the lack thereof.

"Hold up. Stop right there. We ain't goin' do dat," Worl cut in, throwing his hand up, "because if anything da liquor goin' have you ready to knock her hip out, so don't blame it on dat. I know what it is…" he indicated, looking towards Scrap shaking his head, "you' on Shorty's line!" he smiled, knowing that his partner was feeling China, because if it was anything less, he would've gotten his nut and kept it moving.

"Whatever, nigga!" Scrap replied, trying to convince himself that, that wasn't it, but truthfully in his mind, he knew that Worl was right. It was something about China that made him want to get to know her on a more personal level.

Worl noticed that his right-hand man, more than likely adopted feelings, so he hatred his queries pertaining to China and changed the subject. His focus centered around crossing their and likewise, dotting their I's in terms of preparing themselves for the possible move up New York that could perhaps earn them substantial cash flow. Being on point was key in both situations and took careful planning.

Since it was almost checkout time, the two comrades finalized their conversation and elected to go join the women in the other room.

Chapter 33

"Girl, I had a good time last night and this morning!" stated Ra-Ra animated.

"I wish I could say the same," China lazily countered.

"Say what! Don't tell me that he passed out on you from drinking too much."

"Might as well, 'cause he didn't try his hand; not even after I came out my clothes and got in the bed."

"So you basically gave 'em a free invite to the golden gates and…"

"He didn't accept," China cut in, finishing Ra-Ra's statement. "And that's kinda hard to believe, 'cause who can resist this," she proclaimed, getting up to spin around as if she were a model. Being sassy, she then smacked her own butt cheeks, making it jiggle.

"What did he do after you got in the bed?"

"Nothing! He just sat there looking cute as ever and continued talking, until I eventually fell asleep."

"So why didn't you make the first move?"

"Ra-Ra did you not hear what I just said! I took off my clothes, and then got in the bed! I did make a move, but he didn't accept it!" she answered.

"Maybe it's a good thing that he's not tender at the zipper."

"What the hell does that mean, and where did you hear that from?"

"Well it means that he's not just thinking with his you know what, and I heard if from Big Mitch that be hanging around Hanover Place."

"That figures, but you know what?"

"What!"

"Him not comin' on to me made me want 'em even more. I'm not gon' front, it's just something about 'em!" she confessed.

"Let me find out. Scrap got my girl trippin' without even touching her," Ra-Ra commented, tapping her on her arm.

"I wouldn't necessary say all that, but I would say that he…," she began before they heard a knock on the door.

Ra-Ra instantly got up to open it and gave Worl a quick peck on his cheek upon entering.

"What y'all in here gossiping 'bout?" he casually inquired.

"Nothing, just girl talk," Ra-Ra replied.

"Yeah, I bet. Well anyway, y'all ready, 'cause it's 'bout dat time," Worl stated, tapping his watch to indicate that it was checkout time.

"We been ready. We were just waiting on you two."

"Let's be out then," Worl instructed as all four gathered their belongings and headed out the door. Before they went their separate ways, Scrap made sure to get China's information with the hopes of hooking back up with her soon. China had no problem accepting their offer.

Chapter 34

Lil Kent was in the house boasting about the Xbox One that Ode had given him. To say that he was elated was an understatement. He was so enthusiastic about the gift that he could barely sit down.

"Can you take me to get a game?" asked Lil Kent, eager to play the game station.

"Ask your sister first because you know I'm all for it," said Ode, pointing towards Tyshelle.

"Yeah, and when you get back, make sure you clean up that messy room," she replied.

"Sis, thank you," Lil Kent smiled, walking over to give her a hug and kiss.

"Don't keep him out too long," she told Ode.

"I won't,"he assured her. "Go get ready," he told Lil Kent, who quickly jumped up to go do just that. Five minutes later, he was ready to go. Ode handed him his car keys. "It's the blue two door car with the tinted windows. It's parked by the corner. While I use the bathroom, would you please go start it up for me," he instructed, heading to the commade to relieve himself. Lil Kent gladly took the keys and rushed out the house to handle that small task that was asked of him.

Chapter 35

Blac was towards the back of the caravan assisting Reggie with Patricia's body, when Black glanced up and noticed a male, walking in the direction of the Monte Carlo.

"I think we got action!" Blac said, tapping Reggie on his shoulder.

"Hell yeah! Let's go!" He quickly replied, zooming in on their mark. Reggie immediately placed a sheet over Patricia's dead body before grabbing an AK 47 from underneath the second row seats. Blac quickly rushed back to the driver's seat.

"What the fuck is he doin'?" Reggie inquired, noticing that their target stopped at the passenger's door.

"It don't really matter. You ready?" asked Blac, putting the van in drive.

Reggie never responded, he simply racked a bullet in the chamber, indicating that he was prepared to add another homicide to his body count. As Blac reached the intersection, Reggie placed one hand on the sliding door, preparing to open it so he could get a clearer aim at his target

Chapter 36

As Lil Kent was sticking the key into the passenger's door of the vehicle, he halted after hearing his sister call out to him.

"Yes!" he shouted, answering her.

"Don't leave without your house keys!" Tyshelle instructed. Ode slid up from behind, grabbed her by her waist and pulled her in for a kiss on the nape of her neck. "I'll give 'em to him," he whispered in her ear, taking the keys out her hand. "I told you we were comin' right back anyway."

He noticed Lil Kent walking back to the house, when he held the keys up signaling for him to go back. While doing so, he observed a dark colored caravan creeping up with their side sliding door ajar. Out of instinct, he quickly rushed towards Lil Kent, shouting for him to get down. Their aggressors fiercely opened fire, muffling Odes utterance. The loud uproar caused Ode to take cover behind a parked car, while scanning the area trying to pinpoint Lil Kent's' whereabouts. The deafening sound followed by the onslaught of bullets ricocheting off the vehicles hindered his attempt to locate Lil Kent. Everything happened so fast that Ode hadn't realized that the shooting had ceased. After a slow reaction, Ode leaped up, and ran in the middle of the street and returned fire. He was able to strike the van as it sped up the street.

"Fuck!" he cursed, sprinting around the dismantled vehicle's in search of Lil Kent. When he made it around the last vehicle, he found Lil Kent lying in a pool of blood. He was face down, and awkwardly positioned. "No... No ... No!" he blurted out, rushing to his aid. "Please don't let dis happen!" he pleaded, placing his smoking gun on the ground. He turned Lil Kent over to cup him in his arms. "Stay wit me!" he cried out, trying to get him to keep his eyes open.

Lil Kent was struggling to catch his breath, so Ode knew Lil Kent was in trouble. Tyshelle emerged from her house hysterical. After seeing her little brother in Ode's arm, she wildly dashed towards the two. As she continued towards them, Ode tried to signal for her to get help, but the only thing on her mind was reaching them. Lil Kent tried, but he couldn't fight it anymore. Suddenly, his body went limp. Seeing him take him his final breath immediately placed Ode in a dark state of mind. Tears started to flow down his face as he closed Lil Kent's eyelids.

"Get off him! Get away from him!" Tyshelle screamed as she stormed up to pull her brother away from Ode. "Come on baby, get up!" she cried as if he'd overslept. "Let's go baby! It's time to go!" "she yelped, horrified. Once he didn't respond, reality set in. "I love you," she stated, kissing his forehead. She then looked towards with fury in her eyes. Ode was in shock standing their loss in another world, until she jumped up and stormed towards him with a flurry of punches.

"This all your fault!" she snapped, screaming at Ode.

"I'm sorry," he pleaded, picking his gun up off the ground," I'm so sorry, but I can't stay here," he said, knowing the authorities would arrive at any moment. He looked around and noticed some of the neighbors emerging from their homes. As they zoomed in on the chaos, he took one final look at Lil Kent's lifeless body, and took off running towards his vehicle.

Chapter 37

"Good morning. This is Connie Sue from Fox 5 News, reporting live from 5th and Rittenhouse, Northwest. Just over an hour ago on this street, a thirteen-year-old male by the name of Kenneth Jackson was brutally murdered. The small framed teenager suffered multiple gunshot wounds to his upper body, while standing outside of his home. Witnesses claim to have seen a dark colored minivan that sped off seconds after the shooting. They also reported that a young male fled from the scene minutes later that allegedly returned fire," explained Connie Sue, as the news camera zoomed in on the detriment that the assault rifle caused. "Standing here with me is Detective Merrett from the Fourth District Homicide Division."

"Good morning, Mrs. Sue," the detective greeted stone-faced.

"Good morning, Detective. Is it too early to pinpoint the ulterior motive behind this horrendous act? Are there currently any leads on the suspects?" asked Connie Sue, placing the microphone near his mouth.

"At this very moment, the department has yet to learn the identity of the suspects. As for an ulterior motive, one could theorize that it was mistaken identity, or Kenneth Jackson was caught in a cross fire between the suspects in the van and the male individual who witnesses say returned fire," he speculated.

"Are there any leads on the dark colored caravan that was reportedly spotted leaving the crime scene shortly after?"

"Not as of yet, but authorities are canvassing the area, hoping to find any leads and the department would appreciate it if anyone who has information regarding this case to contact us at our toll free number. There will be an award posted later-on today for anyone whose tip leads to a conviction," assured Detective Merrett.

Connie Sue exchanged views with the Detective for several more minutes, hoping to leave nothing unanswered as she proceeded to conclude her interview. "One last statement Detective…," she paused. "I'm sure the people of Washington would appreciate it if the Police Department kept us updated. This is the exact kind of heartless act that causes the parents of today to be apprehensive about allowing their children to go outside and freely play," she stressed.

"The people will be updated. Also, the department is quite aware of the callous act that has transpired. This will be an ongoing investigation, and we can assure the people of Washington that we are doing everything in our power to put an end to these crimes. We are also going to catch these senseless criminals," he promised, wrapping up the interview to finish attending to his official police business.

"There you have it. I'm Connie Sue, and this is Fox 5 News at eleven. Back to you Dave."

Chapter 38

After hearing loud repeated knocks, at his front door, Ty jumped up off his couch and hurried to answer it. *Who da fuck!* he thought as he looked through the peephole. Immediately he saw Ode on the opposite side, looking jittery. It was as if he was a performer who caught a sudden case of stage fright.

"Slim, why you knockin' like you the police?" Ty questioned, after opening the door. Ode simply rushed in the house, disregarding Ty's question.

"What's wrong with you, and why you looking all noided!" Ty questioned.

"Slim, you not goin' believe what just happened!" Ode stated, holding his head as if he had a migraine.

"From the way you're actin' somethin' is telling me I might need to sit down for this," countered Ty.

"Yeah you might just need too," assured Ode as he began explaining what happened.

He gave a detail explanation of the complete incident, leaving nothing out. Ty was sitting there dumbfounded.

"So why would you drive dat hot ass Monte Carlo over here right after some shit like dat!" Ty suddenly blurted out.

"I know, slim, but I parked in the alley around da corner, plus I lost my phone in da midst of all this shit," he stated, trying to rationalize his action.

"Where you lose ya phone at?"

"Slim, I couldn't even tell you, 'cause dat shit happened so fast… Fuck! Lil Kent!" he barked angrily, replaying the event over in his mind. "It's on now! I promise!" he proclaimed, abruptly standing and pacing back and forth.

"Slim calm down! First, we need to get rid of dat car, and then go get you another phone."

"When?"

"ASAP! You won't make it another day riding in dat hot ass jo'nt. Let's handle this first, then we worry 'bout dem clowns later on."

"Yeah, you're right. Hurry up and get dressed so we can take care of this shit."

"Bet!" Ty replied, rushing off to go get dress.

Chapter 39

Ra-Ra was almost at China's house when China decided she wanted to make a stop at the Beauty Supply Store.

"You need anything?" asked China, getting out.

"I'm good," replied Ra-Ra.

"I'll be right out," China assured her, grabbing her new Jimmy Choo bag to head into the store. It didn't take her long to grab the items she needed. On her way to the counter she heard her name being called, "China!" the voice called from behind.

"Kita," China replied unenthusiastic.

"Hey girl! I haven't seen you in a while. What you been up to?" Kita inquired.

"Workin' and staying out the way, that's all," China countered, keeping the conversation brief.

"I know that's right. It looks like you've gained some weight. You not pregnant are you?"

"Child no. Not at all. In my ass maybe," China joked, spinning half way around to flash her baby bump.

"Ooh girl! You might be havin' twins," Kita laughed, noticing China's bag. "That's a Jimmy Choo bag?" she inquired.

"Sure is," China smiled. "You know your bags, huh?"

"Kinda sorta, but the reason I know what kind of bag it is because my girlfriend had the exact same one," Kita confessed.

"Had?" China questioned.

"Yeah! Some dudes came around the way last night and robbed everybody in the area," Kita explained.

"You said last night!" China inquired, thinking she received the bag the night before.

"Last night," she assured her.

"What else did they take?"

"Mmh," she thought for a split second, "Besides everybody money and jewelry, they also took another bag from one of the other females that was with her."

"Girl, y'all need to be careful. Did you all see their faces?"

"No 'cause they had on wigs and scarves," Kita confirmed, noticing China being too questionable. It seemed to her as if she knew or suspected something. Kita decided to dig in a bit further, just to see. "How long have you had your bag?"

"Oh, long before last night," China lied, picking up on Kita's skepticism. "Why you ask?"

"Cause when I question her about where she purchased the bag from, she told me that her father who was overseas sent it to her as a gift," Kita expounded.

"Are you insinuating that it's possible that this is the same bag?"

"Only you would know," countered Kita.

"Well like I said before, I had this bag prior to last night, so it's impossible. You could get that out of your head. But anyway, it was nice talking to you. I gotta get going. My ride is out front double parked," China retorted, rushing off to pay for her items.

Once she got back into the car, she wasted no time explaining what had just transpired.

"Girl, you not gon' believe what happened!"

"What?" inquired Ra-Ra, pulling off.

"I ran into this girl name Kita and she told me how some dudes with wigs and scarves robbed everybody around my way last night."

"For real. Did anyone get hurt?"

"I didn't ask, but she did start running her mouth about how they took two females' bags that were out there," stated China.

"Why she tell you that?"

"'Cause she was tryin' to insinuate that this might be one of them," China replied, pointing to her bag.

"Are you serious? What you say?"

"I basically told her it was impossible, cause I had my bag long before last night's incident," China explained, looking at Ra-Ra funny. "But we both remember when we got these bags. Do you think it's the same ones or a coincidence?"

"Don't know," Ra-Ra shrugged her shoulders. She then recalled thinking she'd seen Scrap place a wig on his head. As she was replaying last night in her mind, China shouted her name, snapping her out of deep thought.

"Ra-Ra!" shouted China a second time.

"Girl what!"

"I know you didn't just enter the twilight zone while you were driving!" China looked at her like she was crazy.

"China be serious."

"I'm serious as death, and that's where we gon' end up instead of my home if you don't straighten up."

"I'm so sorry. I didn't realize I'd done that," Ra-Ra apologized.

"Well get it together, and drive. I got a lot to live for, and if we weren't two blocks away, I'd tell you to pull over so I could drive."

Ra-Ra simply laughed her off and continued driving to her destination while making a mental note to question Worl about the incident.

Chapter 40

"Tell me what just happened didn't, and even if it did, y'all wasn't responsible!" Maurice barked once Blac and Reggie entered his home.

Moments before his two trustees showed up, Maurice had been flicking through his television channels when he was stopped by the alarm of breaking news. He was livid after hearing about the aftermath he knew they caused. The slaughtering of an innocent teenager was surely going to bring all sorts of heat. He told his two henchmen to explain everything that transpired and leave nothing out. Reggie spoke first, and then Blac finished. Once he analyzed the information that was told to him, he quickly began to strategically plan his next move. He still had confidence that his two trustees could handle the situation, but after the recent event, he decided to get more involved.

"Sometimes when dealing with the streets, we gon' encounter a lot of mishaps. But that move you two just did was real reckless, and nothing like that can ever happen again. Understood!" he scolded.

"Understood," they accepted.

"Good," Maurice replied. "Now I think I came up with a plan that'll help destroy them youngsters' fo'good", he assured his henchmen, who stood there listening to his careful methods for achieving an end.

Chapter 41

Bo, who was one of Maurice's workers, was in the comfort of his own apartment, conversing with his partner Reno about a very touchy subject. He couldn't overcome the humiliation of being stripped naked, and smacked on his rear end in front of everyone. He was already feeling horrid about another incident that revolved around Maurice placing the barrel of a gun in his mouth in front of a crowd of onlookers. So the recent incident caused him to be disgusted beyond his wildest imagination, and now he was tired of being the victim. As him and his partner shared a blunt, he was formulating a plan to get even. The only problem was that he needed to convince his right-hand man to roll with him. Normally, he wouldn't have a problem, but this plan involved the one person that he knew he feared, Maurice. He couldn't trust anyone else, so he had no choice but to try to get him on board, because without him, it was a dead issue.

"Know what, Reno?" said Bo, passing him the blunt.

"Wassup."

"I'm tired of niggas treatin me like I'm nothing!" he proclaimed. "I'm tired of being da victim! It seems as though every time a situation occurs, I'm da one taking da embarrassment. Niggas startin' to look at me sideways. All I hear is a bunch of lil slick shit coming out they mouth to me, like I'm a sucka or somthin!" he expressed

"Yeah, I've been jive noticing dat myself," Reno replied, passing the blunt back to Bo.

Bo took a quick pull, before he continued, "See, you even noticed it. That shit gotta cease, 'cause I ain't gon' like dat! Ya feel me?"

"Most definitely, plus dat shit jive got me lookin' crazy, 'cause I'm ya man."

"I know and wit' dat being said, I think it's time we turn this negative into a positive," Bo suggested.

"How so?" Reno inquired.

"By using da beef between them youngins and Maurice to our advantage."

"How do you plan on doin' dat?"

"I'm glad you asked," Bo stated, passing the blunt back to Reno, who was flashing a devilish grin. When Bo clarified his scheme, Reno was apprehensive, but he ended up agreeing.

"You gon' fuck around and get us both killed, but I'm all for it," he assured Bo. He put the blunt out, and gave his partner some dap to seal the deal.

"Trust me, just play ya part and everything gon' work out," Bo concluded.

Chapter 42

Still feeling the aftermath of her brother's death, Tyshelle was being questioned by the detectives that were handling his case. She was awkwardly rocking back and forth, while looking like a junkie in need of their next fix. She cried so much that her hair was in shambles, her eyes had swollen up, and her beautiful complexion seemed to have disappeared. At that moment, she could easily have been mistaken for psychotic. She was lost and emotionally detached from society because the one person that kept her striving to be a better individual was taken away. Everything she worked for, and every thought she considered revolved around making a better lifestyle for her little brother. Now that he was gone, she didn't know what direction she was heading. After a series of questions, the detectives figured they weren't getting the correct answers. Therefore, due to the current situation, they decided to wrap things up and wait for a better time.

"One final question," asked the detective. "Did your little brother own a cellphone?"

Teary eyed, Tyshelle shook her head no.

"Thank you Ms. Jackson, I know this is a difficult time for you and our family, but we do plan on keeping in touch," he stated, passing her his personal card. "And if you have any questions, please feel free to call at anytime," he sympathetically offered as him and his partner stood up to leave.

Tyshelle simply accepted the card, and walked them to the door.

Chapter 43

Ty and Ode were leaving out of City Place Mall, in Silver Spring, Maryland. They were coming from buying Ode another cellphone. Ty disliked driving in Montgomery County, but after the recent episode, the pair thought it would be safer to shop outside of D.C.

"It's been a wild day so far," spoke Ode as Ty drove out the parking garage.

"Yeah, I know what you mean, slim," replied Ty, turning onto Spring Place to head back towards DC.

As Ode was sending out text messages to give certain folks his new number, images of Lil Kent lying on the ground, begging him to, "please not let him die," replayed in his mind.

"Fuck!" Ode cursed, feeling somewhat responsible.

"You aight, slim," questioned Ty, as he unintentionally cruised through a red light, trying to check on Ode. A police officer, who was parked in the lot of 7-Eleven across from the Greyhound Bus terminal, observed the incident.

"Damn!" Ty exclaimed, noticing the police cruiser pulling out the parking lot.

"What?" Ode asked, noticing his partner throwing on his seat belt.

"Don't look back, but I think the Po-Pos might press us out," Ty answered irritated.

"Fo what? We ain't do shit."

"I might've ran a red light when you were over there cussing and shit,"Ty reorted.

"You might've or you did?" Ode queried, witnessing the patrol vehicles closing the distance fast."Fuck dat! You dirty?"

"You dirty?" asked Ode.

"Nigga, we beefin, and you askin' me if I'm dirty. I got da hamma under my seat," Ty informed, approaching the next intersection.

As they neared the light, two out of the three vehicles eased off to the left, and the third car made a right turn, leaving no congestion between the police cruiser and themselves. Once the officer closed the gap, he immediately clicked his sirens on.

"Shit," cursed Ty, seeing the red and blue cherrys flashing in his rearview mirror. "I knew it. Every time I come out here, these crackers stay fuckin' wit a nigga," he said, trying to figure out his next move.

"No sense in wrackin' ya brain over there. Under these conditions, it's only one thing to do," Ode expressed.

"And what's dat?"

"Bust his ass!" Ode stated in reference to ending the police.

As Ty was about to step on the gas, they entered a narrow two-way lane that hindered him from doing so. The two-way street led to Montgomery Community College and too many students were roaming around.

"Too many muthafuckas out here on this lil ass street," said Ty, passing by a storage building on his right hand side.

As they passed the storage place, another police cruiser appeared from the opposite direction, 'causing Ty to make a left turn directly in front of Montgomery College. Groups of students were congregated in various areas, including the street they turned on.

"Look at this shit! It must be lunch time or somethin'," said Ty, pulling over to the side, because of all the students roaming around.

"Fuck is you doin'? I know you ain't pullin' over!" Ode scolded.

"Chill out! I got this. They might don't press us out in front of all these people, and I'm legit," Ty replied, trying to shed some light on the situation.

Once he finally came to a halt, the officer that initially pulled him over, pulled up inches from his bumper. While the second squad car that he turned in front of swung around, then pulled closer to the front of Ty's vehicle, giving him little room to flee if he chose to.

"Driver cut the engine off, then place your car keys on the roof, and keep your hands where I can see them," instructed the officer through his cruiser's intercom.

"And you thought they wasn't gon' press us out, huh?" Ode asked, sarcastically. Meanwhile, more students gathered to see what was occurring as if a scene from a movie was being played.

"Better yet, on second thought," Ty uttered, putting the car in reverse, and revving the engine.

Once his car gained power, he released the brake, and rammed into the first patrol car, pushing it a few feet backwards. He quickly put the car in drive, and then sped around the second squad car onto the sidewalk. He was driving reckless and barely missed a group of students. The first officer's vehicle he smashed into immediately drew his service weapon and aimed for the tires, but quickly dismissed that idea to avoid injuring some of the large crowd of students standing around. He instantly hopped back in his damaged vehicle and proceeded with the chase. The second officer put his car in reverse and drove that way until he reached the crossroad. He quickly put his car in drive, and continued his pursuit, closely trailing the first patrol car. As he approached another

120

crossroad, Ty made a sharp right turn at the stop sign, and quickly smashed the gas pedal, rapidly gaining speed. Closing the distance to the next upcoming stop sign, a vehicle was slowly pulling into the street. Ty topped his speed and immediately began to honk his horn, trying to alert the driver of the slow moving vehicle that he wasn't slowing down. Once Ty got within a few feet, the driver of the vehicle backed out of the way in a nick of time. Avoiding a possible deadly collision, Ty saved himself some time, because the closest squad car had cautiously slowed down. Never letting up off the accelerator, Ty sped around the curvy, two-way street, zooming past the play ground on his left hand side. Rounding the curve at top speed, he came upon a much more occupied road. As he approached the traffic light, he anxiously waited for it to change. Piney Branch Road was so busy that it seemed almost impossible to get away from the pursuit of the officers that were closing in. With no time to spare and only seconds to make a pivotal decision, Ty did the unthinkable.

"Hold on!" shouted Ty as he floored the gas pedal.

Ode held on for dear life, because he knew it was a strong possibility that their lives were on the brink of extinction. The closer they got to the intersection, the tighter Ode's eyes became. Out of nowhere a dump truck emerged in the crossing lane of the intersection, and that's when Ty knew they wasn't going to make it through.

"Fuck it!" he shouted as he shot around the vehicle that was sitting at the light, then pressed the emergency brake, while making a sharp right turn, fishtailing into traffic. As he fishtailed into traffic, the entire driver's side smashed into the dump truck, damaging it completely. Ty managed to somehow keep control, and continued driving southbound on Piney Branch Road right into Washington, DC to escape the police. The officers immediately stopped their pursuit after witnessing what took place. At that very moment, they realized whoever was driving the car would do anything to get away, and they were not willing to do what it took to catch them.

"Scared ass nigga, open ya eyes!" joked Ty, realizing they'd gotten away.

"Fuck you mean scared!" Ode countered, glancing behind them feeling jittery. "I wasn't scared," Ode lied.

"Oh yeah! Then why you have ya eyes shut tight the whole time?" inquired Ty.

"I had my eyes closed 'cause I was meditating."

"Meditating my ass! You had images poppin' outta ya forehead from ya eyes being shut so tight," laughed Ty.

"Slim on some real shit, I was just prayin' 'cause when I saw dat big ass dump truck, I just knew it was over. I gotta give it to ya, though. You one drivin' muthafucka, 'cause I would've killed our asses in dat situation! No bullshit!"

"Bruh, dat was some wild shit?"

"No question," agreed Ode.

"I ain't neva drivin' my shit thru Mo.County again. Plus, this the second time I fucked a car up, bullshittin' wit' them hot, racist crackers!" Stated Ty with anger.

"I feel ya, slim. My bad for havin' you take me out there and for your new car getting fucked up in the process of bustin' them people's ass," Ode voiced with sincerity.

"It's all good. Shit ain't bout nothing. I'll buy another car tomorrow. We still here to talk about it, dat's all dat really matters."

"Guess you right. It ain't even night time yet, and a nigga already been thru too much. Ain't no tellin' what else may happen. I'm stayin' in da house for da rest of da evenin' so I can get my thoughts together."

"I'm a drop you off first, then I'm a go ditch my car somewhere. I'll call you after I handle dat to check on you," Ty explained.

"Dats a bet," Ode replied as thoughts of the day's events gave him a headache.

Chapter 44

Maurice received an urgent phone call shortly after his trustees left his home. The caller not wanting to meet in the neighborhood requested they meet up somewhere else. Since he hadn't had a bite to eat as of yet, Maurice decided to meet up at the Blue Duck Tavern on 24th Street, NW Washington. He and one of his cohorts arrived a bit early, so they decided to order while they waited. After surveying the menu, he settled on the Chesapeake Crab in lemony, caper-studded cakes and raw Path Valley brussel sprouts into a cider spiked salad, while his associate ordered a serving of light-seared scallops with stewed tomatoes and pickled okra.

"My man Reno!" Maurice uttered, taking a sip of his water.

"Wassup, Maurice" Reno replied, taking a seatand getting comfortable. Reno had a weary look on his face, and Maurice instantly picked-up on it. "So...what was so important that we had to meet away from the neighborhood?" Maurice asked. Before Reno answer, Maurice and his cohart's food suddenly arrived. The waitress placed their meal in front of them and left. "She's kinda fine," Reno complimented, then got back on task.

Since Maurice began to dig into his food, Reno figured he didn't want to talk in detail in front of company. Maurice caught on and casually instructed that his associate briefly remove himself, so the two could converse.

Once the gentleman excused himself, Reno began to speak. Not knowing what to expect, he nervously explained the details of Bo's plot. Maurice didn't seem surprise that one of his foot soldiers was plotting against him. His reaction to Reno's information was expressionless, and that alone had Reno skeptical. Waiting for a response, he gave Mariuce direct contact.

"Damn, this is one good crab salad!" Maurice stated, placing his utensils down, then wiping his hands and mouth with his napkin.

Reno wondered if Maurice heard anything he'd just explained to him, because that was most definitely not the response he expected. Yet, Reno kept his game face on even though he was nervous, feeling almost as if he were entering unknown territory.

"You and Bo been friends for how long?" questioned Maurice, staring directly into his eyes.
"Since third grade," Reno answered uneasy.
"So my question to you is…What's ya reason for tellin' me this, cause I can't see how somebody could be friends wit someone so long, and then basically throw'em head first into da Lion's Den," he asked sternly.
"Don't get me wrong, I love Bo like a brother, but I just love my life more," he naturally stated.

Maurice sat there staring at Reno for a few seconds, trying to analyze his story. He thought back on the fact that Bo had been acting distant since he'd been humiliated in front of everyone. He also knew that Bo understood the consequences of double crossing him.

If what Reno was stating was true, then the aftermath would be death. Yet if he were lying for whatever reason, then his fabrication would be the death of him. Either way, death was the outcome. For the moment, Maurice decided to put some eyes on Bo to see what kind of moves he made. Normally, he would've made the call and had him dealt with, but it was always three sides to a story, the one he was hearing, the one that was being accused, and the truth.

"Who else knows about this?" asked Maurice

"No one dat I know of," Reno replied.

"Good. Keep it that way. Is there anything else I need to know?" Maurice boldly inquired.

"Nah, that's it," Reno answered.

"Well I guess we're done here," Maurice stated, indicating that their brief conversation was done.

Reno simply excused himself from the table.

What the fuck did I just do? was his final thought heading out the door.

As Reno exited, Maurice signaled for his sidekick to join him back at the table.

Chapter 45

Once he dithched his vehicle, Ty ended up over Block's house after having him meet up with him. After a long morning, Ty was in need of some exotic weed to calm his nerves.

"You still got some more of dat good good we got from Big Lyn?" Ty asked, flopping down in Block's recliner seat.

"Yeah, I still got some short shit left," answered Block, readying himself to lift some weights. "Look in my bottom drawer," he directed commencing to do chest presses.

"You got some rollin' paper?" Ty inquired.

"Stop askin' so many damn questions, and grab da shit out da drawer! It's some Backwoods on my T.V stand too."

Ty got up to grab the weed, and when he opened the drawer, all he saw was a stack of porn D.V.D's. Ty pulled one out, and burst out in laughter.

"Fuck you laughin' at?" Block questioned, looking up from the weight bench. "Nigga, put my shit back, and get what I asked you to get!" Block barked, noticing what Ty was holding in his hand.

"Now I see why every time niggas go over a bitch's house to chill, you stay in, because you got in-house pussy," Ty joked.

"Yeah, whatever! Roll-up!" Block ordered, reaching over grabbing the Backwoods and tossing them to Ty. "Nosey-ass nigga!"

"How da fuck I'm nosey? You shouldn't have told me to go in your drawer if you didn't want me to see your stash."

"I ain't trippin'," stated Block, continuing to do more bench presses.

"You need to be. Dat's why you stayed in last night. Talkin' bout you stayin' in where it's safe. Nigga please! Dat's not even your MO. You stayed in 'cause you don't have no bitches... Oh my bad, I almost fo'got, you fuckin' every last broad on dem DVD's!" taunted Ty.

"Nigga stop playin' wit me before I beat ya lil ass in here!" Block aggressively barked.

"Beat my ass!" Ty reiterated, mocking him. "Slim, you ain't do enough beatin' last night," he joked while unraveling the Backwoods.

"Dats it you lil muth-a-fuc...!" Block bellowed, jumping up.

"Whoa... Whoa big fella! I'm just messin' with ya. You getting all rowdy and shit! Calm ya big black ass down before you pull a muscle "Ty quipped, extending his arms out, halting Block's approach. "I see you ain't gon' be satisfied until I step on your lil ass!" stated Block, as he went back to weight lifting.

"Yeah, yeah whatever," Ty said, brushing Block's comment off. "On some real shit, what's up wit dis beef? Shit startin' to get out of hand, especially since da incident dis morning with Lil Kent."

"Yeah dat was fucked up, 'cause I know how much Ode cared fo Shorty. But fo'real, fo'real I'm just relieved he didn't get hit," said Block conveyed.

"Yeah, dat definitely was too close to home," Ty replied, putting some fire to his neatly rolled Backwood.

As Ty was taking a few puffs, Block was giving some thought to the current situation. After mulling over it briefly, Block's mind was set on one thing, vengeance. Block knew his partners would share the same mindset. Once he recieved the tightly rolled Backwood, he inhaled deeply and then envisioned a tragic outcome as he blew out a cloud of smoke.

"Here take dis!" he insisted, passing the Backwood right back to Ty while shaking off his thought.

"What's wrong?" inquired Ty, passing the Backwood back.

"Ain't nuthin, I'm cool. You go ahead and smoke da rest of dat."

"You sure?" Ty questioned shockingly.

"Positive," assured Block.

"Fuck it, more fo' me," Ty nonchalantly said, continuing to cloud his natural mindset.

Block went back to weight lifting. *Are my thoughts premonitory?* he thought, realizing either way, he didn't endorse it. When Ty asked him what was wrong, he didn't want to speak his thought into existence. One thing he knew for sure was sooner than later their beef needed to be handled before someone in his immediate circle ended up catching a bullet. That's a thought he couldn't fathom, due to their brotherhood. Block thought about Big Lyn's forewarning about Maurice's long arms and Bg Wig status in the streets. Ode's near death experience was a wake up call for them all. The situation had become grave and the odds were stacked against them. As the underdogs in a game of street wars, there was only one way to come out on top and that's to be the aggressor.

"We need to have a meetin'," stated Block.

"Fo what?" questioned Ty, feeling the effects of the exotic marijuana.

"Cause dem bammas ain't playin' wit us, and we need to get on top of these niggas, so we can go back to getting' dis money!" Block explained.

"Make it happen. Plus, I don't think Scrap and Worl know what happened, yet unless Ode hipped 'em already."

"I'm 'bout to get on top of it," assured Block, knowing the situation had to be resolved ASAP.

Chapter 46

Back at the Fourth District Police Station, Detective Merrett and his partner were examining the one piece of evidence that they hoped would bring them one step closer to concluding the Kenneth "Lil Kent" Jackson, Jr. case. Cathy Lanier, the chief of police, was pressing the issue and expected immediate results. The detectives was tinkering with the cell phone that was discovered in the area of the crime scene. They were hoping to gain some form of helpful information from it, such as numbers, pictures, text messages, etc., but they had two problems on their hands. The lack of a passcode, and the shattered screen was not much aide in trying to identify its owner. They thought if they could somehow break the lock code that they could still possibly obtain some form of Intel from the phone. Detective Merrett had a strong feeling that the phone belonged to the individual who returned fire according to witnesses. He was their key and if they could find him, then they should be able to unlock the rest of the conundrum. He was there focal point and to find him, they had to either get into the phone, or put some eyes on Tyshelle. Being as though they weren't having luck with the phone their second option was their best choice.

"Detective Merrett!" said a female officer, interrupting the two detectives.

"Yes, Officer Windbush?" Detective Merrett replied.

"There's a detective that's been trying to reach you from the Fifth District Homicide Division. He claims to have found a burned up Caravan. It's possible that it's the same vehicle used in the Kenneth Jackson slaying. But there's more."

"Well, I'm listenin." Spit it out," he stated in a rushed manner.

"There was a Jane Doe also in the van," she added.

"Hmm, A Jane Doe," he reiterated. "That's interesting you have the Detective's phone extension?" he asked the female officer.

"Right here," she replied, handing him the piece of paper with the information.

Detective Merrett quickly took the piece of paper and dialed the number. He instantly got an answer, said a few words, and was transferred. Once the detective from the Fifth District got on the line, the two spoke briefly, before concluding their conversation.

"Bingo!" retorted Detective Merrett, hanging up. "Come on let's go," he instructed.

"Where to?" inquired the partner.

"We gotta go identify the van to see if there's a possible connection to the suspects who witnesses say drove away hastily from the crime scene shortly afyer the shooting," Detective Merrett explained as he gathered his things and headed out of the precinct with his partner in tow.

Chapter 47

Worl was at home spending time with his younger brother, which was something that he hadn't done as of late, due to the impulsive desires pertaining to his street dealings. As the two were watching the Teenage Mutant Ninja Turtles movie, their mother walked into the house with two grocery bags.

"Y'all go grab the rest of those groceries out the car," she commanded Worl and his eight-year-old brother. "I need to speak with you when you come back," she told Worl. They both did as they were told and when they came back in, she immediately began to speak her mind, "so what happen up there earlier today?" she questioned.

"What happened up where earlier?" Worl reiterated, not comprehending what she was asking.

"Boy don't play stupid! I'm talking about that little boy who was gunned down on the street you call yourself hanging on!"

"What! I didn't hear anything about dat!" he replied, shocked.

"I don't see how not, it's been all over the news," she added.

"Ma,' you serious!" he inquired.

"As a heart attack!"

"Did da news say who it was?"

"Some Jackson kid."

131

"Jackson... Jackson," he repeated to himself, trying to figure out whose last name that was.

"Kenneth Jackson! That's his full name, and it happened on 5th and Rittenhouse," she confirmed.

"5th and Rittenhouse... Kenneth Jackson," he thought for a few seconds. "I think dats Lil Kent's real name," he replied.

"And who's that?"

"Dats Ode's female friend's baby brother."

"Well if so, your friend Ode might be who the police are looking for 'cause on the news, they claim they want to question the boyfriend who fled from the scene right after the shooting."

"Damn! Dat's crazy! I need to find out what's goin on."

"Watch your mouth in my house," she demanded.

"I'm sorry Ma," he apologized, pulling out his cell phone to try to reach Ode. After a few rings, Worl was greeted with a recording.

Worl was finally able to reach Scrap, and the first thing Scrap asked when he answered was, had he heard about the situation. They both became concerned and decided to contact either Block or Ty. They agreed upon one calling the other, and then checking back in with an update. Worl immediately dialed Block's number and was a little relieved when he answered on the second ring.

"Slim, I was just about to call you. You must've read my mind," said Block upon answering.

"You heard from Ode?" questioned Worl.

"Dat's what I was callin' you fo. He's straight. Ty dropped em' off not too long ago. You need to come over so we can holla at you about what transpired, 'cause shit jive got outta hand," explained Block.

"Say no more, I'm on my way," Worl ended the call. When he turned to leave, his little brother was standing in his path.

"You ready to finish watching the movie?" asked his little brother.

132

Worl immediately cursed himself for having to cut their brother time short. Worl not wanting to disappoint or lie to his younger brother kneeled on one knee and genuinely explained his reason for him having to leave. He made up for it by promising to take him to the Monster Truck Show that was coming to town for the weekend. His brother was so excited that he jumped towards him giving him a big hug, and then ran off to go tell their mother. Worl was pleased with the fact that he didn't upset his brother. He smiled to himself and relished in the excitement his brother displayed, then quickly grabbed his keys and headed for the door.

Chapter 48

When Maurice left the restaurant after conversing with Reno, he stopped through the neighborhood to check on a few things. He wasn't staying long, due to an important business meeting he had within the next hour. He had a lot on his mind that was stemming from the episode as of late. His mind was full of thoughts associated with him getting shot in the foot, to one of his immediate circle leaking information, to his henchmen, slaughtering a thirteen-year-old, and the news about the one person that he'd decided to mold as his number one hood distributor plotting against him. He turned Bo into a hood superstar over night by giving him the work to spread to everybody in their hood, and all received their fair share. The game had levels, and Maurice was the (H.N.I.C) Head Nigga in Charge. Bo reported to Blac or Reggie and they reported to him. After all he'd done for him, he was a little stunned that Bo would overstep his boundaries, considering that Bo knew what he was capable of doing to him.

Maurice always said that betrayal was worst than slaughter, so if the allegations against Bo proved to have any merits, then he would be dealt with accordingly. The funny thing about it all was how they surfaced. He didn't have to cut any grass to find the two snakes in his yard, 'cause they were stupid enough to expose themselves by sticking their heads out to get them chopped off. Time was passing by just as fast as his thoughts were evolving. He glanced at his Romain Jerome time piece, realizing he had to get to his business meeting. He signaled for his cohort to come, so they could leave. As the two were getting into Maurice's Benz, they noticed a female flagging his car down.

"You want me to stop?" said his cohort.

"Nah you good, I'll catch her later. That ain't nobody but Kita gossiping ass," Maurice replied, as he zoomed in on who he was disregarding, so he wouldn't be late for his meeting.

Chapter 49

Bo and Reno hooked up shortly after Reno met up with Maurice. They had made plans to party later on and wanted to buy themselves some outfits to wear for the club. They were at Sports Zone, located on Georgia Avenue by Howard University in Northwest, D.C.

"Big Brian wassup?" said Bo to the manager of the store.

"What's good Youngsta? How can I help y'all today?" Big Brian replied.

"I need a size ten in these," stated Bo, holding up a pair of 990 New Balances.

"And grab me a pair of these in a size 9½," add Reno, showing a pair of Foam Posites.

Big Brian immediately directed for one of his assistants to get the shoes they requested.

"You heard from Tarji?" inquired Bo.

"Not lately, but you know he opened up a barbershop on K St. by the Rouge Lounge," explained Big Brian.

"Oh yeah! Dat's wassup! I might stop thru and holla at 'em."

"Well if you do, tell 'em I said bring me my money for them Go-Go CD's he got from me."

"Same 'ole Big Brian, still slangin' CD's, huh?"

"You know it. Got some now. Gotta keep our culture relevant," Big Brian stated as his worker came back with their shoes.

"Would you two care to try them on?" asked the female sales rep.

"No need," Bo replied.

"Will that be all?" asked the female rep.

"Yeah dat's it," Bo said, walking the shoes to the counter.

Bo couldn't help but admire her firm figure as he and Reno trailed behind. As they reached the counter, Bo looked towards the entrance, catching a glance of a somewhat familiar face slyly peeking through the window. He couldn't completely grasp who the individual was, due to him walking off.

Fuck, where I know that face from," Bo thought to himself as they were paying for their items.

Big Brian interrupted his thoughts when he asked him if he wanted to purchase any Go-Go CD's.

"Yeah you already know," stated Bo, answering Big Brian's request.

After the two headed out of the store, Bo peeped out of the entrance before stepping out.

"You alright?" questioned Reno, noticing his partner's guarded behavior.

"I'm cool," Bo replied, quickly heading to his car.

"We need to hurry-up and get on top of that other situation," conveyed Bo, as the two comrades climbed into his vehicle

"What's da rush?"

"Cause opportunity can't tell time, and we gon' end up losin' out if we don't hurry up'," explained Bo, starting his ear before pulling off.

Chapter 50

Big Lyn had been into real estate for some time, but he recently expanded into commercial and industrial properties. Him and his realtor were currently at a piece of property, which he was sure would elevate his flow of currency when he finalized the deal. All the pros of the property were like music to his ears, but Big Lyn wanted to know all the cons that came with it before making a final decision. As the realtor broke down the possible challenges that could arise, Big Lyn analyzed the good and the bad and was basically sold on the benefits. As he was reaching out to shake the realtors hand to confirm the deal, the door buzzard alerted the two.

"Expecting someone?" asked Big Lyn.

"Actually, I am. Hope you don't mind, but I had another potential buyer stop past. No need to worry cause you have the authoritative assertion on the property," assured the realtor, as he walked to the entrance to allow the other buyer in.

When he opened the door, the other buyer was instantly surprised upon witnessing the two males.

"Mr. Zeleski," greeted the client.

"Mr. Jefferson," replied the Real Estate Agent.

"Hope I'm not late," stated Mr. Jefferson.

"On time as usual, but as I previously stated, the other investor is the primary contender on this property," the agent said.

"And why is that?" questioned Mr. Jefferson in reference to not having the first say.

"No particular reason, only because his name came up on my contact list first, but I do believe it'll be beneficial if you two met," Mr. Zeleski proclaimed. "Mr. Jefferson, I would like for you to meet Mr. Grey," he expressed, formally introducing them.

When Mr. Jefferson finally looked up at the massive figure standing before him, his facial expression went from normal to displeased. The agent had a smile on his face as if he were introducing Rick Rivera to Chuck Myers before noticing both men eyeing one another vengefully. It was an awkward moment, and the agent felt foolish for trying to link up his top two investors for his benefit.

"I take it you two already know one another?" asked the agent.

"Yeah we've met before," replied Mr. Jefferson, not losing any eye contact. Mr. Jefferson was standing his ground even though Big Lyn was almost twice his size. Mr. Zeleski, aware of the tension between the two tried to think of a way to defuse the situation before it escalated.

"We are all businessmen here, so please let's conduct ourselves as such," he verbalized, stepping between the two.

"It's funny you mention that, when you're the reason we're standing here in the first place," scolded Mr. Jefferson, glancing towards Mr. Zeleski, who was looking startled. He made a mental note of his associate's actions and planned on addressing it soon.

"You're absolutely correct, and I sincerely apologize. I might've been wrong for introducing you two, but I can assure you that my intentions were logical. I have personally dealt with both of y'all on a high scale level, so I know what you two are capable of. I figured if I could somehow get the both of you to do some business together, the outcome could've been epic. Excuse my actions, but don't fault me for thinking I could make us a lot more money," explained Mr. Zeleski.

"It's kinda strange that you thought just because we had some similar ideas years ago, that this would be a good connection for me," stated Big Lyn. "But needless to say, your actions today caused you to lose a good client. Thank you for everything, but I'm going to decline on the proposal. Hopefully it'll work out between you two," he calmly said, shaking the agent's hand, tilting his hat towards Mr. Jefferson, and then casually headed for the exit. Big Lyn felt his old rival burning a hole through his back as if he were Cyclops from X-Men himself.

Disappointed from Big Lyn's statement, the agent turned towards Mr. Jefferson to inform him that the property was available, which cause Mr. Jefferson to stare at the forms.

"You hold on to that, then next time you'll think to call me first, 'cause I don't come second to no one, especially that dude," he boldly emphasized, disregarding the paperwork as he turned to leave.

"You sure?" the dissatisfied agent asked.

Mr. Jefferson never responded, he simply continued walking towards the exit with his associate trailing close behind.

What have I done, Mr. Zeleski thought, standing there dumbfounded as his two top investors walked out on him.

Chapter 51

Everybody met over Block's house with the exception of Ode whom was staying in the comforts of his home. He was out of harms way, so he called and told them that he would catch up with them some other time. He felt as though he had escaped two more deadly altercations and wasn't going to allow the streets to get a third attempt in the same day. The others continued to prudently outline a plan. Once Ty explained to them the earlier events, they were relieved to be concocting a plan for revenge, rather than a funeral. The stakes were definitely high, actually it was just as Big Lyn had warned them. Their adversaries proved to be heartless and out for blood. The incident was a wake-up call that consumed the life of someone that was dear to a member of their circle. They intended on handling the situation.

"No more hidin' out! No more slidin' thru our own neighborhood, and definitely no more being da prey, especially when we hunters ourselves!" Block coldly voiced.

"Yeah, I'm tryin' to work! Them clowns don't put no fear in my heart! Whatever happen is gon' happen!" Ty added, getting animated.

"Aight, everybody calm down, and lets not get beside ourselves. Big Lyn already hipped us to what we were up against, so we're gon' get at' em without movin' recklessly," declared Scrap.

141

"Since Ode on the feds radar… Let's just chill out for a few days. This will allow me to shoot up New York to holler at these folks," Worl suggested.

"Dat's a bet. Do what you gotta do, but when you get back it's on!" commanded Block, eager to retaliate for Ode's lost.

"Say no more," countered Worl.

"When you plan on goin' up top?" asked Ty.

"I was gon' go up there some time next week, but under da circumstances, I'm a hit baby girl in a lil bit, and have her set it up for tomorrow," answered Worl.

"Cool wit me. Handle ya business. In the meantime, I'll probably hook back up with shorty until you get back," stated Scrap.

"Do ya'll, Im'ma beat da block up, so I could make up for some of this bread a nigga been missin," assured Block.

"I'm wit you, besides I ain't drivin' anyway," added Ty.

"Whatever ya'll do, just be careful," said Worl.

"I'm good. I ain't duckin' nuthin'. Fuck dem niggas!" barked Block.

"I ain't just talkin' 'bout dem niggas! I'm talkin 'bout da Po-Po's, too, cause you know it's been hot as shit up there since Lil Kent got smashed," retorted Worl.

"You right. I got you, I'm a make sure I be on point," assured Block.

"You do dat, and hit me if any of ya'll need me," Scrap told them, grabbing his things to leave.

"One more thing," Worl said, as the others stopped to hear what he had to say. "I need dat bread dat we got up off dem clowns da other day to take wit me. Block can you go to that money?"

"Yep." he left for a second and came right back. "Here you go," stated Block, handing him a brown paper bag full of money.

"Bet. I'm gone. Im'ma get things situated for tomorrow," Worl relayed, dapping his men before heading for the door, followed by Scrap.

Chapter 52

The following evening Block and Ty hit the neighborhood like they said they would. For the most part, everything seemed normal. There were additional police cruisers roaming around. That was already expected, due to the prior incident. When they walked on Georgia Avenue, they ran into two other neighborhood associates. Silk and Devin were out there fooling around, and kicking the Bo-Bo as usual.

"Wassup with y'all?" inquired Silk.

"Where y'all been hidin' at da past few days?" added Devin still laughing at something Silk said before they walked up.

"Ain't nobody been hidin'... We just been chillin,'" Block replied somewhat defensive.

"My bad big boy, I didn't mean it like dat," replied Devin.

"Ay, some dudes came thru here yesterday evenin', and not too long ago lookin' fo'Ode," stated Silk.

"How they look?" questioned Ty.

"Some slim, brown skin nigga, 'bout ya height. He said his name was Bo. Plus he left a number," said Silk, reaching for the info.

"He left a number," he reiterated stunned.

"Let me see dat," Ty gruffed, snatching the number out of his hand. "You know who dis is right," said Ty, showing Block the number.

143

"Nah, who is it?" Block inquired.

"Dis dat clown from da other night, Ty said, reminding him.

"Which one?"

"Stripper man." Ty smiled.

"You serious! Oh Slim must want some work or somethin!" Block barked.

"I don't know, but why would he leave his number," Ty curiously replied curiously.

"How 'bout just find-out. Call dat nigga," Block demanded.

Ty pulled out his phone and dialed the number. After a few rings, a voice came through on the other end.

"Hello?"

"Can I speak to Bo."

"Dis him. Who dis?'

"I heard you been slidin' through, tryin' to holler at my man, so what's up!" Ty scolded.

"Oh yea! Look man, I come in piece. I'm not lookin' fo no trouble. I'm just tryin' to put a bug in his ear about somethin' dat could be beneficial to all of us," Bo replied.

"Aight look, just come back thru and talk to me face-to-face, and if I think you on any kind of bullshit, Im'ma fuck you around. Simple as dat!" Ty threaten.

"Understood. I'll be back thru there in about twenty minutes." Bo informed.

"I'll be here waitin' on you. Just hit dis phone when you get close," Ty instructed, ending the call.

"I don't trust da nigga, especially knowin' how we humiliated him," Block expressed.

"Me either, but we gon' find out what he's up to soon, 'cause he's on his way."

"Make sure you meet 'em on da side of the street just in case, and Im'ma stand in da cut," stated Block.

"Bet," confirmed Ty.

Twenty minutes came around fast. By the time they briefly conversed with Silk and Devin, Ty's phone was ringing.

"Dis slim right here," stated Ty, looking at his incoming call. "Its been twenty minutes already?" Ty asked, answering. "Wassup?"

"I'm on Georgia Avenue, passing the McDonalds," Bo informed him.

"Aight, bet. When you get to Sheridan Street make a right, and you'll see me standing by the alley," Ty directed.

"I'll be there in a minute."

"Bet," replied Ty, ending the call. "Come on, let's hurry up, cause he by da McDonalds," he quickly stated to Block, as the two trotted off.

Literally a minute later, Bo was turning the corner. Ty's phone rung again.

"Dat's you in the Lex?" Ty asked.

"Yeah dat's me," verified Bo.

"Who is that wit' you?"

"It's my man, he's cool."

"I'm not even sure if you cool, so find somewhere to park, and get out by ya'self," instructed Ty, ending the call.

"Aight," Bo agreed, finding a place to park and then exiting his ride.

Bo slowly walked over. As he got closer, he lifted up his shirt, then spun around to reveal that he was unarmed. Ty swiftly pulled his pistol, while standing at an angle so it wouldn't be visible.

"You good right there," Ty told Bo once he took a few steps into the alley. "So wassup?"

"I was hopin' to speak to Ode," said Bo.

"Slim, as of right now you ain't in no position to make any request. Whatever you gotta say to him, relay it to me, and I'll make sure he gets the message."

"Look! I know there's some tension between us, but I'm comin' wit a peace offering," Bo proposed.

"Peace offerin'!" barked Ty, brandishing his pistol. "What da fuck could you offer us! Nigga blood was shed, a life was lost! What da fuck can you offer!" he scolded venomously.

"Man, I swear I'm takin' a helluva chance by doin' dis, but dis is what it is," he stated, as he began explaining, hoping to convince them of the plan he'd concocted. Lurking from a distance was someone other than Block surveilling the meeting and taking pictures unbeknownst to the rest in attendance.

Chapter 53

J-Rock had been trailing Bo ever since Maurice put him on 'em. He managed to snap a couple of pictures of the two conversing, before forwarding them to Maurice. He immediately called J-Rock's phone after receiving the photos, and realized who Bo was talking too.

"Wassup, Boss Man?" J-Rock answered.

"How long ago you took these pics?" questioned Maurice.

"A few minutes ago. Why what's good?"

"That's the lil nigga who shot me in the foot!" he shouted. "Where they at now?"

"They still in the cut, hollerin' at each other," he assured him.

"Handle that lil nigga for me! Don't worry about Bo. I'll deal wit' 'him myself!" he ordered.

"Say no more. It's done," he guaranteed, ending their call.

J-Rock removed his pistol, switching the safety off, while he waited for Bo to leave. He noticed whoever was in Bo's vehicle was focused on them and not paying him any attention as well. *These youngin's too sweet,* he thought, knowing if given the order, he could've easily eliminated the person sitting in the car, Bo, and his primary target.

Moments later, Bo started walking back to his vehicle with a grin on his face.

"Laugh now, cry later, 'cause ya time is most definitely about to expire," stated J-Rockto himself, referring to Bo's lifeline.

Once Bo pulled-off, he quickly sprung into action. He checked his surroundings before stepping out. He had to move a certain way, cause he was aware that Ty had a pistol. J-Rock didn't look suspicious due to his attire. He was casually dressed, but quickly slipped-on a pair of track shoes that were on the passenger's floor. Ty was on his cellphone, unaware of the danger that was approaching. J-Rock was pretending he were on his own cellphone when Ty glanced at him, then discounted him, after he didn't pose as a threat. J-Rock seemed to be in an in depth conversion when he neared Ty.

Once he was within twenty feet of Ty, everything unfolded. J-Rock pulled his 40-caliber pistol on Ty quicker than a marksman. Before Ty realized what was taking place, a bullet ripped through his shoulder followed by others. The first one spun him around, and caught him off-guard, causing him to drop his phone. He immediately tried to reach for his pistol as he turned around, but the bullets manipulated his course of action and sent him crashing backwards. As J-Rock continued to walk him down, out of nowhere, shot's rung out from behind him. His attention quickly changed due to the hail of shots fired. J-Rock aimlessly returned fire, scooting behind a dumpster as he tried to see where the shots were coming from. He felt a burning sensation, but his adrenaline was pumping so much that he disregarded the feeling. He glanced at Ty, noticing he was squirming around on the ground, before suddenly, jumping up and firing shots in the direction from where the furtive shooter unleashed his assault.

J-Rock let off several rounds that caused his assailant to take cover while trying to finish his initial obligation. Once he made it to Ty, he lifted his head off the ground, placed the pistol to his temple, and squeezed the trigger three times. When Block emerged, he noticed J-

Rock holding a gun on the side of Ty's face. While Block charged towards him frantically shooting again, J-Rock released Ty, and then took-off running down the alley, in the opposite direction.

"Ty!" shouted Block, kneeling down to help his partner. Ty was in a state of shock after feeling the cold steel press against his head, but luckily for him his attacker ran out of bullets.

Chapter 54

Silk and Devin was standing in front of Food Barn when they heard multiple shots. A few bystanders either rushed off in their vehicle, or on foot.

"Dat shit sounded too close," said Silk.

"I know," agreed Devin, Where da fuck Block and Ty step-off to?" he asked when out of nowhere a vehicle shot across Georgia Avenue, almost colliding with another vehicle that was traveling southbound. The incident alone drew suspicion, and they took off running in that direction. They turned right on Sheridan Street, almost sprinting past the alley when Devin spotted two individuals.

"Right there!" Devin pointed towards the two.

"Oh shit, it's Ty!" stated Silk as they rushed over to help. When they approached Block and Ty, Block immediately tossed his keys to Silk and told him to quickly go grab his car and pull it around. Once Block told him where his vehicle was parked, Silk darted off to retrieve the car.

"Slim we gotta move fast, 'cause it's a matter of time before the police get here!" Devin suggested, just as Silk was turning into the alley. Block quickly picked Ty up, and carried him to the car.

"Go... Go!" Block bellowed after getting in the backseat.

"What da fuck happen?" questioned Silk as he pulled off. Block never responded, because he was focusing on Ty who kept going in and out of consciousness. "Stay wit me, soldier, we almost there!"

With the help of Devin, Block begun to peel Ty's top layers, exposing the one thing that possibly saved his life, other than his attacker running out of bullets. One of the bulletproof vests that Big Lyn had given them worked, yet a few bullets managed to still find three marks.

"Anyone of y'all dirty?" Block inquired, hoping the two didn't have any weapons or drugs on them.

"I'm clean," Devin replied.

"Me too!" added Silk, pulling into the hospital.

"Good, 'cause y'all gon' have to take 'em in and stay wit 'em while I go get rid of dis shit," Block instructed.

"Bet!" Silk replied, pulling up to the entrance before throwing the car in park and jumping out. The three swiftly rotated positions. Block pulled Ty out, handing him to Devin and Silk as he jumped into the driver's seat. "I'll be back as soon as I clean up," stated Block, speeding off as Devin and Silk rushed Ty into the hospital.

Chapter 55

Feeling the effects of his wounds, J-Rock was zipping through traffic, trying to make it to his destination. After phoning Maurice, and relaying to him what had happened, Maurice quickly informed him where to go. Lucky for him, Maurice had a doctor that he paid greatly for such situations. Even though he was feeling light headed and the pain had spread, he still managed to make it. Maurice was satisfied knowing that J-Rock made it safely. Once he hung up, Kita walked up on him with a huge smile on her face, "Ay, Maurice," she greeted, flirting a little bit.

"Wassup Kita?" he asked half-heartedly, disregarding her flirtatious approach.

"You pulled off so fast yesterday when I was tryin' to catch you. I wanted to talk to you about something," she said.

"About what?" He asked.

"About uhm…" she thought for a moment on how to relay her message. "This might sound kinda crazy, but when I ran into your niece yesterday, I noticed something that seemed sorta suspicious. I'm not quite sure, but I'm bringing it to your attention," she explained.

"What you tryin' to tell me, Kita?" he asked, tired of the beating around the bush.

"Some bags, two of the females were carrying the night of the robbery, I think your niece was carrying one of them bags when I bumped into her at the Beauty Supply Store yesterday."

"You think or you know," he questioned glaring at her.

"Not quite sure, but I spoke to the girl who the bag belonged to and she assured me that if it is her's, her father had her initials, N.P., engraved on the inside pocket," she explained.

"Maurice mulled over what she said while rubbing his chin. "So if what you saying is true, then how did she get it?"

"Exactly," Kita said.

"Aight, I'm gonna look into it, and make sure this stays between your friend, you, and me."

"I'll make sure," she guaranteed before walking off, putting an extra sway in her step.

Chapter 56

"This is real nice! I never knew this park was here," China blushed, taking in the view.

"This da National Arboretum. You never been here before, huh?" Asked Scrap, surprised.

"I must say this is the first time," she admitted. "But I do appreciate you showing me," she stated, kissing him on his cheek.

"Well I'm glad you appreciate it," he smiled.

"You probably bring all your female friends here, huh?"

"Believe it or not, you da first. I use to come here once a month by myself just so I could get some peace of mind and reflect on everything dat's goin on around me. Dis where I find peace at, right here, dis very place," he explained, looking into her eyes sincerely.

"That's sounds emancipating, so my question to you is, why me?"

"What do you mean?" he asked confused.

"Why make me the first female you ever brought here, especially since this your place of peace?" she inquired as she stared deeply into his eyes as if she were a mind reader.

Scrap kneeled down to feed the fishes, as he thought deeply about her question. After a moment of deliberating, he stood up and looked directly in her eyes. "Listen, I'm not goin' to stand here and feed you no

154

corny lines. What I do know is dat I like you, I like talkin' to you, I like ya smile, looks, ya smell and most of all how you carry ya'self. Dis might sound out da norm, but…" he hesitated, "I'm tryin' to further dis friendship."

"How you know you not going to change your mind tomorrow or the next day? I mean, we barely know one another."

"Dat's a chance I'm willing to take. I can only express how I feel. Unless I find out later dat you a serial killa or somethin'," he joked, causing her to laugh. "You not a serial killa are you?"

"Boy, no!" she blushed, tapping him on his shoulder.

"Nah, but on a serious note, dis a gamble I'm willing to bet my money on," he confided.

"I'm glad to know you feel that way. I must say, I sense a strong connection, plus I'm a risk taker myself," she concluded with a smile on her face.

At that very moment everything just seemed refined. The temperature, the wind, and trees all seemed to furnish a fresh breath of air. Scrap used the perfect opportunity to close in for a kiss, which she blissfully accepted. By the time the long passionate kiss had ended, it appeared as though the fishes and turtles were gathered together cheering them on.

"So I guess that means we both willin' to give dis relationship a chance and see where it take us, huh?"

"I guess so," she confirmed.

Scrap simply held her tight, while taking in her euphoric aroma, *damn she smell good*, he thought. Everything he had anticipated was coming to head. At that moment everything seemed complete, then that familiar ringtone he knew so well sounded.

"Excuse me fo' one second," he stated, answering his phone. "Ode, what's good?"

Hearing that name immediately caused her to reflect back to her uncle ordering his two henchmen to find someone. *Ode...Ode,* she thought, *I wonder if he's the same person.* She glanced at her bag, and remembered the conversation she had with Kita in the store. She was sure, it wasn't coincidental. *Maybe I should ask him, or should I warn him about his friend. Maybe he has nothing to do with it, but I can't say anything 'cause it's my uncle I'm warning him from, which could backfire. Either way I'm in a crossfire, between my uncle who I love dearly, and to the man I just committed to.* All sorts of emotions overcame her as she contemplated what to do. When she snapped out of her daze, she heard Scrap telling Ode that Worl had went to New York, but he was on his way.

"Not tryin' to be rude or anything but we have to go," he stated with a bit of anger in his tone, as they grabbed their things and left.

Chapter 57

Bo and Reno were just pulling up in their neighborhood. They found some place to park so they could finish eating their honey barbecue wings. As the two devoured their wings, the topic of Bo and Ty's conversation popped up.

"So, do you think we could trust dem nigga's?" Reno asked.

"Nah! Dem fools ain't to be trusted," replied Bo, enjoying every bite of his meal.

"So how you know this plan of yours is goin' to work?"

"I don't, but what I do know is everything in dis world revolves around money and who wouldn't wanna get a bank roll while eliminatin' their enemy at da same time?" Bo construed.

"I feel ya, but how you know they don't think you on some bullshit?"

"To be honest, dats a question I can't answer, but I did slip slim a photo of how Blac and Reggie look just to gain some kind of trust," Bo admitted.

"And you think that'll work?"

"Hope so. I know one time, you askin' a lot of damn questions!" he retorted, looking at Reno dubiously. "Wassup wit dat?"

"Nothin' up wit it, but if dem niggas don't get on board, then we hit!" Reno expressed.

Bo thought about what his partner was saying. He knew he was right, but it was too late to turn back. Two moves were already made, and he had to make his very next move his best, or they were sure to lose.

"I got us, trust me," Bo assured him, but was he actually convinced that he could pull it off? Bo could tell his man wasn't up for this discussion so he switched the subject. "Slim you crushed dem wings, you must've been hungry as shit," Bo teased.

"Me! You da one wit honey barbecue sauce all in ya mustache, like you were over there tryin to snort dat shit," countered Reno.

"You got jokes, huh?" Questioned Bo, wiping his hands and mouth.

"Nah, it really looks like you were hittin' a line of some red shit."

"Fuck outta here! You sicin' it now," Bo while smiling.

"Yeah OK, if you think so. All you had to do was look in da mirror before you wiped it off."

"I believe you fool. Grab dem cups out da glove box, it's time to pour up," Bo instructed grabbing the Rémy Martin 1738 from the backseat.

Reno retrieved the cups, passed one to Bo, and they both poured their own troubles. Soon as Reno place the cup to his lip, he noticed Maurice standing a short distance away engaging in a conversation with a female.

"There goes bossman over there," Reno pointed.

"Where at?" Asked Bo looking in the direction that Reno had pointed. "Oh yeah I see'em," he assured him. 'I should go holler at'em."

"Fo' what?" Replied Reno.

"Cause I'm trying to find out da next time he's going to be straight. What you worried about?" Bo question getting out, heading towards Maurice.

"Dis nigga trippin'," Reno uttered to himself hopping out trailing behind Bo.

Maurice had just finished talking to Kita when Bo walked up with Reno close behind.

"What's good Boss Man?" Greeted Bo.

"Same fight, different round," countered Maurice. "I see you got ya side kick with you."

"What's good?" Asked Reno feeling uneasy, but managing to keep his cool.

"Y'all tell me what's good. Yall sipping good. What yall celebratin'?"

"We not celebratin' nothin', dis just what we do," answered Bo, holding up the cup of Rémy.

"That's cool, I assumed you two were celebratin' since y'all seem to be in a good mood. Where you two comin' from anyway?" Maurice asked, already knowing the answer.

"Shid we just came from over these lil broads house," Bo responded.

Maurice simply looked at him, then at Reno, he knew Bo was lying.

"So what is it you wanted to holler at me about, I gotta be somewhere soon?" Maurice was ready to end the conversation, before he messed around and allowed his nefarious ways to take over.

"I wanted to know when da next time everything is goin to be straight again?"

"I'll make sure Blac or Reggie contact you soon as," Maurice replied, thinking he won't be alive long enough to receive the info.

"I appreciate it."

"No problem, you know I got you," said Maurice with a shiesty look on his face

"Bet," countered Bo turning to walk away.

As Reno turned to follow, he caught Maurice pointing towards his phone. Reno didn't understand what Maurice was trying to say until he got back into Bo's vehicle, and received a recreant text message, that immediately left an unsettling feeling in his gut.

Chapter 58

"I'm about to call my uncle, Papi to let him know we'll be pulling up soon," Ra-Ra conveyed.

"Dat's a bet," Worl replied as he continued to drive.

"Get in the right lane, so you can take the George Washington Bridge," Ra-Ra instructed right before her folks answered.

Merging into the far right lane, he couldn't help but respect how she switched from amicable to straight business. Her business savvy was one of many qualities he loved about her. She was speaking in Spanish, but he could still see she was handling her part.

"Everything is good, Papi," she assured him. "He said for us to park on 175th and Audubon Avenue once we get off the exit."

"Den what?" Asked Worl.

"Then call him and wait," she answered as they rode on the George Washington Bridge.

15 minutes later they were coming up to their exit. "That's the exit," she directed, as Worl veered towards the exit, going around the bend.

"Where to next?" He asked after coming up on the main road.

"Make a left here, then a right on 175th, and find someplace to park on the one-way street," she informed, dialing her folks number. She spoke in Spanish momentarily before informing Worl that her Uncle

161

would be pulling up in ten minutes, he'd been getting the two a hotel room as she requested. They had made plans to stay for the duration of the night, then hit the road bright and early.

"I see you on ya A-game, makin' sure everything is straight," he complimented, leaning over giving her a kiss.

"You know I got your back, plus that's my family he's going to make sure that I'm good, Papi," she stated with confidence.

The two sat and talked for a few minutes, when a dark green Laredo Grand Cherokee pulled up directly across from them.

"Is dat ya' folks?" Asked Worl

"Not sure, he's always driving something different," she replied just before her phone started ringing. "This is him calling me now." She talked for a few seconds, before telling Worl it was time to get out.

"Dat must be him, huh?"

"Yes, grab your things so we can go. He wants for you to get in the front with him," she relayed.

"Aight hold on so I can get this money out," he told her retrieving the money from under the backseat.

"Hola, tio!" Greeted Ra-Ra getting in her uncle's backseat.

"Qué pasa, sobrina? ¿Como esta mi hermana?" Her uncle greeted before inquiring about her mother.

"Ella muy bien," she replied, then politely introduced him to Worl. "Tio este es mi amigo, and Papi this is my Uncle Fito."

"Pleased to meet you. I've heard a lot about you," Fito said, extending his hand.

"Like wise," Worl replied, returning the handshake.

"You must be very special to my niece if she wants me to meet you. She's been raised with morals and principals, and she knows not to bring random people around," Fito stated, driving off.

"Yeah she's my heart," Worl smiled at her. "Also, I like to think of myself as a man with da same ethics."

The two continued conversing throughout the course of the ride, mainly grasping a feel for one another. Fito resembled the Latin pop singer, Romeo Santos. He didn't look anything like a drug dealer, more like a preppy collegian. Fito wore a brown Santiago Roberto Graham button down, blue Calvin Klein denim jeans, and a pair of leather, suede trim Cole Haan Oxfords Loafers. He sported no jewelry, but he did showcase a Brera Sottomario Diver Watch. Worl liked his inconspicuous manner, for the mere fact one could've strolled past him a million times and never figured him to be in the drug game.

Fito finally made it to his destination, a thirty floor high rise apartment building. He parked in a garage, then motioned for Worl and Ra-Ra to follow. He entered the opulent building, taking the elevator to the sixteenth floor. He'd choosen that floor because it gave him opportunity to make a hasty escape to his penthouse suite.

Once inside, Worl instantly admired the layout. Exquisite Gregory Bolden paintings hung on the walls. A Capelloti Luxury Italian living room set completed the beautiful look. The view was a designers dream.

"Dis a beautiful place you have here," Worl complimented.

"Thank you," Fito smiled, thinking, *if he only knew the apartment wasn't anything more than a stash house.*

As Worl mentally examined the glamorous settings, he couldn't help but to notice a laptop stationed on an end table displaying a four way split screen. It seemed to be monitoring two different entrances, an entire hallway, and what appeared to be the rooftop.

"Raquel, you or your guess care for anything to drink?" Asked Fito.

She looked towards Worl who nodded his approval, "Si, qué tienes?"

"Sobrina tu sabes que sólo bebo jugos naturales."

"Orange juice for both," she answered.

"Coming up," he replied. "La Beba!" he called out.

Emerging from the backroom was a georgeous Dominican female that looked as if she were created by Constantin Brancusi himself. Worl had to catch himself from gazing so hard.

"Por favor, tráeme dos vasos de jugo de naranja," Fito requested as La Beba strutted off to retrieve the drinks.

Fito and Ra-Ra briefly chatted and got caught up on one another. La Beba casually strolled back into the dining room placing the drinks on the coasters in front of them. Worl, once again, couldn't help but take one move quick glance at her natural beauty.

"Raquel, do you mind excusing us for a moment?" Fito asked, standing.

"Not at all tio," she assured him.

"Gracias," replied Fito, signaling for Worl to follow him to the Balcony.

When Worl stepped outside he was amazed by the view before him. The overlook of the Hudson River was emancipating. Worl immediately made a promise to himself that one day he'd have a similar view from his very own home.

"You like the view?" Asked Fito.

"No question! Dis da life right here. Hopefully someday I'll be able to have a view like dis," Worl stated.

"Places like this aren't hard to come by, but opportunities are. Time waits for no one, and I'm here today on behalf of my baby niece, to offer you a chance at a better life," he stated candidly.

"I accept, who wouldn't want a chance at a better life, but I must be honest wit' you about somethin'," Worl hinted.

"Speak your mind."

"I've never dealt wit' a large quantity before" Worl stated honestly.

"Don't worry yourself, it don't take two hours to watch sixty minutes," Fito smiled. "I got you," he assured him, patting him on his back. "You in good hands trust me. It'll all work itself out."

"I'm wit' you. Imma follow your lead," Worl said, shaking Fitos hand.

"Good," countered Fito, excusing himself and leaving Worl to enjoy the view. When he came back, he handed Worl a John Varvatos shopping bag. "That's half of kilo of El Chapo's finest. You can tap dance on that fifteen times and it'll still be a ten," he assured him.

"I told you, I only have twenty. That's not even half," Worl stated.

"And I told you that I got you. Keep your money. This one is on me, next one on you. I have a good feeling about giving you an opportunity. Any time my niece left from up here, where she needs for nothing, to go four hundred miles away just to be with some young man, I figure something has to be worth me taking a gamble. Either way I still win," Fito explicated nonchalantly.

Worl thought about what Fito stated about Ra-Ra leaving all this luxury behind just to be with him. That alone convinced him that she was down for him 110%. He felt compelled to express his concern for Ra-Ra father who had recently come into some health issues, "Hope I'm not being too personal, but I just wanted to ask about ya brother. How's he holdin' up?"

"Who, Raquel's father?" Replied Fito.

"Yeah, I heard he recently fell ill."

"Kno what, I'd rather leave that discussion between you two," he stated brushing off the question, then handing him the key card for the hotel. "How you plan on storaging the package for transportation?"

Worl elaborated on his so called stash spot.

"That's not gonna work. You have to stay on top of your A-game if you plan on succeeding in these streets: Mi Amigo. I wouldn't feel comfortable allowing you to drive on the road like that, especially with my niece riding with you. That vehicle you drove, are you making that one of your permanent highway cars?"

"Most likely," Worl replied.

"Hand me your key's and leave me five of that twenty you brought with you," he insisted, Worl casually complied with his demands. "I'm going to allow you to keep my Cherokee, so you two can make it back safely. When you return, your vehicle will have all the necessities that it will need for your travels. You always need a secure stash spot amigo, stay ahead, not on the same level of the game," Fito expressed.

"Thanks for everything," Worl stated shaking Fito's hand.

"Don't worry about it. Now let's be going, so you two can go get some rest."

They passed on a brief message to La Beba before leaving. When they got into Fito's jeep, he carefully showed Worl how to use the hidden compartment. He slid the package in before concealing it, then pulled off. Fito suggested that Ra-Ra drive after he got dropped off, since she was familiar with the area. Once they made it back to Worl's vehicle, he told Ra-Ra the location of the hotel, before saying his goodbyes.

"Be safe," he concluded, walking off.

Ten minutes later they arrived at the Corona Inn right across from the Bronx Zoo. Both were exhausted and just wanted to relax. When they entered the room, the both of them zoomed in on the heart shaped hot tub and bottle of champagne sticking halfway out of an ice bucket.

"Dat's wassup! Your uncle is full of surprises, huh," Worl stated, lifting the bottle out the bucket. "Dom P! I definitely can use a sip of this right about now," he said with a smile on his face.

"Me too, Papi," she countered wrapping her arms around his waist. "We can relax even more in this jaccuzi," she said turning on the water.

"Sho'nuff," he replied giving her a kiss. "Thanks for everything. Your uncle really looked out... Speakin' of your uncle, wassup wit' your pops. I asked about 'em, and he told me to discuss it with you," Worl explained.

Ra-Ra sat down on the bed gathering her thoughts, then quickly decided to be straight foreward. There wasn't any need to hide anything any further, "Mi padre murio hace cinco anos!"

"Speak English, I don't understand," he stated uneasy, sensing she was divagating,

"My father died five years ago," she admitted cutting her eyes then turning away.

A mixture of shock, anger and disappointment began to overtake Worl.

"Died five years ago?" He uttered in a grim tone. "So you been lying da whole time?"

"I was goin to tell you, I just didn't know when."

"I thought our relationship was built on trust. You got a nigga feeling like he can't trust you," he proclaimed.

"Don't say that! I promise you can trust me," she assured him.

"Yeah dat's what ya mouth says!"

"No, that what my heart says," she said, standing up, looking directly into his brown eyes. "Papi at the time it wasn't meant for you to know. I was protecting my family, but I don't have anything else to hide from you. Bringing you up here to meet my uncle was me introducing you into my world. I couldn't tell you I was moving back to New York so I could help my uncle with his drug business," she sincerely explained.

After he thought about her story, he wasn't mad anymore. He actually respected what she did to keep him out of their family business. He simply shook his head trying to suppress a smile closing the gap between them. "What's understood don't need to be explained, you done da right thing in dat situation," he said kissing her passionately on the lips.

When they pulled apart she had a kool-aid smile spread across her face. "The water is ready," she blushed, shutting the nozzle off.

He popped the cork off the champagne and took a sip, then handed Ra-Ra the bottle, "Go ahead and get in while I go feed da fishes," he said rubbing his stomach.

"Ughh, well you better not bring no fish food back to the sea," she, joked.

"Never dat," he replied placing his phone on the bed, then taking off majority of his clothes, heading to the bathroom.

Ra-Ra switched the jets on, peeled off her clothes, grabbed the bottle and got into the Jacuzzi. The bubbles from the champagne mixed with the vibrations from the jets seemed to relax her after the long ride.

"Baby girl turn my phone on and see if I have any messages," Worl requested from the bathroom.

Ra-Ra went to do what she'd been asked, and carefully placed his phone on the arm rest of a chair by the Jaccuzi. Almost immediately his phone began to show that he had multiple messages.

"Papi, your phone lighting up like crazy," she called to him.

"On my way," he said coming out the bathroom. "I see you started without me," he smiled.

After he read his first set of messages, he almost dropped his phone in the Jacuzzi. "What da fuck," he barked, dialing Ode's number. "Ode, what happened?"

Ode explained what had happened since he'd been gone. Worl couldn't believe what he was hearing. Ra-Ra noticed the change in his mood, but could sense from Worl's tone that it wasn't the right time for her to ask questions.

Worl talked for a few more minutes before assuring he'd be back in town first thing the next morning. With frustration plastered over his face, he peeled off his clothes, then stepped into the jaccuzi. Without a question ever slipping from her lips, Ra-Ra strattled Worl, hoping to help him get rid of some built up tension.

Chapter 59

"Dat was Worl, he said keep'em posted, and he'll be back first think in da mornin'," Ode told Scrap and Block. They were at the hospital, along with a few of Ty's family members. Everyone sat worried awaiting the doctor to return with news. Ty was rushed into surgery after being shot three times. One of the bullets went clean through. One of the others was lodged in his shoulder and the third bullet had settled somewhere near his spine.

The doctor emerged from the back causing everyone to approach apprehensively.

"May I speak with you alone?" The doctor asked, Ty's mother.

The two stepped away from everyone as the doctor updated her on Ty's condition. When the doctor had left, Mrs. Dixon walked back to the group, teary eyed. Everyone stood around to hear the outcome.

"The doctors couldn't remove the bullet near his spine. They said it was too risky. He needs another surgery, and they hope to remove it then. We just have to hope the bullet stays put for now, until the procedure," she explained wiping the tears from her eyes. "Which should be in the next few days."

"Can we see 'em?" Ode asked.

"The doctor said he needs his rest, the anesthesia hasn't worn off yet," Mrs. Dixon explained.

"I hope he'll be okay," Ode sympathized.

"Do you? Then why put yourselves in these situations?" She'd caught Ode off guard.

Ode broke eye contact, looking towards the floor.

"Ode!" Mrs. Dixon exclaimed.

"Ma'am."

"Do you hear me talking to you?" She questioned, cupping his chin in her hand.

"Yes ma'am. Truthfully I don't think anyone wants to be in these situations, but the environment we grew up in basically placed us here," he answered.

"Excuses are the most crippling disease. You have to expand your mind. There are so many others that came from the same environment and made something of themselves," she said staring directly into his eyes. If Tyrone makes it through this, who's to say if this happens again that the outcome won't be gravely. I'm no preacher but I would appreciate if you three would give some thought to what I'm saying. No mother wants to get that call saying their child has been hurt. Do you understand?"

"Yes ma'am," the three of them spoke in unison.

"Good," Mrs. Dixon said giving each of them a hug and a kiss on the cheek. "Now y'all go 'head home, get some rest. I know you can use it. I'll keep you all informed if anything changes."

As the trio started to leave, Mrs. Dixon spoke again, "One last thing," they stopped to hear her out. "Live life to see another day, not to take one away." What she didn't know though, was the three of them were too deep into the situation, and there wasn't anything anyone could say to change that.

Chapter 60

Maurice finally rounded up his crew. The meeting was held at a place only Blac and Reggie knew about. It was a lowkey detached two level single family home. The rear entrance led to an alley only that house was connected to. It was the perfect place to solidify his alliance.

Besides Blac and Reggie, there were a few selected men that he dealt with for different purposes. For instance, Marcell was a street dude who had paid his own way through school. He became a successful Electrician and Maurice's go-to when it came time to make an enemy talk.

Black Moe was a street pharmaceuticals, and hands down had 14th street on lock.

Ka'von "Dizzle" Copeland was the one individual that actually took his street dealings to another level. He'd mastered the stock market, specifically trading foreign currencies, he could take a portion of Maurice's money and quadruple it.

Young Scooter, was the youngest in the room, and also the gun connect. No one, not even Maurice knew how he managed to get his hands on almost any kind of weapon.

Denzel 'Toby" McKinnie also made his way through school, finishing with a degree in business management. Maurice invested in an up and coming club about five years ago, that wasn't doing so well. Toby convinced Maurice to hire him and with Toby's ideas and a few upgrades, the club slowly but surely became the spot to be. Maurice's business partner, Mark Barnes couldn't stop thanking him for making Toby manager.

Finally, there was Nick. Toby introduced Maurice to Nick, and Nick was responsible for referring Maurice to his latest connect. After quite some time of getting to know Nick, Maurice brought him into the circle. Their union proved to have been beneficial for both individuals. For Maurice, when his connect got knocked, and everything seemed to be at a stand still, Nick came through. When Maurice casually walked into the room, followed by his dog, all the idle talking seemed to come to a complete halt.

"How y'all gentlemen doin'? Glad to see everybody doin well for the moment," he stated.

Everyone greeted him back, except for Toby, speaking on Maurice's company, "Damn boss man! Why you bring her with you?"

"Nigga, who is you to be questionin' me about my bitch!" Maurice barked as Toby received cold stares, not only from Maurice but everyone else as well.

"My bad, I didn't mean it like that," Toby apologized.

"Then why you open your mouth about it! She's with me and that's all that matters," he hissed walking over to the mini bar and pouring himself a glass. "One thing I can say about Remi, she never once crossed me," he said, holding his glass in the air then taking a drink. "There's an issue that's been brought to my attention, that needs to be addressed," he stated placing the glass in the center of the table. "As we all know, I recently got myself into a minor situation that's just about done and over with, so that's not my concern. My concern is to make sure that I keep my surroundings strong," he said, stopping behind Toby.

"I haven't been anything but fair to and straight up with y'all, so I expect the same in return," he proclaimed scanning the room. He moved from behind Toby and continued walking through the room, speaking to his associates about his definition of loyalty. While Maurice spoke, Nick quickly sent out a text, telling someone to meet up with him in the hour at the Rouge Lounge. Nick was able to go unnoticed as everyone focused on the guest who strolled behind Maurice.

"Now, that glass of Rémy symbolizes us as a whole, being able to get this money without worryin' about treason between any of us," he said pointing to the glass. "Now this is the time to come clean about everything. Before takin' a sip, I want you to tell me if there's anything that I don't know, that I should. If you don't come clean and I find out, then the consequence is Death!"

"Marcell you start, then pass the glass around."

"I don't have anything to say. I've never hid nothin' from you," Marcell assured him taking a sip and passing the glass to Young Scooter.

Young Scooter thought briefly before taking a sip, "I only do wrong to my enemies," he commented passing the glass over to Dizzle.

"Unless you call receiving money from the rich to get richer doin' something wrong, I'm in the clear," he said taking a sip and handing the glass to Black Moe. He immediately took a sip along with Blac and Reggie, who really didn't have to prove their loyalty.

Reggie passed the almost empty glass to Toby who with his cocky attitude, looked at it with a huge grin and said, "Shit I been A-1 since Day 1," he happily stated tilting the glass to his lips.

"Hold up for a sec!" Maurice said, stopping Toby right as the glass touched his lips.

"What's the problem?" Asked Toby.

"It's one minor thing," hissed Maurice walking back behind Toby. "You being apart of this circle led me to take your judgment for face value," explained Maurice.

"What judgment?" asked Toby.

"Nigga you brought a snake into the house," he stated with a devilish grin.

"What you mean, I don't know what you talkin' bout," he said confused. The nervousness in his voice caused Maurice's guest to react in an aggressive manner.

"What's up with your dog?" He questioned, jittery.

"Who, my bitch Remi? Unlike others, she's never let me down," he declared, pointing his finger towards Toby. "Watch'em," he instructed Remi, who was now showing all her teeth.

"Maurice please don't!" He begged, throwing his hands up.

"Drink!" Maurice signaled for his dog to attack.

Remi immediately leaped towards Toby's neck, like a lion taking down his prey. Toby tried to shield himself but it was no use, the militant Pitbull forcefully connected with his mark. Everyone jumped out the way, watching as the vicious dog brutally mauled his target to death. The gruesome scene only lasted a mere two and half minutes, but left the occupants in the room appalled, with the exception of Blac and Reggie. Dizzle and Nick seemed to be displeased by the ordeal, mainly because they dealt with Toby a little more.

"Who the fuck is the snake that made you kill'em?" Dizzle blurted out, looking back and forth between Maurice and his dog.

Soon as Maurice uttered something in a foreign language, Remi immediately halted her onslaught. The group stood stunned at the dog's obedience.

"If you listen, Im'ma tell you. Sit down," he insisted, disregarding the dead body lying only a few feet away.

"I think I'll stand," countered Dizzle.

"I'm not goin' to ask you again," threatened Maurice. "Have a seat! The rest of ya'll too," he demanded, before telling Blac to hand him his cellphone.

Dizzle took a seat along with the rest of them as Maurice dialed the code for Blac's voicemail, pressed speaker and placed the phone in the center of the table so that everyone could hear.

"I can't talk long, but your lil' man came through Riggs Park and layed down some of his workers, not to mention put one in the hospital from pistol whippin' and stomping him out. That nigga on some other shit, so let them youngins know to stay from up there temporarily, or at least don't be out in the open," spoke the voice on the voicemail.

"Who that 'pose to be?" Asked Dizzle, not able to decipher the voice.

A split second later Nick rushingly pushed his chair out and jumped out the closest window, making an attempt to get away.

"I guess that answers your question, huh," Maurice said to Dizzle, before ordering his two henchman to go after him. The two didn't have to do much, when they made it to the ground level, Nick was squirming on the ground wincing in pain.

"There go that fool right there!" Pointed Reggie, rushing towards him.

"Get ya bitch ass up," blurted Blac, snatching him off the ground.

Nick tried to put up a fight, but the two put down a slight beating that quickly calmed him down. When they finally dragged him back into the house, Dizzle looked towards him as they placed him into a chair.

"Hold ya dog," Dizzle said to Maurice, springing out of his chair, grabbing the liquor glass off the table and busting Nick upside his head with it. "Bitch nigga I trusted you! Had you around my family and the entire time you was a fuckin perp," he snapped in disbelief. To say that he was pissed off was an understatement. He felt as if his family's lives had been jeopardized by having him around.

"Got damn Dizzle you done knocked the nigga out!" hissed Reggie.

"Fuck that clown," countered Dizzle, hog spittin on his face.

"How we 'pose to question a nigga that's knocked out cold?" Reggie replied.

"Don't trip! Grab that bamma's phone. He was textin' somebody earlier when I was talkin'," ordered Maurice. Blac went through his pockets, retrieving his phone and handed it over to Maurice.

Maurice scanned through his contacts, call logs and messages. He noticed a recent text as, he suspected, that read for him to meet up with someone at the Rouge lounge within the hour. Checking his watch, he realized time was wasting and decided to go to the Rouge Lounge to try and figure out who Nick was texting. Nick wasn't no fool, he only had a few numbers programmed into his phone, and the majority of those were women.

"Blac and Reggie, take Nick to the basement and tie 'em up. Scooter I need you to stay and watch that fool until we get back. Marcell and Black Moe, you two to dispose of Toby's body. Dizzle grab the bleach out the hallway closet and clean this mess up," Maurice commanded and everyone went their separate ways.

Once Remi had been dropped off at Maurice's house they began to make their way over to the Rouge Lounge.

Chapter 61

Just like previous nights a couple of Maurice's people had gathered in the schoolyard. Maurice made a pit stop through his neighborhood telling his workers to be careful just in case the same youngins that came through and robbed everyone slid through again. Lil' Skip assured him that they'd be on point in case that issue arose. Pleased with what he heard, Maurice left to head to the Lounge.

For the most part, it was a chill night. Not too much traffic, just people hanging out, joking, laughing and reminiscing. Skip and Fatz had the stage as if they were performing a comedy show. Their jokes rolled off their tongues as if they were speaking Spanish. One of the onlookers noticed a yellow cab double parked a little longer than normal with his inside light on.

"Is it me or has anybody else noticed how long dat cab been sittin' over there?"

"He probably waitin' for someone to come out," claimed Fatz.

"Dat bamma been sitting there fo' bout ten minutes," he assured him.

"Man dat clown got da car light on wit' his head down like he readin' something. Fuck dat nigga!" Barked Skip, turning his attention back towards the group of people that were standing around.

"I'm about to tell'em he has to move just to make sure it ain't da popo," said the concerned onlooker.

"Do you!" Skip replied going back to clowning around.

The young teenager stood up then walked towards the parked cab, "ay cab driver," he shouted walking closer, "ay cab driver! You lost or somethin'! You need to move this hot azz ca…" he tried to say, but was interrupted by a muscular arm flying out the window. The guy inside the cab grabbed the teenager then placed what looked like a horse gun to the side of his face.

"Now!" roared the cab driver pulling the trigger. The trunk of the cab flew open, a masked gunman popped out, aimed towards the group in the schoolyard and opened fire.

The first shot startled the group, but the raid of bullets that followed, began knocking down members left and right.

Fatz tried to retaliate, but was quickly met by a trail of bullets. Skip, on the other hand, managed to return fire but not much good came from it. When the masked gunman's Mac 90 finished spitting, he rushingly jumped from the trunk into the passenger side. The driver sped off, leaving a bloody massage behind.

Chapter 62

Maurice and his two trustees finally arrived at the Rouge Lounge. Reggie quickly parked in the lot across from the club before heading towards the entrance. They entered, then walking up a flight of stairs before reaching the actual lounging area. The Rouge Lounge was more like a strip club. It stood on 5th and K Street in the down town area. As they reached the top of the steps, the bouncer stood waiting to pat search them. Blac slipped him three one hundred dollar bills and he simply stepped to the side. When they entered, the first thing they noticed was a tall thick red bone on the center stage, dancing to one of Tupac's classics, "*How Do You Want It.*" Maurice did a brief scan through, then directed Reggie to grab a couple of bottles while he and Blac found someplace to sit. He saw that the seats and both pool tables in the rear were occupied. Then he glanced at the single stage next to the restrooms, and still didn't see any available seats. He was about to sit at the bar, until he noticed a familiar face at the far end of the club. He made a quick pit stop to tip a dancer before strolling over, in hopes of clearing the air on some past issues.

The entire time Maurice's old nemesis sat in the corner watching his every move. He was locked in from the time they walked in. He wondered if it was a coincidence or intentional that Nick hadn't shown up. The minute he saw Maurice and his two cohorts he dialed Nick's cellphone number to tell him not to show, but didn't get an answer.

"Do you mind if I sit?" Asked Maurice.

"I don't see why not," Big Lyn replied.

Maurice told Blac that he wanted a one on one with Big Lyn and Blac respectfully sat one table away to allow the two their privacy.

"So what you doin' here all by yourself?" Maurice questioned.

"Who said I was here all by myself," countered Big Lyn. "Everything isn't always what it appears to be, not even us two sitting here pretending to be friendly. Especially since you made it perfectly clear where we stood."

"True enough, but you have to admit, it was kinda awkward to realize we were dealing with the same real estate agent," he said as Reggie walked up handing him a bottle of Clicquot, leaving them to talk amongst themselves.

"It wasn't awkward for me. You must've forgot I tried to go into business with you. You turned down a once in a lifetime offer that would've put us both in a position to make millions!" Big Lyn expressed.

"I'm doin' quite well for myself now, plus I'm already a boss, so there's no need to be a partner in anything!"

"My bad bossman," Big Lyn smiled, taking a sip of his drink. "I thought the reason you shot me down was because you felt some resentment from our past encounters."

Maurice smiled before answering, "Oh you mean back in middle school when you used to used your size to scare off us little guys," he laughed. "You were actually chargin' the kids fifty cents to cross the bridge to get to school."

The dancer that was on the center stage walked up, thanking him for the tip. Maurice introduced himself, while complimenting her on her beauty and a few other features he admired. After a brief talk and a few blushes she offered him her number. He mistakenly grabbed Nick's phone instead of his but quickly tucked it away before grabbing his own. He concluded their conversation with another tip before sending her on her way, admiring how her azz shook as if it were an earthquake.

"You a tricksta, huh?" Big Lyn asked with a hint of sarcasm.

"They say if you got it, buy it or if you can't afford it, ignore it. I don't do no window shoppin'," he hissed pulling Nick's phone back out his pocket and pressed send on the missed call he noticed. Maurice watchied Big Lyn's phone ring, *don't tell me this who the nigga been talking to the whole time*, he thought.

"Excuse me for one second," Big Lyn stated, getting up.

As Big Lyn distanced himself from the table, Maurice hung up the phone, denying him the chance to answer.

Maurice continued to watch from a distance as Big Lyn gave the impression that someone had hung up on him. Nick's phone rang in his hand and when he didn't answer, a text followed shortly after, stating to not come inside.

Big Lyn was making his way back to the table as Maurice closed out the message. "So where were we?" Big Lyn asked sitting back down.

"It wasn't important, but um…" he paused for a split second, "you mind if I ask you somethin'?"

"Not at all," assured Big Lyn taking another sip of his drink.

"How do two people on our level manage to be close in some ways, but stay so far apart in others?" Questioned Maurice.

"Probably cause I chose to take another route and get out, while you chose to stay in the game."

"So you're tellin' me that you're done with the game?" He laughed. "I find that hard to believe."

"I've always been a firm believer in never goin' past the mark I aimed for," Big Lyn answered.

"They also say preeminence and over confidence can push someone past there ambition," countered Maurice.

"One thing about me is I'll never let my success go to my head. There's no substitute for careful planning. If I reach my goal, there's no reason to further my chances of losin' everything I grinded for," he proclaimed, looking directly into Maurice's eyes.

"If that's the case, why does it seem as though I'm always a part of your plans," expressed Maurice.

"How are you a part of my plans," Big Lyn frowned.

He stared at Big Lyn attentively, choosing his words carefully before speaking again, "It's been brought to my attention that one of my associates has been playin' both sides of the field. Would you happen to know anything about that?"

Big Lyn threw his hands up, baffled at the question. "I mean, why would I?" He answered trying not to sound offended.

"You know what," he rubbed his chin, "that's why us goin' into business together wouldn't have worked out," he calmly stated.

"And why is that?"

"Cause my last memories of you reflected nothin' pleasant, and ever since then I've never trusted you," he retorted. "Enjoy the rest of your night."

Maurice left his half full bottle of champagne on the table, while signaling to his two trustees that it was time to leave. As Maurice and his men exited, Big Lyn quickly pulled out his cellphone so he could try to reach Nick one more time. He had a feeling that Maurice knew of their dealings. He wanted to warn Nick, tell him to fall back from Maurice before something happened to him. Pressing send to dial Nick's number, he noticed the table was vibrating. He moved the champagne bottle to the side and seen a cellphone in plain view. Once he grabbed the phone and turned it over, his eyes lit up when he surveyed his own number clear as day.

Chapter 63

Detective Merrett and his partner received a call for a shooting in Riggs Park around twelve thirty in the morning. When they arrived, there were people scattered all around taking in the blood ridden scene. Some were in tears, some were frantic, others were arguing, and roaming about.

"What do we have?" Asked Detective Merrett, flashing his badge to the leading officer on the scene.

"It's a mess," assured the officer, walking over to the dead body in the street, slightly lifting the white sheet. "Twenty-year-old, identified as Calvin Stewart."

Detective Merrett and his partner shook their heads at the sight of the victim with half of his head missing.

"Had to be a high caliber gun to do this much damage with a single shot," said the leading officer.

"I agree," replied the detective.

"Now, over there in the schoolyard," he pointed, while heading in that direction, "we have three more deceased. Two males and one female, and three more rushed to the hospital with gunshot wounds."

"Were any of these victims identified, and did anyone see the shooter?" Asked Detective Merrett.

"Not yet, but one of the gunshot victims that was rushed to the hospital claimed the attackers shot from a yellow cab," he explained. "Oh, one more thing… there was a clipboard found near the first victim in the street."

"Where is it now?" Questioned Detective Merrett.

"I personally retrieved it, it's in an evidence bag in the backseat of my cruiser," he confirmed.

"Send it to the lab ASAP and have it dusted for fingerprints. When the results come back make sure I'm the first to know," ordered the detective.

"Detective, Detective!" called out a female officer.

"How may I help you officer?"

"I just heard over the radio, that a stolen cab was abandoned, around Chillum Road," she informed.

"I bet you that's our vehicle! Tell the officers don't touch anything until we get there," instructed the detective.

"I'm on it," assured the female officer.

"Try to identify the other victims, locate thier families, then have this area cleared out," he ordered.

"I'm on it," said the leading officer immediately doing what was requested of him.

Chapter 64

Maurice and his two men finally made it back to the house they had Nick bound at. Now that Maurice knew that Nick and Big Lyn were dealing with each other, he was determined to find out what was up. Different images ran through his mind of what it could've been, but it was only one way to find out.

"Y'all left a nigga in here long as shit! I hope it was worth it. What y'all find out?" Asked Young Scooter.

"I found out more than enough, but now I need to know why," stated Maurice, heading down to the basement after pouring himself a glass from the mini bar. Once he reached the basement, he saw that Nick was passed out in the chair. He walked over to him and poured the alcohol from his glass over his open wound.

"Agghhh!" Yelled Nick.

"Get ya sucka azz up!" Barked Maurice.

"Shit! Fuck! Man this shit burning like..." he snapped, but was interrupted by the back of Maurice's hand smacking him across the face.

"I'm not tryin' to hear that cry baby shit," he scolded and grabbed another chair, sitting it directly in front of him. "From here on out I'm not tryin' to hear ya mouth, unless I ask you somethin'!"

"Man it's not what you thin…" was all he managed to say before Maurice began to punch and kick him, knocking him to the floor.

"I thought I just told your azz not to speak unless I ask you somethin'," Maurice barked angrily as he stood over him.

Nick laid there defenselessly, coughing up blood. He knew it was only a matter of time before they killed him. He had no choice but to try his best to keep his mouth closed, even though the pain he was feeling made him want to holla badly.

"Pick that clown up," ordered Maurice. Blac and Reggie both helped to lift him off the floor, sitting him back upright in the chair.

Maurice's phone began to sound off and he noticed it was Skip from the neighborhood.

"It better be a damn good reason you callin' me in the middle of the night!" Maurice answered.

After a few minutes of listening to the person on the other end he hung up the phone with an expressionless face.

"Slim, wassup?" Asked Blac.

"Them youngins came through a little while after we left and shot the whole jo'nt up," he explained.

"Damn! Did anybody get hit?"

"They smashed Lil' Kenny, Fatz, Stu' and Kita," he said rubbing his temple, "plus put some others in da hospital! Not sure if they in critical or not."

"Da hood goin' to be hot as shit," said Reggie.

"Yeah I'm hip," replied Maurice, standing back up, "we need to head over there."

"What we goin do with this nigga?" Asked Reggie.

"Leave his azz in here until later, he can't go nowhere," he said grabbing Nick by his face. "When we get back, if you don't tell us what we want to know, we gone start choppin' ya sucka azz up until we do, you hear me? Put his azz in da corner!" Blac and Reggie forcefully dragged Nick into the corner before they headed up the stairs, and out the house.

Chapter 65

Block and Ode's adrenaline was still pumping after their recent episode. The two rushed into Block's basement. Ode was boasting about their encounter. "Fuck dem nigga's thought we weren't bout dat lyfe! We put dat work in too," he stated, removing his coveralls.

Block was in deep thought, and Ode picked up on it being sure to ask what was on his mind.

"I think I messed up, Slim," he proclaimed.

"How you do dat?" Asked Ode.

"Dat damn clipboard! Dat muthafucka flew out da window when I pulled off," he explained.

"And?" Questioned Ode, free of worry, "we had gloves on da whole time."

"Yeah I know, but I brought dat board wit me, cause I planned on burning it up with da car."

"Why would you bring dat board anyway?"

"Cause I was fakin' like I was readin' somethin'."

"You sure it flew out da window?"

"It had to, cause I don't remember seein' it when I got out."

"Slim, I hope you wrong but you know what..." he paused for a moment, "you've never been locked up nigga, so basically they don't have no fingerprints in the system fo' you," Ode said trying to defuse the situation.

As Block sat and thought about it, he felt a little relieved by what his man said, "relax ya'self big boy, you straight, plus we might need to keep this between us, cause this ain't no bullshit matter," Ode suggested.

"Yeah you might be right," he agreed.

"Once we get rid of the rest of this stuff, we all da way in the clear," stated Ode, patting Block on his shoulder as to say that everything going to be alright.

Chapter 66

Back at the police station, Detective Merrett and his partner were reviewing the evidence they had gathered from the crime scene. They'd been trying to peace together some things but were coming up short. They eventually found out from word of mouth that a beef recently started with some dudes that usually hung around Rittenhouse, right-off Georgia Avenue. That immediately led him to believe that the incident that occurred around Riggs Park was a form of retaliation, from the Kenneth Jackson Jr. case. Even though things were slowly forming, no arrests were made, and the citizens wanted answers. It was seven o'clock in the morning and the detectives had yet to get a sniff of rest. The clipboard that was found at the crime scene still hadn't given them a lead, the print that came back didn't have a match to it. When they left the scene and headed over to where the cab was found, it wasn't anything to inspect, the cab had been destroyed from the fire. Detective Merrett had to take a seat to gather his thoughts. He was rubbing his temples trying to figure out his next move when his partner asked about the shooting that transpired in the alley behind Uptown Auto Parts.

"That's it," he yelped, "how did I forget? We need to get over to the hospital and question that young man, I bet all this is tied together somehow. Let's finish up here then head over there and see what we come up with!"

Chapter 67

It was ten in the morning and Worl was finally back in the city. Jumping on New York Ave. from off of Baltimore Washington Parkway, he stopped at Checkers to get Ra-Ra and himself a bite to eat. Once they pulled away from the drive thru, Worl decided to check into a near by Days Inn Hotel. Once he pulled into the the parking lot he had Ra-Ra run in to get the room while he turned his phone on to let his men know he was back in town. When she came back, he drove around to the other side of the parking lot where the rooms were located. He cautiously followed the necessary steps to open the hidden stash before placing the package into his Checkers food bag and heading to their hotel room. Even though the jeep had the stash spot, he still didn't feel comfortable riding around with it.

When the two entered the room, Ra-Ra admitted to still being a little restless from the night before and driving half the way back to the city.

"I need a change of clothes if we going to stay here until tomorrow, Papi," she stated.

"Im'ma stop at a store and pick you up an outfit, and panties to put on," he assured her.

"You better," she smiled, "you kow women don't wear the same thing two days in a row. They better not anyway."

"I would hope not. But let me go handle a few things then check on my man, and I'll be back shortly," he said giving her a kiss.

"Papi, I need to ask you something before you leave."

"What's dat?"

"Where did you and Scrap get them bags from?"

"What made you ask me dat?" He asked, trying not to sound offended.

She went on to explain the Beauty Supply Store incident, but left out the part of her thinking she saw Scrap in the same area that night, placing a wig on his head. To her relief, Worl didn't lie about how they obtained the bags, he actually broke down what had taken place that night. It meant a lot to her, knowing she could trust him. It was one more thing she wanted answers about, but decide against it. She wanted to ask about Ode. She figured she'd bring it up later. He had important things to handle and she didn't want to be annoying him with a lot of sudden question.

"Thank you for being honest, Papi," she said expressing her gratitude.

"Baby girl I told you, our relationship revolves around honesty and I meant dat, so don't ask me nothin' you don't really wanna know da answer to," he stated.

"Understood," she agreed.

"Bet," he countered giving her another kiss, before walking into the bathroom. By the time he came back out, she was passed out under the quilt.

Damn she must've been tired fo'real, he thought to himself while quietly leaving out, so he wouldn't disturb her.

Chapter 68

The two detectives finally made it to the hospital to question Ty. Presenting their badges at the front desk, the detectives were easily directed to Ty's room. As the two entered the room, they saw Ty sitting up eating pretzels.

"Mr. Dixon, how you doing this morning, sir?" Greeted Detective Merrett. "I'm Detective Merrett and this is my partner Detective L.P," he said extending his hand.

"Shaking hands, spreads germs, and I'm eating," Ty replied, giving the two detectives a stern look.

"Is that so?" Countered Detective Merrett.

"Pretty much!"

"OK," he stated sensing the sarcasm. "Look here Mr. Dixon, I'm only here to do my job, not to get acquainted. Let's get that straight before I continue!"

"Dat's good to know," he smiled, "but Mr. Ferrett..."

"Merrett," he corrected.

"Whatever," he said before continuing, "you're probably wastin' ya' time, cause I have nothin' to tell you."

"Like I said before I have a job to do. Rather you answer the questions or not is on you. But I must assure you that there's an ongoing investigation that involves multiple homicides, including a young man gunned down just five blocks from where you were shot. That said, just hope that your name doesn't end up on my desk for being involved in any of it. I'll see to it that I bury you for being a smart ass!" He growled, standing only inches from Ty's face.

Ty basically unfazed by the threat simply gave a satisfied smirk, "Thanks for da heads up, but its obvious I don't have nuthin' to worry about, cause I have no idea what you talkin' bout Mr. Ferrett."

Detective Merrett didn't correct him, he just smiled at his slick remark. "So neither incident had anything to do with you?"

"I don't have any answers for you detective, so unless you have somethin' on me, which I know you don't, our conversation is over," Ty meaning every word he spoke.

Detective Merrett stared at Ty with fire in his eyes, but he was right, if he didn't have anything on him he couldn't really press him. He knew he wasn't getting anywhere questioning Ty so he decided to wrap things up with the promise of seeing him again shortly.

"Well until then, take care," stated Ty.

"You do the same Mr. Dixon and try to stay out of trouble, whom ever tried to take you out the first time will probably be back," he said walking out of Ty's room.

"Pigs," hissed Ty as they shut the door.

Chapter 69

Big Lyn summoned an emergency meeting amongst three of his business associates. They were at a car dealership off of 18th Rhode Island Ave, which was ran by Shaka. Shaka was a Nigerian that Big Lyn had known for over twenty years, and the other two, Big Shay and Lil Steve were two good men he connected with on a brief jail bid. The three just clicked and since Big Lyn was the first to get released, he kept his word and looked out for the two for the remainder of their stay. By the time they'd gotten released, Big Lyn was officially the man and he decided to take them in. It was understood that Big Lyn was the head of the alliance, and no one bothered to contest.

Big Lyn chose to have the meeting at Shaka's establishment, because his recent matter involved Shaka. With the exception of Big Lyn, the other members were seated waiting to hear what was on his mind.

"Jeff do you mind steppin' out, and assisting any customers that might come in?" Shaka asked.

"Sure, no problem," replied Jeff stepping out of the office.

Jeff was Shaka's nephew who worked there at the dealership keeping the vehicles detailed. When Jeff left out, Big Lyn got down to the situation at hand.

"First of all I appreciate everyone making it here in such short notice, but I have a serious issue that needs to be dealt with," he stated, scanning the room as he continued, "I have a relative that's in some serious trouble with someone we having close dealings with. My guess as of right now, is either he's already dead," he stated bowing his head, signifying the father, the son and the Holy Spirit, "or some place badly hurt, either way I plan on finding him."

"How do you know for sure that the person you're speaking of actually responsible for what he's being accused of?" Asked Big Shay.

Right away, Big Lyn spoke on the incident from the Rouge Lounge the night before.

"So why wasn't it dealt with at the time?" Asked Lil Steve.

"It's a time and a place for everything, and technically I can touch the dude whenever I'm ready," Big Lyn explained.

"And how is that?" Questioned Big Shay.

"Cause what the fool don't know is that I'm the one supplying him his product through Shaka," he clarified.

"Who, me?" Shaka pointed to himself, making sure he wasn't mistaken.

"Yeah, you," he stated confidently.

"Who you talkin' about?" He asked eagerly, sitting up straight.

Big Lyn looked at Shaka for a few seconds, before revealing who it was.

"Don't tell me you talking 'bout Maurice from Riggs Park," said Shaka.

"Yeah that's him," he confirmed.

"That's bad for business, he alone is bringing in a shit load of money!" Shaka hissed standing up.

"One thing about this game, it's always a bench player waiting to compete for a starting position," Big Lyn stated.

"True! But you can't just take a player off the bench, throw'em in the game and expect 'em to fill the shoes of a franchise player," he countered.

"This situation is not debatable. Like I stated earlier, it's family involved and all the money in the world can't come between that!"

"You're absolutely right," he replied as he thought about it, "and excuse me for thinking past the importance of the situation. So how did all this happen?" Shaka questioned with interest.

Big Lyn got off the edge of the desk and walked over to the window to collect his thoughts before he spoke. Big Lyn told his story, leaving nothing out. About how he'd taken advantage of Maurice back in their middle school days. And how several years later, both were simultaneously blowing up in the drug trade. Big Lyn searched to find out who his competitor was, wanting to present an offer that was sure to prevail both men in the game. When he finally caught up with 'em he was shocked to see who it was.

With all the bullshit behind and money on his mind, he still approached him. Maurice listened to what he had to say, but it didn't take long for him to turn it down. Big Lyn let the offer go for the time being. It wasn't that Big Lyn was desperate, but he did figure only two things could happen in the long run, either they were going to break bread, or bump heads. He didn't bring the offer up again until he bumped into Maurice at a function, Big Lyn figured he'd might have a change of heart. He approached him one last time, but like before, Maurice shot it down. But, come to find out, Big Lyn had a cousin that was close with the manager of the club Maurice had invested in and was introduce to him. Big Lyn, with his creative mind used that as bait. He offered his cousin fifty thousand if he could get in good with Maurice and a lot more if what he had in mind panned out. Shockingly, he got in way more than expected. He was hanging out with Maurice on the regular. When time presented itself he stepped to him, claiming to have a connect with good prices.

"But the nigga never entertained the thought," Big Lyn explained. "He was as hard as stone to turn, but after about eighteen months, the fool's connect got knocked.

He decided to lay low for a while, and during that time, I sky rocketed. I also formed this alliance we have here today. Instead of him being a partner, he ended up being a high buying client in the same enterprise he'd turned down. When my folks made the call I knew I couldn't show my face, so that's when I called you to deal with 'em," Big Lyn concluded.

"So you mean to tell me you baited that man in from the very beginning," said Shaka rubbing his chin astoundingly.

"Yeah and it paid off abundantly, but now I'm paying for it cause my folks been exposed," stated Big Lyn.

"Sorry to hear about your folks but you had to know that this could've happened at anytime… But why did your cousin continue to be around him after Maurice took the bait?" Asked Big Shay.

"My folks convinced me that he was cool with sticking around. Not only was he getting a percentage off of each brick that Maurice purchased from me, but he was also getting hit off by Maurice for hooking him up. Dude was eating real good by sticking around without havin' to put work in for nothing," Big Lyn clarified.

"So, what did you have in mind? You already said the majority of that next shipment was for him," Shaka said.

"I know," Big Lyn said beginning to lay his plan out.

Chapter 70

Maurice found out what happened in his neighborhood and that his name had been dropped in the investigation. It was time to get some distance between his neighborhood and himself, at least until things died down. He wasn't scared, just cautious, he knew when bodies started dropping it would bring a whole different kind of heat that he wasn't trying to face. His first priority was the safety of his niece, Charity. He promised that he'd never leave her without support, especially after she lost both parents.

Thanks to his realtor, he had a vacant five-bedroom home in Accokee, Maryland. He knew his niece would be able to get around without any worries there. As he rode to his current residence in Riggs Park, he was being followed by Blac in his niece's newest gift. He didn't want to alarm her with the sudden move, but under the circumstances he had no choice. He called out to her as he entered the house.

"Yes," she responded from the bedroom.

"Come here for a quick second," he hollered back while walking into his den with Blac and Reggie trailing behind.

When they entered the den, Charity was walking down the steps. He immediately noticed what she was carrying when she walked in.

"Hey Blac and Reggie," she greeted.

"Wassup Charity," they spoke in unison.

"Look, I need to speak wit' you 'bout somethin'," he stated, eyeing her bag before continuing. "I umm... saw Kita yesterday and..."

"I saw her myself the other day," she interjected, figuring she'd ran her mouth about the bag.

"You know she was killed late last night in the schoolyard," he said, straightforward.

"Oh my God! Are you serious?" She covered her mouth with both hands.

"We need to move from here just to be on the safe side," he said candidly.

"Move? Where? How soon?" She asked frantically.

"Within' the next few days," he said. "It's out in Acokee," he confirmed. Truthfully he'd been wanting to move, but knew she was content where she was.

"What about my nursing classes? How I am supposed to get back and forth from out there?" She questioned.

"You know I thought about that," he voiced holding up a set of car keys.

"What are those?" She asked with a bit of excitement.

"They're yours if you want 'em," he smiled, glad to see that her mood had change for the better.

She glided over, grabbing the keys out of his hand, giving him a hug and a kiss on his cheek. "Thank you Uncle Moe, but I thought you were going to wait until I finished nursing school?"

"I was, but under the circumstances I think that it's best if you had it now, besides you deserve it," he stated.

"Where is it?" She beamed.

"It's out front, all cleaned up for you," he told her.

She brushed past Blac and Reggie, disappearing to admire the new Lexus from the window at the front of the house.

"Once you showed her those keys she forgot all about Kita," stated Blac.

"Yeah I know," Maurice agreed, "but to be honest I don't think she was close to her. She used to say all Kita did was run her mouth."

"She ain't lyin'," Reggie agreed.

"Speakin' of Kita, when I saw her yester..." Maurice started.

"And it's my favorite color!" she yelped, cutting Maurice's conversation short. "I was about to walk to the store, but not any more! Do you mind?"

"I bought it so that you can do as you please, just be mindful of what I told you. Don't go parading through the neighborhood," he said.

"I promise I won't," she said sincerely, marching upstairs to change into an outfit to compliment her new ride.

"Oh, Charity!" Maurice yelled out to her.

"Yes, Uncle Moe?"

"Before you leave, pile some of your important things on your bed. We gonna head over to the other house to drop off a few things."

He went on to explain what Kita had told him about the bag Charity was carrying. While they conversed, Charity came back downstairs looking as if she was entering a fashion show. Her hair was already cut short with precision, each layer in its place. She looked clean and refined, sporting her Gucci shorts set with the matching sandals.

"I know I said that I was on my way to the store, so I figured why not do a drive by and kill me a few onlookers on the way," she joked, heading for the door.

"She's definitely your niece," stated Blac.

"Who you tellin'," smiled Maurice, shaking his head.

"Might have to keep eyes on her before one of them creeps try to snatch her up," stated Reggie.

"Don't say no crazy shit like that. The street hasn't seen physical force, until someone even thinks of layin' a finger on her," he countered in a dead pan tone. "One of y'all grab them boxes out the car, so we can pack some of this shit and drop it off before we go deal with this fool Nick again."

Chapter 71

Worl went straight to work with that hustler ambition. After making a few pit stops, he found out that the prices were ranging anywhere between sixty-five to one twenty a gram. It didn't take a rocket scientist to know that the higher price was supposed to be high quality. But the current quality was too mediocre to get those that had been snorting since the 70s. If what Fito told him panned out to be true, then he was 'bout to bring the 70s back.

His last stop was in his area. He was on his way to Takoma Station to meet up with this old head, Big Mike, who sold anything he could profit as long as it didn't assassinate his character. On his way there, he reached out to Scrap and told him to meet 'em at the same location so they could talk. While driving he couldn't help but think about Ra-Ra and her family ties. He had a lot of respect for her, and not because of her connections. It was how she carried herself through the whole situation. She never once led him to believe that her folks were well off, though, she would casually drop a hint from time to time. He should've been paying more attention to the small things. Not only did she not work, but she drove a new Benz CLK, plus she's always sported the lasted fashion. He brushed it off, figuring that she was spoiled, and to an extent she was, but how could she not be when her uncle's the man. Now he saw why she was always good when he offered her money, she had her own. *Her father probably left her a nice piece of change when he passed too,* he thought pulling up to his destination. Even if he did, it didn't matter because it wasn't his to spend. Ra-Ra had done enough with the introduction, and now he was more determined than ever to get his own and make sure he and his partners wouldn't need for nothing.

He quickly called Big Mike and told him that he was outside parked in a Cherokee. Three minutes later, Big Mike was hopping in, "Why you didn't just come in nephew?"

"I was tryin' to talk to you in private," Worl replied.

"I was at the bar by myself, but that doesn't matter now. Talk to me," Big Mike said.

Worl, with his smooth demeanor told him everything and awaited Big Mike's response.

Big Mike digested what was said before speaking, "Nephew I'm more than twice ya age, and I haven't heard of no torch like that since I was ya age. Ya feel me? So if what you're tellin' me is accurate, then you could slow walk it, step on it half as much, and practically be a millionaire before this time next year."

"Ya think so?" Worl responded.

"I know so. Trust me, and if it is what you say it is, Im'ma help you move it and get rich wit' ya."

"Say no more. Im'ma meet back up with you this time tomorrow and drop something off," he assured him, as his phone came to life. "Hold on fo' one sec," he said before answering. "Scrap wassup?"

"You. Where you at, 'cause I'm pullin' up," informed Scrap.

"I see you, you're directly in front of me. I'm in da Cherokee behind you, hollarin' at Big Mike."

"Well go 'head and handle ya business, Imma be right here. And tell Unc I said wassup," said Scrap.

"Bet," replied Worl, ending the call. "Scrap said wassup. But like I was sayin' we gonna hook up tomorrow so we can get da ball rollin'," Worl stated, extending his hand and ending their discussion.

"Like I said, I'm waitin' on you. I'm not making any calls until I hear from you," he replied, returning the handshake and getting out of the car.

"Got you," Worl countered, also getting out.

He heard Scrap finishing up a conversation, telling someone he'd see them soon, as he got in the car.

"Who was dat?" Worl asked looking at the smile across his partners face.

"First of all bruh, how was ya trip? Secondly, that was China," he answered, giving him some dap. "She tryin' to see da kid."

"I see y'all gettin' well acquainted. Dat's wassup," he congratulated. "But Slim, you ain't goin' to belive this shit," he hissed.

"What," countered Scrap, curiously.

"I think we finally hit da jackpot!" He went on to explain what had happened in New York.

"Are... you... fuckin'...serious," Scrap managed to blurt out. "You mean to tell me shorty connected like dat?"

"Sho' nuff," Worl smiled, leaning back in his seat.

"Shid, it's time for da take over, ain't no sense in bullshittin'! We all need to meet up and get some things in order, plus get on top of this Maurice situation. Like Big Lyn said, it ain't but so much you could make while you beefin'," said Scrap.

"Let's do da muthafucka then," retorted Worl.

"Bet," he countered. His phone lit up and another smile spreaded across his face before he answered, "Sup Ms. Lady?" He spoke for a couple of minutes before ending the call and directing his attention back to Worl. "You already know who dat was. I'm bout to go meet up with her right quick, so get at me later on."

"Dat's a bet. I gotta get back to this hotel anyway, tell her I said wassup," he said giving Scrap some dap, exiting the vehicle.

Chapter 72

Worl finally made it back to the hotel, and as promised he stopped past a few stores to grab the items Ra-Ra needed, including some good ole Jerk Chicken from Tropicana. When he entered the room Ra-Ra was wide awake watching Lifetime. When she saw that both his hands and mouth carried bags, she instantly went to help out.

"Papi! What, you bought the entire store?" She joked taking a few bags and shut the door.

"Thanks," he said, placing the food on the table. "Not really, just a few things for you and my little brother, since I promised 'em that I was takin' em to da Monster Truck Show this weekend.

"Aww I think that's sweet," she proclaimed, giving him a kiss. "I've never been to one of those before."

"Me neither," he confessed, pulling out three tickets with a smile. "I guess it's a first time for all three of us then."

A smile stretched across her face, "Oh Papi, you're taking me with you! I finally get to meet your little brother," she expressed, pushing him back on the bed and lying on top of him, covering his face with soft kisses.

"Don't start nothin' you not goin' to finish," he warned.

"I finish everything that I start, Papi," she countered, pulling her shirt over her head, exposing her espresso colored nipples and perfectly round youthful breast.

Worl passionately began sucking on her twins. He gave them both his full undivided attention, not wanting to make one jealous of the other. He cupped them both together in the palms of his hands, squeezing them gently, causing her libido to increase. He quickly spun her around, laying her flat on her back. He swiftly removed both of their clothing and spread her legs, took his finger, parted the rose folds of her pussy then stuck his tongue deep inside her. He continued to suck her clit, sending her into a realm of ecstasy, "Oh my God, Papi I'm about to cum for you," she moaned, as her body became rigid then lunged forward in a spasm. "Right... there... Papi," she blurted, reaching her first climax.

Worl got up, then briskly slipped his swollen manhood into her pussy. She was so wet, that his love muscle slip into place, as if he were driving into his very own personalized garage. The way he was pumping, grinding, and rotating his hips, he couldn't tell if she was screaming from pleasure or agony. Her moans were enticing him more and more with each stroke. The way her pussy was clinching his dick made him lose control, he could feel himself on the verge of busting.

"I'm 'bout to cum!" He exclaimed, exploding deep into her.

Once they were done, they slumped back, glistening with sweat, taking a deep breath of satisfaction. After the pulsating between her legs subsided she casually got off the bed, then went into the bathroom to shower, with Worl behind her. As soon as they finished bathing one another, they sat down to enjoy their Jerk Chicken. While eating, Worl explained his plans on getting rid of the dope, and that the only problem was to finding out how or who to cut the dope. Ra-Ra raised an eyebrow to him.

"Why you look at me like dat?" Worl questioned.

"Cause it's simple, I can show you how," she answered, continuing to eat.

Worl gave her a sly look, "You full of surprises huh," he stated. She simply smiled and continued to finish her meal.

Chapter 73

When China and Scrap eventually met up, she stepped out her new car feeling like a princess easing out of her golden carriage. Scrap looked at her like she was an entrée at an all-you-can-eat buffet. She walked right up and gave him a welcoming hug, as he kissed her cheek.

"Damn! You lookin' and smellin good," he complimented examining at her from head to toe.

"Thank you," she blushed, spinning around to give him a full view.

"Dat's ya new ride?" He asked, noticing the paper tags on the vehicle.

"Yes," China replied in her sweetest voice. "You like it?"

"Yeah dat's real nice, plus dat color is perfect for you," he compliments, grabbing her hand and taking a closer look at the car. "When you goin' to take me for a ride?"

"Whenever you ready," she smiled, taking in his handsome features.

Scrap smiled kindly, pulling her close. He stared deep into her beautiful oval eyes like he was trying to see into her soul.

"Women like you don't grow on trees. I think you're special," he said closing in for a kiss.

She closed her eyes, relishing the moment. The two had a strong connection that was surely forming into something special. Their kiss sent a chill down her spine, and when their lips finally parted she found herself in a slight trance, like when Lois Lane first kissed Superman.

Scrap couldn't help but smile as she opened her eyes, "You good?" He asked.

What has this man done to me, she thought. "I'm straight," she said with a smile. She pondered the fact that they'd never had sex, and he still had her mind gone. Also the fact that he hadn't pursued her when she was more than willing, made her admire him even more.

"Come on lets walk," he said, grabbing her by the hand.

They went for a nice long stroll with no destination in mind. Walking hand and hand like a married couple, China was loving every moment. Every word that Scrap spoke was like music to her ears. By the time they made it back to their vehicles, an hour had zoomed past with ease. As he embraced her, she felt so comfortable that right then and there she knew that's where she belonged. She rested her head on his chest, listening to his heartbeat as he held her as tight as humanly possible. While leaning up against his car, his phone started to ring snapping her out of her comfort zone.

"'Cuse me for a sec," he suggested reaching for his phone. "Ode, what's good?"

The sound of Ode's name caused her to look up. It was the first time she'd heard his name since overhearing her uncle mention it at the house. Not wanting to jump to conclusions she gave him the benefit of the doubt, hoping that it was a different Ode. But her mind couldn't help but go to the bag she'd received from him, plus her encounter with Kita at CVS instantly popped in her mind. She didn't want to seem obvious, but she semi tuned into his conversation to try and decipher if it was actually the Ode her uncle mentioned or not. As their conversation seemed to go more indepth, her phone started to ring. By the sound of the ringtone, she knew it was her uncle. She stepped away from Scrap answering her phone. By the time she ended her call Scrap, had already finished and was patiently waiting on her.

"So what's da plan for da evenin', you wanna go out?" He asked after she put her phone away.

"I would love too, but I'll have to call you after I take care of something important for my uncle," she responded.

"Alright dat's cool, I'm just goin' to hang over my man's house until you call me," he said giving her a hug and a kiss. "Don't forget, I got someplace special dat I'm tryin' to take you."

"I won't," she blushed walking off to her car, with a walk that could've stopped traffic.

Chapter 74

Maurice was just about finished unloading a few things at the house in Acokee when he got a call.

"Didn't expect to hear from you for another few days," answered Maurice.

"I wasn't expecting to call you for another few myself but the clothes came early. The only thing is, if you can't meet me in the next forty-five minutes I'm gonna have to get backup with you in two weeks, I have a family emergency and I have a plane to catch," explained the caller.

"What time is your flight, I'm on the other side of town, I'm gonna need a little more time than that," Maurice replied.

"I don't have more time," he assured him.

"I really need them outfits, my inventory is low," he stated. "Matter of fact I'll be there. Same place right?" Maurice desperately changed his mind.

"Yeah, same place," he confirmed.

"Aight cool. I'm gonna drop the bread off, then have your co-worker meet back up later to drop off the merchandise."

"I can do that."

"I appreciate it, and have a safe trip."

"Will do," said the caller.

Maurice quickly dialed his niece to find out where she was. She told him she was about 15 minutes out. He instantly gave her directions to go into the basement, grab the two duffel bags next to Remi's kennel, and then gave her instructions on where to drop them off. He didn't think he was putting her in harms way, all she was doing was dropping the bags off, that's it and that's all. Once he sent her on her way and finished unloading everything, he, Blac and Reggie went to finish with Nick. Now was the time for Maurice to find out what connection he shared with Big Lyn. When they walked in, on cue Maurice walked over to the mini bar and poured himself a drink.

When they opened the basement door a strong odor forced its way out.

"Damn," hissed Blac, stepping back, "it smells like straight up shit down there!"

"What you expect! The bamma been tied up for damn near a whole day," replied Maurice. "It shouldn't matter, since you always talkin' shit anyway," he joked, stepping down the steps.

When they got down the stairs, they looked towards the corner to see Nick passed out. His once, light tan linen pants, were dark brown and smelled of urine.

"That nigga looks dead," said Reggie.

"It damn sure smells like it," added Blac.

"Well let's find out," said Maurice, backhanding Nick across his face.

"Fuck!" yelled Nick, his voice faint from the loss of blood and lack of food.

"Fuck what nigga! Get your snake azz up," Scolded Maurice.

"Look at me man! I'm weak as shit," he pleaded, "I can barely hold my head up, plus, I'm suffocating, and smothered in my own shit and piss!"

"You don't expect me to feel sorry for you, do you? You brought this on yourself! I trusted you. I made you part of my circle, and you snake me! I don't have no sympathy for you. You made your bed, you lie in it," he expressed, lifting Nick's head up by his chin. "Now what I wanna know is what dealings did you and Big Lyn have?"

"I don't know anyone by that name."

Maurice released his chin, then glanced at both of his henchman with a grin of his face, before giving Blac a head nod.

Blac immediately put on a pair of brass knuckles and hit Nick in his midsection, eventually causing him to spit out a sizeable amount of blood. He felt like his insides were being crushed.

"Did that help jog your memory?" Asked Maurice, lifting his head back up by his chin.

"I swear I don't know what you talkin' about," Nick said through clenched teeth.

"Still playing dumb, huh?" Asked Maurice, once again releasing his chin. This time he gave Reggie a head nod. He unhesitantly pulled out a pair of sharp wire cutters, then placed Nick's pinky finger between the blades and clip it completely off.

Nick roared out in so much pain that it seemed as though he was trying to wake the dead.

"I didn't know that somebody lacking so much strength could yell so loud," Marice said, "but the fact still remains the same, I don't know the answer to my question, so please enlighten me."

Nick wiggled in the chair trying to cope with the pain.

"I'm not askin' again!" Maurice hissed, striking Nick across his face again.

So many thoughts were running through Nick's mind, but the main thought was, how Maurice managed to find out that it was Big Lyn he was dealing with. He felt another hand forcefully crash across his face, almost causing him to blackout, but he managed to lift his head up just enough to look Maurice in his eyes.

Realizing he was in a no win situation, Nick finally spoke. "You sure you wanna know?" He asked with a sinister grin.

"Should I answer that?" Maurice, returned the gaze.

Nick began to explain how he and Big Lyn were blood relatives, and how he was sent to him underhandedly to do business. When Nick finished struggling to explain everything, Maurice sat in the chair in front of Nick speechless. He sat and stared at the wall for a moment, looking as if he had missed the lotto by one number.

"Boss man," Reggie said pulling Maurice out of his daze.

"So you mean to tell me..." he started to say, rubbing his temples. "So he been my connect the whole time. This whole fuckin time! This was a gimmick from the beginning. How the fuck could I be so stu'..." he cut his statement short. "Shit!" He barked.

"What?" Asked Blac.

"Charity!" He responded, quickly pulling out his phone to call her. He was met with her voicemail, so he tried again and again until he finally got an answer.

"Now you see what happens when you send someone other than yourself to handle your business," Big Lyn's voice boomed through the phone.

"Where the fuck my niece at!" He barked, instantly feeling lightheaded after hearing a man answer her phone.

"Oh, she's safe for now, but I don't know how long I'm gonna keep it that way. It was obvious who this was meant for, but since that didn't work out, I'm taking the next best thing," expressed Big Lyn.

"I'm sure we can work somethin' out," stated Maurice.

"All of a sudden you want to negotiate, but when I tried to, you never entertained the thought. See your arrogance got you in this predicament. Now it's my time to let you know that I don't wish to work anything out with you! I'm sure by now you know that Nick was my blood relative, and since she's yours, I'm taking what you took from me!"

"Ho..ho..hold on!" Maurice stuttered, placing the phone to Nick's ear. "Say something," he ordered.

"Cuzz I'm messed up but I'm breathin'," he managed to say before Maurice snatched the phone back.

"So is it safe to say, fair exchange isn't a robbery," Maurice rationalized.

Feeling relieved that his cousin was still alive, Big Lyn agreed.

"When and where?" Asked Maurice.

Big Lyn paused momentarily before giving him the location, "In exactly one hour, she'll be in a dark blue Chevy Conversion van in the alley of 14th and Allision, but just like Nick, don't expect for her to be in perfect condition," stated Big Lyn hanging up.

"I swear the first chance I get I'm shootin 'em right between the eyes," he berated, turning towards his henchman." Clean this fool up so we can go get my niece back, and call Scooter, it's time to strap all the way up."

Chapter 75

Scrap eventually linked up with Ode and Block shortly after leaving China. It was dark and well past the time they agreed to meet backup. After calling twice and not getting an answer, he figured he'd just wait to hear from her.

The three were merely finishing a fifth of Patron when Ode decided that he had enough valor to call Tyshelle.

"Slim you might wanna call from a different number just in case them people monitorin' her phone," Block suggested from the passenger side of his Cadillac.

"Yeah dat's ya best bet," Scrap agreed, taking a sip from his cup.

As they drove to drop Ode off, Scrap brought up the topic of going through Riggs Park since Worl had made it back. Normally Block and Ode would've jumped in the conversation, but there was an awkward silence. Scrap knowing his two men like the back of his hand, immediately picked up on it.

"Did ya'll hear me?" Asked Scrap.
"Yeah we heard you," they said in unison.
"Then why y'all ain't say nothin'?"

"Ain't nothin' to say, we heard you," Ode responded.

"See dat's that bullshit I be talkin' bout," he stated, looking back and forth between them both. "I know y'all, and there's somethin' y'all ain't tellin' me."

"There's nothin' to tell you, but dat jo'nt probably goin' to be shut down for a minute," Ode stated, as Block pulled up to his destination. "So what y'all bout to get into?" Ode asked, changing the subject.

"We'll probably cruise around for a minute, plus I'm waiting on my shawty to hit me back, but fuck all dat! Don't try to change da subje..." Scrap tried to say before being interrupted by the slamming car door. When he looked, Ode had a big smile on his face treading off.

"Don't be slammin' my door, like that no more!" Block shouted towards Ode. Block had a slight smirk on his face when Scrap turned towards him, he knew what was coming, "So where we going?"

"It don't make a difference, but you can stop past the spot on 14th Street, so I can grab us some more of dat Orange Sniper from Big Lyn's folks, while you bring me up to speed on what da fuck you and Ode actin' all secretive about," Scrap said, leaning his seat back.

Block explained everything, leaving nothing out. From the time they pulled off, to the time they arrived at there destination.

"I thought we all agreed not to do anything until Worl made it back safe from New York," said Scrap, point blank.

"I'm hip, but one thing lead to another and we decided to go through wit' it."

Scrap knew it wasn't any sense in debating about it. What's done is done, so he decided to leave well enough alone.

"Fuck it! It is what it is," he said. "Pull over right there, I should be in and out."

Scrap walked through the gate, then went around back to knock on the door.

"Who is it?" A voice called from inside the house.

"This Scrap!"

"Hold on for a second."

"Hold on…" Scrap said to himself. They never told him to hold on, before plus they knew that he had the green light to come and go as he pleased. Two minutes later the door opened.

"Lil Scrap wassup?"

"Damn Elmo, you had a nigga standin' out here like some kind of fiend or somethin'!"

"My bad Slim, but a nigga jive in the middle of somethin'," explained Elmo.

"Well look, I was just slidin' through to find out if y'all had some of dat Orange Sniper left."

"Yeah, but this not a good time. We handling something for big boy, so you goin' to have to come back later on."

"Ay Elmo I'm jive twisted. I ain't tryin' to be runnin' back and forth down hot azz 14th Street."

"Noooo!" Shouted a female voice from the far end of the house.

"Bitch!" Shouted a male voice from the same direction, followed by a loud slap.

"What da fuck was dat?" frowned Scrap, not really concerned, but leery to some degree.

"That ain't nobody but Gizz, Zay, and some dizzy azz broad. That shit ain't 'bout nothin'. I'll tell you what… Imma run in the back and grab somethin' for you, so I can finish takin' care of this situation," he said, rushing towards the back.

When Elmo disappeared to the back, Scraps curiosity got the best of him. He wasn't known to be nosey, but the liquor had him acting out the norm. He proceeded in the direction that Elmo went, turned back around to go back by the door, and then turned right back towards the noise. When he advanced closer, he noticed the first bedroom on his left cracked open just enough for him to peek inside. The moment he glanced in, it immediately ignited the fuel to a fire that had been burning on the inside for so long. Without a second thought he pulled out his forty-five caliber pistol, just as Elmo was emerging from the other room.

"Scrap what the…" Elmo managed to say, before Scrap lunged forward, striking Elmo on the side of his face, forcing him back into the room he came out of. Scrap quickly snatched Elmo back up, then used him as a human shield forcing his way into the other room.

"Y'all need to back away from shawty!" Scrap threatened, after bursting, into the room, startling the two males inside.

"What the fuck," Zay spat, reaching for his gun on his waist.

"Zay don't do it," warned Scrap, aiming directly towards him.

"Don't do what Scrap," he shot back, "You need to act like you got some sense and put that hamma away, before you get ya'self into somethin' you can't get out of!"

Scrap glanced towards the female and noticed she was out cold. Zay followed his glare and went off.

"You mean to tell me that's what this all about! A broad! You willing to sacrifice ya life and loyalty for the big homie over some female!" He barked. "Man fuck that bitch," Zay scolded, pulling out his pistol, then aiming towards the young woman, but was met by three shells to the chest before he got a chance to let off a single shot.

"Ho…ho…hold up Scrap!" Gizz stuttered, jumping out the way from Zays falling body. "What is it that you want?" He panicked, throwing both his hands high above his head, to show Scrap he didn't pose any danger, "Scrap you know we like family. This ain't for us," he pleaded. "I tell you what, it's eight…"

"Gizz shut the fuck up!" Blurted out Elmo, cutting Gizz's statement off, "Don't say shit!"

"Don't say what?" Hissed Scrap, now pressing his gun against Elmo's temple. He glanced over towards the female and instantly knew she was in desperate need of medical attention. Whatever he was going to do, he had to think fast if he was going to get her some help. Instead of keeping his gun pressed against Elmo's head, he aimed the gun back towards Gizz who was shaking like a leaf in the wind.

"You have exactly three seconds to say what you gotta say," Scrap said. "One."

"Gizz don't say nothin'!" Shouted Elmo.

"Two," he continued.

"Gizz fuck this nigga!"

"Three…"

"Man it's eight hundred and forty thousand in them two duffel bags by the door! Take the money just don't kill us!" Gizz spatted frantically, hoping to persuade Scrap from shooting them.

When Elmo noticed Scraps reaction after hearing how much money was in the two bags, he immediately tried to grab Scraps arm and knock the gun out.

"Grab the money and get out of here!" Yelped Elmo, as he tussled with Scrap for the gun.

As Gizz snatched the two bags and rushed out the room, Block appeared in the threshold pointing his gun in Gizz's direction, stopping him dead in his tracks.

"Where you goin', and Where's Scrap?" He questioned, and almost simultaneously heard a gun shot. Block's eyes darted past him, then right back to Gizz, before pulling the trigger, shooting him directly between his eyes. Block rounded the corner, quickly noticing Scrap on his knees with a gun pressed against the back of his head, "Scrap watch out!" Shouted Block, startling Elmo just enough for Scrap to lay flat on his stomach, while he got a clear shot to unload on Scrap's assailant.

"Right on time big boy," hissed Scrap, jumping up holding the side of his face, causing Block to rushed over to assist him. "I'm good. Get her, she's hit!"

"Who's dat?" Asked Block.

"I'll tell you in da car, but let's get out of here first!"

Block scooped her up, then headed out the room towards the backdoor. When Block darted out the house, Scrap stood back briefly making sure he wiped down anything that he might have touched, and to check and see if he dropped anything that can link him to what had happened.

Oh shit, he thought out loud, halfway to Block's car.

"C'mon!" Shouted Block, noticing Scrap turning back around.

"Hit da trunk," he countered, rushing back towards the house.

When he stepped back inside, he noticed how Gizz's head had swelled to the size of a basketball before pulling the two bags from his grip. Rushing back outside, he quickly threw the bags in the trunk, then hopped in the passenger side.

"Washington Hospital!" Bellowed Scrap, reaching in the backseat to check on China, while Block accelerated to the hospital.

Chapter 76

Big Lyn had pulled up almost right after Scrap and Block drove off. Two minutes sooner, and they would've ran right into each other. It was nearing the time for him and Maurice to make the switch, so Big Lyn was in a rush to grab Maurice's niece. Big Lyn phoned his nephew Elmo to tell him to bring the girl to the exchange spot, but never got an answer.

"It's still twenty minutes left so we good, plus the spot is down the street," commented Shaka, from the driver's seat.

"I guess you right. Come on," stated Big Lyn, walking towards the house. He entered through the front door and walked through the living room, towards the back where the two bedrooms and basement were located.

"These fools probably in the basement smok…" he started to say until he spotted the backdoor wide open with Gizz's body sprawled out on the floor. He swiftly removed his .357 Smith & Wesson from his shoulder holster, while holding his index finger up to his lip to hush Shaka as he took the corner. On cue, Shaka whipped out his weapon as well. The two quickly pointed their pistols like two marksmen as they went. They didn't have to search far, the first open door they came upon revealed everything. Big Lyn's heart dropped when he saw his nephew lying on the floor, dead. He walked over to make sure, as Shaka checked the other rooms.

"We need to get outta here," retorted Shake, storming back into the room with Big Lyn.

Big Lyn slowly stood up, glanced over at Zay's dead body, then left out the room. Big Lyn thought about the money, but had enough sense to know whomever committed these homicides, more than likely took the money.

"What are we goin' to do now about the switch?" inquired Shaka, as the pair stormed out the house, into Shaka's vehicle.

"It's obvious that whatever happened with his niece hasn't reached him yet, he wouldn't still be meeting us if he did. Once we get them into the alley, we have to make damn sure they don't make it back out, until we get my peoples," Big Lyn fumed, as they pulled off.

Chapter 77

Once Block arrived at the hospital's emergency entrance, Scrap wasted no time hopping out, grabbing China, and rushing her in.

"Stay wit me baby girl! Stay wit me!" He pleaded, hurrying through the double doors. "We need a doctor! We have an emergency!"

Seconds later, help came rushing out with a stretcher.

"Sir, what happened?" Asked one of the nurses who came out to assist China, also noticing a gash on the side of his face.

"Don't know, I found her like dat," he replied, slowly back peddling in the opposite direction. He knew he couldn't hang around, it was just a matter of time before the authorities showed up asking questions. He wanted to stay badly, at least to make sure she pulled through, but when the nurse's vanished around the corner so did he.

"Slim this a crazy situation. Da question is how your folks end up in dat house," said Block, as Scrap got back in the car.

"Your guess is as good as mine, I don't have a clue," Scrap replied, holding his head. "Thanks for saving me big boy, dat definitely was a close one."

"Dat goes without sayin'. I'm just glad I made it on time. Somethin' told me to go check on you. You were takin' too long, and dat's not like you."

"Slim, I fucked up!" He admitted, coming to his senses. "I zapped da fuck out when I seen her in there, and because of that, Elmo, Zay, and Gizz's are dead behind dat shit!" He expressed.

"I know," Block agreed. "And if he have da slightest idea dat we had anything to do wit dat mess, we hit. But you know me, Big Lyn or not, if it comes down to it, I'm goin' smack at' em! Period!" Block candidly stated.

"Even though it's all my fault, I would hate for it to come down to dat, he's damn near like a father to me," Scrap said regretfully, "but fo' da time being we just gotta play it by ear. In da meantime go past my jo'nt so we can see what we got in da trunk," he stated, sitting back and thinking about China.

Chapter 78

"Clear!" Shouted the doctor using the defibrillator to revive China. They managed to stabilize China and start her on oxygen.

"Her heart beat is strong," announced one of the physicians, "we have a fighter on our hands!"

The attending physician came into the room asking for an update. One of the residents quickly caught her up on China's condition.

"How much blood has she lost?" The attending asked, walking over to view the victim. As she surveyed the victim injuries, one thing noticeably stood out.

"A lot," replied a resident, looking in the direction of the attending who seemed to be in a minor daze. "Doc!"

"Yes," she answered, snapping out of her mental fog.

"Did you hear me?"

"Of course! Listen, I'm going to page Dr. Yuman. Let's get her in an OR."

"Sure thing!"

She quickly left out the room to page Dr. Yuman, one of the hospital's top surgeons. She knew the victim had a better chance of surviving with Dr. Yuman's assistance. After contacting Dr. Yuman who quickly obliged, she had to make one last important call before zipping to the operating room.

Chapter 79

"Listen up, I'm a need for y'all to be on point just in case they try somethin' when it's time to make the switch," spoke Maurice as they neared the location.

Reggie drove, Blac rode in the passenger seat, while Nick sat, tied up, between Black Moe and Maurice in the backseat. Young Scooter was positioned in the hatchback of the Ford Bronco, ready with twin Chinese AK-47s on his lap.

"Make a right turn on the next street, while I call this fool to let'em know we pullin' up," ordered Maurice, dialing his niece's phone. "Keep your eyes open," he stated, just before Big Lyn picked up.

"You here?" Answered Big Lyn.

"I'm turnin' on the street now," he assured him.

"Good. You'll see the van in the far end of the alley. Have one of your associates get out with my folks, while I do the same with yours. Have them meet midway and do the switch. We both get what we want, then go our separate ways," instructed Big Lyn ending the call.

"Aight y'all stay on point and watch all angles, this nigga is a snake!" Warned Maurice.

Besides the light from the street that lit the front part of the alley, it was completely dark. The darkness played to Big Lyn's advantage, their angle made it easy for his men stationed throughout the alley, hide from their targets. Big Lyn's plan was simple, under no circumstance were they to leave without his cousin.

"It's dark as shit in that alley," voiced Reggie.

"Yeah I know," Maurice agreed. "I tell you what, back into the alley, then roll the rear window down a little less than halfway, so Scooter can have them choppas ready, just in case. Black Moe you do the exchange. Reggie watch our front, and Blac stand outside so you can cover Black Moe," he orchestrated, as his phone kept buzzing back to back from an unknown number.

When Reggie backed into the alley, Scooter held one of the AKs just above the window in case something went wrong.

"Black Moe when you get out, make sure you stay directly behind him, he's your shield, and don't forget, move slow," he instructed, once again looking down at his phone to see the same number popping up.

"Got you," assured Black Moe.

"Well Nick, I must say that you taught me a valuable lesson; the more you show someone, the more dangerous they become to you. It was a bad decision on my behalf, I can admit. Let me assure you though, if we ever cross paths, I'll kill you right where you stand," he said through gritted teeth. "Now get out my sight," he ordered, giving Black Moe the signal.

Black Moe cautiously stepped out, weapon in hand, and scanned through the alley before pulling Nick out with him.

"It's dark but it looks like they getting out the van now," uttered Black Moe, holding onto Nick with a firm grip.

Seconds later, someone flicked the flashlight three times, indicating for them to proceed.

"That's the cue," Maurice ensured. "Like I said keep 'em in front, and move slow," he said. He then turned his attention towards Scooter, telling him to not let them out of his sight. Scooter, clutching the assault rifle, firmly watched as they footed up the alleyway. When the two got about a quarter of the way away, Maurice's phone sounded again for the umpteenth time.

"Damn, somebody blowin' ya phone up," Reggie noticed.

"Yeah, I know," Maurice replied, a bit irritated glancing down at his phone, still trying to focus on Black Moe who was midway up the alley.

"It has to be somethin' important for them to be hittin' yo' jo'nt back to back like that," Reggie suggested.

"This is important, but you know what," he stated, finally answering his phone. "Who's this!"

"This is Ms. Cathy; why haven't you been answering your phone? I know you've seen my calls!"

"Ms. Cathy! Ms. Cathy! Hold up, slow down because right now isn't a good time. I'm in the middle of somethin' very important, so whatever it is, is goin' have to wait."

"Well you need to stop what you are doing and get your tail over to this hospital, as soon as possible!"

"Ms. Cathy!" He started to speak before being interrupted.

"Boy! Damn, stop what you doing and get over here. Your niece is in one of my emergency room as we speak, fighting for her life," she said.

"What!" He shot back.

"You clearly heard what I just said! I need to get off this phone and try to help this poor child," she concluded, ending the call.

Not wanting to believe what he just heard he quickly realized he was walking into a trap, "Shit!" He cursed.

"What?" Asked Reggie, causing Scooter to lose focus.

"Black Moe come back! It's a set up, ya hear me, it's a trap!" Maurice hollered from the window, prompting his soldier's to spring into action.

Blac Moe heard Maurice's voice from a distance, just as he was about to make the switch. He looked back at Maurice and then forward again. He was met with guns pointed in his direction from Big Lyn's man and the female he'd suspected to be China.

"Don't take another step!" She demanded, revealin her true identity.

"You don't take another step!" he threatened, quickly wrapping his forearm around Nick's neck in a choke hold, while pressing his pistol to his dome. He began back pedaling towards the car but out of nowhere several infrared beams were aimed in their directions. For the next few seconds it seemed as though everything just stopped. He kinda paniced after measuring the distance between himself and the Bronco, he knew from that length that his men couldn't help him. He made a split second decision by shooting towards the female impostor and Big Lyn's man, forcing them to take cover, then frantically shot Nick in the back of his head. It seemed as though his body fell in slow motion. Black Moe swiftly tried to turn and dash towards the Bronco, only to have bullets trailing behind him. Black Moe only made it a few feet before getting gunned down. The flashes from Black Moe's assailants caused Scooter to view in on his demise. Scooter, furious, quickly aimed the AK-47 towards the direction the flashes came from and squeezed the trigger. The ear piercing explosion from the assault rifle lit up the alley like a severe lightning storm, chopping down everything in it's path. All of a sudden, a silhouette emerged from the driver side window aiming towards Reggie.

"Get down!" Shouted Maurice, reaching over the seat, snatching Reggie down.

The attacker let off two rounds, before Blac decorated his chest from the opposite side of the truck. Once Scooter's slaughted halted, he quickly reached for his other assault rifle. But Big Lyn's coops returned fire. The short burst from their returned automatic fire riddled the Bronco making it look like Swiss cheese.

"Pull off! Pull off!" Barked Blac crawling back into the Bronco.

Reggie managed to spring back up just enough to put the truck in drive and accelerated out the alley, unharmed with the exception of Scooter who was lying in the back motionless.

Chapter 80

When Block departed from Scrap, he drove straight to Party Time Liquor store off of New Hamphire Avenue to purchase himself a personal bottle, before heading home. The two duffel bags full of money were embedded in his mind, as he got back in his vehicle and immediately poured himself a cup. He downed the first one, then fixed another one to sip on while he drove. Even though him and Scrap agreed to stash the money until things cooled off, just the mere fact of knowing that it was in their possession had him stimulated.

"If I don't do nothin' Imma ball
I'm countin' all day like the clock on the wall
Now go and get your money lil duffel bag boy
Said go and get your money lil duffel bag boy," Lil' Wayne's voice blared through the speakers. As Block came up on a stop sign, he drifted through and almost instantly saw the red and blue flashing in his rear view.

"Damn," he said to himself, quickly downing the little bit of liquor that he had left in his cup before pulling over. With one hand gripping the handle of his gun, the officer cautiously approached.

"License and Registration?" Asked the officer.

"How you doin' sir," responded Block, reaching in his glove box to retrieve his registration, then handing it over, along with his license.

"Do you know why I pulled you over?" He questioned, disregarding Block's friendly gesture.

"I think I slid through the stop sign," he admitted, not really concerned with the offense, he was just happy he'd left his dirty weapon at Scrap's.

"You think or you know," said the officer.

"I mean I stopped, it just wasn't a complete stop," he replied.

"Which one is it, either you stopped or you didn't!" The officer's voice becoming irritable.

"You right," Block said in defeat not wanting to get on the officer's bad side. "I ran it, but as you can see on my license, I only live around da corner. I'm just trying to get in da house, dat's all."

"Is that so," the officer said, leaning in for a closer sniff, "Smells like you've been drinking."

"Officer all I have is a bottle of liquor under da seat dat I only had a cup out of! You can search da car if you choose to, but I could assure you dat it's nothin' else in here," he pleaded.

The officer stared at him for a brief moment before saying, "I tell you what... Since you're being straight with me and you only live around the corner I'm going to cut you some slack. It's the end of my shift, and I really don't feel like doing any paper work... If everything comes back legit on your license and registration, I'll send you on your way."

"Thanks a lot," he breathed a sign of relief. "You're a true gentleman and your kindness will never be forgotten."

The officer simply shook his head and walked off to run his name and tags through the system database. Once everything came back legit, the officer headed back over to return Block's credentials, just as another squad car pulled up.

"Is everything alright out here?" Questioned the second officer, walking over to the car.

"Man I know dat ain't Burt s hot ass! What da fuck is he doin in a regular uniform!" Block whispered to himself, Burt was a well known jumpout.

"Yeah everything is fine, just a little traffic stop. He's legit, so I'm sending him on his way," answered the initial officer.

Officer Burt took one glance at Block, and immediately knew who he was, "Mr. Davon Weems, how are we doing tonight?" He produced a phony smile leaning over towards the window.

"I'm cool, just tryin' to make it in da house. Dat's all!" Said Block throwing his hands up briefly.

"You sure you're going to make it, it smells like you've been drinking! You mind stepping out for a second," Burt asked.

"Burt why you doin' this! I'm three blocks from my house," he sighed. It's nothin' in da car!"

"How do I know that, besides anything can happen in a three block radius. So, can you please step out of the car," he hissed, "and I'm not going to ask you again!"

"Shit crazy!" Block mumbled stepping out.

"You say something? Speak up so I can hear you! Don't be a sissy, be a man and speak your mind son! Burt shot back.

"Burt I don't want no problems. Like I said I'm just tryin' to get in da house."

"Well act like it and put your hands on the car. Don't move until I say so. You hear me?" He shouted, pointing his finger in his face.

"What's all dat for?" Asked Block.

"Shut up!"

Everybody that was in the streets knew about Burt. When he came out, and the word got around, the area quickly went from crowded to vacant. If one thing was for certain, it's when he was on patrol, someone was getting locked up, even if he had to plant something on you. He was a six foot, heavy set, white male that was hated by all dealers because of his nefarious ways. Another thing everybody knew of him was that he wouldn't give chase, he'd simply find out who you were and make you pay later, one way or another.

Block figured that's the reason Burt was harassing him, he wasn't known to mess with people over petty stuff like he was doing at the present time. The initial officer was watching oddly as his co-worker seemed to be doing a bit extra.

"Look what I found! So you have been drinking, huh!" He uttered, placing the liquor bottle on the roof of the car, "Wonder what else I'm going to find by the time I'm finished."

A few onlookers had gathered around while Burt basically put on a show. Twenty minutes later, after searching every possible stash spot, he still came up empty handed.

"Now take everything out your pockets, and place them on the hood," he ordered, closing the trunk and walking towards him. "What y'all looking at? Y'all need to step back!" He shouted to the crowd that had formed. "Mr. Malocky do you mind showing these folks the sidewalk!"

Officer Malocky, who couldn't wait for this circus to be over with, casually walked over to the onlookers and in a respectful manner, asked if they could please back up. Block emptied everything out his pockets then placed his items on the hood of his car so Burt could pat him down.

"Man Burt I don't have nothin' else on me," Block assured him.
"Shut up! Did I ask you that, boy? Matter of fact, since you wanna keep talking slick out the mouth, I'm taking you in for D.U.I. smart ass!"
"Smart azz! I ain't say shit disrespectful to you! So I don't know why you actin' all petty and shit! What ya wife found out you was gay or

somethin', cause you sho-nuff actin' like a real homo right about now!"
He lashed out as Burt placed the handcuffs on him.

"Oh I got your homo!" Berated Burt, punching Block in his
stomach, forcing him in to the back of his squad car.

"Burt you leaving my money, keys, and phone on the hood!" He
said as they drove off.

"Does it look like I give two shits?" Burt laughed driving towards
4th District police station. Lucky for Block, Officer Malocky grabbed
everything and took it to the precinct.

Chapter 81

The next morning, Tyshelle and Ode met up at the Capitol City Diner, off of Bladensburg Road. It took some persuading, but she eventually agreed to meet up with him. When he arrived, she was already seated towards the rear of the diner. "How you doing this morning?" asked Ode, walking up to her, giving her a kiss on the cheek before taking a seat.

"I could be doing better," she replied, glancing up towards him for the first time. "You know I really don't want to be here, but I am, so talk."

"And I appreciate you taking the time to meet up with me," he said looking deep into her eyes. "When we spoke briefly yesterday on the phone, I told you I was sorry, but I would like to take dat back."

Tyshelle frowned in confusion.

"I didn't mean it like dat," he assured. "Just hear me out. I was always taught to never say dat you are sorry unless you can make it better, and I can't do dat under da circumstances. I can't bring back da deceased. I never meant to bring any harm to either of you and I'm pretty sure you are aware of dat. I mean... I would've done anything in my powers to help him to fulfill his dreams. I always wanted what was best for him. But now because of my past encounters I snatched those dreams away from someone I cared deeply for. I know two wrongs don't make a right, but I promise on my life the people dat's responsible for our loss is goin' to feel my pain!"

"See Ode, that's your problem. You need to let go of old habits and leave that street mess alone. You retaliating is only going to make matters worse. The same umbilical cord that gives you life, can also wrap itself around your throat and kill you," she expressed. "I understand that you didn't mean for any of this to happen, but what you fail to realize is that you brought violence to my home, losing me the life of my little brother who was my everything. I had so much love for you, and still do, but I can't risk being friends with you, because who's to say that it won't happen again."

He could tell that she was mentally battered and scorned, nothing he could've possibly said would've changed her state of mind. He just wanted for her to know that he had so many buried feelings inside and the only way for them to be revealed was to seek vengeance.

"You need to change your ways Ode, you have so much life ahead of you."

"This is who I am," he conceded, "I can't just up and switch off whats been embedded in me."

"I'm not trying to change you, but in order for you not to endure the same pain that you caused, the good in you must overshadow the torment you created! Until then, I wish to no longer have any ties with you," she said as the tears seemed to pour out a bit more. Cutting him completely off seemed to be the second hardest thing she'd ever done, behind burying her younger brother. "The funeral is Tuesday; I'll text you the info before I change my number."

"Tyshelle it doesn't have to be this way," he pleaded, gently grabbing her left hand.

She eased her hand away and told him goodbye in her sweetest voice, before excusing herself from the table and heading for the exit.

He wanted so badly to go after her, but her last statement shut down all hope he had left for them. He watched her disappear into the morning traffic, while sitting momentarily reflecting on everything he'd done that led up to that point. Unbeknownst to Ode, all the while he was being photographed and watched. Tyshelle had unknowingly led the law to whom they believed could be a meaningful piece to their investigation.

Chapter 82

Maurice and his two trustees stayed at the hospital overnight, while the doctors were doing everything within their powers to save China. Ms. Cathy made sure she had the best surgeons available aiding her. Maurice felt like he was being torn in two. He truly condemned himself for what happened to his niece. If he wouldn't have sent her, then none of this would've never happened. Now because of his greed, she was fighting for her life. This was a part of his life's chapter he wasn't willing to accept. He vowed no matter what, he would keep her safe, and he failed to do so. Nothing could settle the torment he felt, and it was transparent by the expression on his face.

China was suffering from a broken eye socket, broken jaw, fractured cheekbone and a gunshot wound in her chest. She was unrecognizable from the swelling and contusions. How could he have allowed this to happen? Had he gotten so comfortable that he actually involved his heart and soul in his business? The weight was bearing down heavily on his mental and taking its toll. Everything that led up to this point seemed to have derived from him acting out of character.

"We're only human with mortal flaws," Ms. Cathy stated, from the door, aware of Maurice blaming himself

"How is she?" He asked, eagerly.

"Her condition is the same. We're still running some tests. I can assure you that she's in the best of care here."

"Thank you for everything, cause I'm nothin' without her," he enunciated.

"It's the least I can do," she countered. "You all look as if you can use a meal and rest. Go and get yourselves regenerated, and if anything happens you'll be the first to know," she guaranteed.

"I'll be the first to know cause Imma be right here, but you two on the other hand, if y'all need to freshen up feel free, just don't be all day," expressed Maurice.

"Yeah I could use me a meal and shower, I smell like death," Blac joked.

"Me too," Reggie added, as they stood up. "You sure you good?"

"Yeah I'm straight. Imma eat somethin' from the kitchen," Maurice assured them.

"Aight cool! We'll see you in about two hours' tops," said Reggie, dapping Maurice followed by Blac.

Once they got into Reggie's vehicle they drove over to Rex's on Riggs Road to grab a bite to eat.

Shortly after, Reggie dropped Blac off on 1st place and Kennedy St.

"Slim hurry back, cause you know how this broad get to trippin'," retorted Blac as they turned onto the street.

"I got you," he laughed. "It shouldn't take me long at all. I'll see you in a minute."

"Bet," countered Blac, hopping out walking into his building.

Reggie didn't pull off until Blac was inside. He took Missouri Avenue to Riggs Road, straight into Hyattsville, where one of his apartments were located. After finding a place to park, he took his time getting out, before walking to the trunk. He heard an all too familiar sound. The cocking disturbance of a bullet racketing itself into a chamber startled him, "Heard y'all were looking for me!"

Chapter 83

Soon after Ode's mind settled, he realized he was being tailed. He skillfully eluded his shadow, knowing the cops must have been following Tyshelle to get to him. Once he was sure he was in the clear, he drove over to the hospital to check on Ty. He parked, then proceeded to walk towards the entrance. Approaching the entry, he saw Blac and Reggie emerge from the doorway. Ode quickly dipped behind a van, observing from a distance. He zoomed in on the vehicle they got in before hurrying to his car, and followed suit.

He stayed a descent length away, carefully trailing them as they stopped to get something to eat. He watched Reggie drop Blac off and made a mental note of his address. He then followed Reggie until he finally came to a stop. While Reggie was taking his time, Ode's impetuous instincts kicked in. His eyes darkened, resembling a lion hunting down his prey.

He crept up on Reggie, aiming his pistol at the back of his skull, then cocked the slide back, "Heard y'all was lookin' for me!" Ode uttered venomously, quickly patting him down and removing the gun on his waist band.

Reggie shook his head, disappointed that he'd got caught slippin, "So what you just goin' to shoot me right here out in the open?"

"I thought about it, but I have a better idea," he stated, knocking him in the head with the gun tossing him in his own trunk.

He quickly ran to his own vehicle to grab some rope and duct tape. When Ode came back, he checked to make sure Reggie was still unconscious. Convinced that he was, Ode securely duct taped his ankles, hands and mouth before jumping in the driver's seat and pulling off. He drove to the nearest gas station, so he could buy a gas container to fill up.

"Dollar on pump ten," Ode told the cashier, rushing off.

An ominous feeling came over him when he glanced up and saw a Prince George's County squad car pull up to the pump directly behind him. The officer in the vehicle seemed to be staring at him attentively. Ode tried to play it cool by casually unscrewing the top off the container, so he could place the pump inside. Ode stood at an angle so the cop wouldn't notice the slight bulge on his hip from the clip of his weapon.

The officer emerged from his vehicle, causing Ode to squeeze his pistol. Ode wasn't taking any chances, cause if the cop made any threatenbing gestures, he was going to let loose everything he had in his grip.

"Excuse me sir but I couldn't help but notice..." the officer started to say as a radio call came through.

The gas pump was just finishing when the officer turned his attention back towards Ode.

"As I was saying, I couldn't help but to notice..."

Don't make me do this, Ode thought, gripping the pistol even tighter.

"You have a slight crack in your left tail light," he stated, causing Ode to let out a sigh of relief. "With a nice ride like that I strongly suggest you get that taken care of," he advised.

"I'm on my way to take care of it, as soon as I finish cuttin' my grandma's grass," he countered, swiftly tucking the gun back into his waistband. "Have a nice evening officer," he smiled as he twisted the top back on the container. He walked around to the driver's side, got in and pulled off. *Stupid azz cop bout to lose his life, having me crash out over a dumb azz tail light*, he thought out loud as he drove to a secluded area.

When he got out and opened the trunk Reggie was still laying there, passed out. His eyes quickly opened after a few smacks to the face.

"Get da fuck up nigga!" Ode snapped coldly, snatching the duct tape from Reggie's mouth.

"Aaaahhhh!" Reggie grimaced, shooting Ode a devilish look.

"Which one of y'all clowns shot that Lil' boy up on 5th and Rittenhouse?" He questioned.

"Don't know what you talkin' 'bout."

"Oh yeah," he countered, shooting Reggie in his shin bone.

"Aaahhh Fuck!" He cried out from the pain.

"Don't make me ask you again!" Ode threatened.

"Man fuck you and that Lil boy!" He fumed boldly.

"Dat's how you feel?" Hissed Ode. He immediately snapped, hitting Reggie repeatedly in his face until it was basically smashed in. Still not satisfied with the outcome, he pulled out the gun that he took from Reggie and emptied the clip into his body. Ode didn't feel a bit of sympathy as Reggie laid engulfed in his own pool of blood.

Afterwards he scrolled through Reggie's phone, finding Blac's number, he sent him a text message telling him to be outside in 15 minutes. Blac immediately text back telling Reggie to hurry cause his lady friend was giving him a severe headache.

Ode simply replied with a, "Lol I got you, just be out front."

"Yeah I got you alright. I got something that's going to take that pain away," he uttered to himself, driving over to Blac's.

Chapter 84

Scrap basically walked around the hospital for nearly a half hour, determined to locate China. He was relieved to some degree, after he'd heard a couple of doctors talking about how she'd pulled through. He'd had a difficult time tracking her down because he didn't know her full birth name. After describing the incident to one of the nurses, she knew exactly who he was speaking of and politely directed him towards a room.

"Thanks," he said rushing off. His heart was beating out his chest as he approached the door. He took a deep breath before entering without knocking. When he first walked in he thought he had strolled into the wrong room. He didn't recognize the patient before him, because of the bandages that covered her face.

"Who's you? Every open door isn't an invitation!" Maurice spat standing up.

"My bad," Scrap said throwing his hands up as if he was stopping traffic. "I didn't mean no disrespect, I was just hoping to find my lady friend dat's all," he apologized, glancing back towards the patient. He quickly zoomed in on the birthmark that covered part of her right leg. He remembered noticing it the night they were in the hotel together, "China!" He exclaimed, moving towards her.

"Hold up young blood," Maurice stated. "I'll appreciate it if you turn around and walk back out that door, cause I don't know who you are!" He expressed seriously.

"You have every right to feel da way you do, but I feel it's my duty to be next to her in her weakest moment," he stated sincerely, as Ms. Cathy walked through the door, causing them both to look in her direction.

"Oh I didn't know someone else was in here with you," she stated sensing the tension between the two. "Unfortunately only family is allowed in here."

The two briefly eyed each other before Maurice decided to speak up, "Ms. Cathy he's good. He's with me," he relented. He stepped to the side, allowing Scrap to walkover next to China.

He gently grabbed her hand saying a silent prayer. As he stood there genuinely expressing his true feelings to China, it seemed as though their connection had some affect on Ms. Cathy and Maurice. Their fingers had somehow become intertwined. Maurice not sure of how to react, just simply went long with it.

A smile formed on Ms. Cathy's face, when Maurice didn't end their connection. She had always secretly cared for Maurice, and this was the first time that she made an attempt to show it. The timing seemed perfect. Not wanting to overdue anything, she whispered that she'd be back to check on them, then gave him a kiss on his cheek, before leaving him there to ponder about what had happened.

Once Scrap concluded his one on one with China, he casually stood up and walked over to thank Maurice.

"They say that the eyes never lie," he quoted. "Even though I don't know you, I could sense the sincerity in you. By the way my name is Reese," he extended his hand.

"I'm Shawn, but my friends call me Scrap," he replied, returning the friendly gesture.

"Have a seat," signaled Maurice.

An hour had flew passed before the ringing of Scrap's phone interrupted their conversation, "You mind excusing me for one moment?" Scrap said, stepping out the room then answering the phone. "Hello!"

"You have a collect call from, 'Davon Weems,' from the D.C Detention Correctional Facility. To accept the call dial one, to decline the call dial two, to block any further calls press--," Scrap hurried and pressed one, wondering how in the world he ended up over in D.C. Jail.

"Slim what da fuck are you doin' over in the jail?" He asked as loudly as he could without shouting.

"You not goin' to believe this shit," he countered, then commenced to explaining the story of every thing that happened from the moment they left each other to the incident that led to him getting locked up.

"Yeah, but dat still don't answer my question of how you ended up over there. If you got arrested for D.U.I then you should've paid your citation and been out," said Scrap.

"Naw you ain't let me finish. I was about to get released when Burt comes back to me talkin' bout I might as well get comfortable cause it doesn't look like I'm goin' nowhere anytime soon, smilin' and shit! So I'm thinkin' da pig jokin' until I saw da other officer dat was on da scene, and he told me dat my fingerprint was found on a scene of a homicide," he explained.

"You serious!"

"Yeah Slim," Block assured him in a dead pan tone. "Oh I need for you to stop by da crib and grab my twin daughters up, and keep 'em with you. Let 'em know daddy should be home soon."

"I'm a get right on top of it. Anything you need just hit me and let me know. You need some money on ya books?" He asked.

"Not at da moment."

"Okay, dat's a bet big boy. Let me go handle dat situation for you, so just hold tight. I got you!" He confirmed.

"Bet, you do dat. Luv nigga!" Stated Block.

"Luv nigga!" Scrap shot back, then ended the call.

Scrap knew that he had to hurry, Block had made sure Scrap understood he needed to go to his house and grab the two guns he had in there, just in case the police decide to search it. Scrap walked back into the room telling Maurice that he had a family emergency, but promised to be back everyday until things got better for China.

He walked over to her, gave her a kiss on her hand and said, "Get well baby girl," before turning to Maurice dapping him up, and stepping out the door.

Chapter 85

"How come you never spend any time with me? You always popping up when you want, then rushing back out after you get what you want! I'm tired of you treating me like that! You better start finding some time for me!" The woman shouted, speaking up for herself.

"Or what! What you goin' to do? Don't forget I'm lookin' out for you, payin' your bills! Don't get me wrong, I do fuck wit' you, but you knew what it was from the jump! I don't stay here wit' you Meka! I pay the bills here, but this still your shit. If you don't like how things are workin' out between us then say somethin', otherwise I ain't really tryin' to hear that shit you preachin'!" Blac shot back.

"I am speaking my mind, and you heard what I said," she scolded.

"Look, what you wanna do? I ain't changing up my program," he replied sternly.

"Well I think you should get your stuff and leave, I'm not going to be just lying around here like I'm your love slave. I have a life and too much time on my hands to be waiting on someone that don't want the same as I do," she expressed.

Blac glanced down at his phone after receiving a text that his ride was outside. "Look my ride out front, so you sure about what you sayin'?"

"Yeah I'm sure," she responded hesitantly, standing with her arms folded.

"Fuck it then, it is what it is! Hope you have some other means of income, cause I'm not payin' for nothin' else in this muthafuck! I'll be back to get my shit later!" He barked, grabbing his keys off the table and heading towards the door.

"So it's just that easy for you to leave, huh?" She snapped in disbelief standing in his path, her hand on her hip.

"Don't try to put this shit on me! This is your choice! Now 'cuse me," he said walking around her so he could leave.

"Blac if you leave out that door, don't come back, and I mean it!" She threatened, as he unhesisantly unlocked the door and walked out, not looking back.

"Ooohhh he make me sick!" She berated. She stormed into her room, grabbed as much of his stuff she could possibly bear, and rushed out the door after him.

By the time she made it out front, Blac was damn near in Reggie's car.

"Blac you better come get this stuff, or Imma leave this mess out here!" She warned.

"I wish the fuck you would leave my shit out here!" he said turning around back towards her. He quickly thought about it and stopped, "matter of fact you could keep that shit!" He spat, back peddling to Reggie's vehicle. "Nigga what took you so long, cause shorty…" he started but was interrupted when he realized the male in the driver's seat was pointing a gun to his head.

"Y 'all chose da wrong nigga to fuck wit'," Ode uttered, shooting Blac twice in his face, point blank range, then kickin' 'em back out the car.

The two shots instantly startled Meka, causing her to look up and witness Blac's body being shoved onto the street. "Oh, God nooo!" She shouted tossing his clothes to the ground and bolting over to him. As she got closer, she prayed the man she had strong feelings for wasn't laying lifeless in the middle of the street. Once she reached him she saw a sight that would remain embedded in her mind for ever.

Chapter 86

As the day started to wind down Big Lyn met up with Shaka at the Penthouse Gentlemen's Club on Georgia Avenue and Park Road. They two instantly turned heads once they entered the clubhouse cause their presence demanded attention. Shaka entered the establishment first, wearing an all black knitted button up and matching tie by Tom Ford. On the bottom, he wore a pair of slim fit denim, Seven Jeans with a comfortable pair of Vallentino slip-ons. His Tom Ford glasses and black rubber BRM watch completed his fit.

Big Lyn on the other hand, was always dressed as if he were attending a red carpet event. He could've been in a room full of Oprah's and Trump's and still stood out. His character was intriguing and mysterious at the same time. He slid in behind Shaka smoothly with his dark Bosalina Fedora tilted to one side like the boss that he was. It was as if Dolce and Gabbana had him in mind when they'd designed the outfit he was rocking.

The loafers by John Lobb Lopez were so comfortable it felt like he was walking on clouds and the watch he sported probably could've took someone's vision.

Out of habit, they chose a table in the top far end corner, so they'd be able to see the whole view of the club. It didn't take long after they sat down for the dancers to flock to their seats. It don't take long for word to spread throughout the club who the big spenders were. They tipped well, but kept conversation brief. Big Lyn didn't show it but he was highly disturbed about the prior night's incident. Losing two blood relatives and four other associates was unacceptable, and one way or another, retribution was inevitable.

"Nothing went right yesterday," stated Big Lyn.

"I can agree, but something will surface soon," assured Shaka. "The word already circulated about your boy," he informed.

"That was quick. We just had that meeting this morning."

"I know, but with that kind of money on someone, word seems to travel fast," countered Shaka.

"I bet it does, especially when it's a concrete jungle full of starving animals looking for a come up," replied Big Lyn as his cellphone vibrated on his hip. He instantly recognized the number, "didn't expect to be hearing from you so soon," "What you got?" He answered.

"It's probably nothing, but I still called to let you know anyway. A neighbor claimed to have seen a white car leave the area, around the time of the incident. Thought it was a Cadillac, or a Lincoln or something of that nature," the caller explained, "which ever one it was, it was a big four door vehicle."

"A big white four door vehicle," Big Lyn said to himself, recollecting to when Scrap and his little men had rolled up in a brand new white Cadillac. "Thanks, you've been more than helpful. Call me should anything else arise. Let's do dinner so I can show you my appreciation."

"Gladly! You pick the time and place and I'll be there."

"Enough said. You'll be hearing from me soon," assured Big Lyn ending his conversation.

"You good?" Shaka asked.

"My inside source was just informing me that a neighbor claimed to have seen a white four door leaving around the time of the incident," he explained.

"Does that ring a bell?"

"Yeah but I hope it's not what I'm thinking," Big Lyn admitted.

"And if it is?"

"Then there's a penalty to pay for treason," he announced.

Chapter 87

As promised, Scrap went to Block's home and got on top of his situation like he'd asked him to. He made sure not to take long, just in case the authorities decided to kick the door in. He also managed to reach out to a lawyer that would hopefully be able to get his partner off. Scrap made a stop to pick up some money, then paid the lawyer. After that he headed to the hotel to bring Worl up on everything that had happened.

"What's good wit' you?" Greeted Worl hopping in Scrap's car.

"A whole lot," Scrap answered.

"Oh yeah, like what?"

"First and foremost, Block's over da Jail," he said.

"For what?" Worl replied.

Scrap shook his head, leaned back into his seat and relayed to him what Block had said and also what had happened around Riggs Park while he was in New York.

"I thought that we all agreed to wait until I came back!" Worl proclaimed.

"Yeah I know but they took it upon themselves to slide through, and now da shit back firing on them," said Scrap.

"Them niggas movin' too fast! This shit messed up!"

"I did manage to get 'em a lawyer," Scrap confirmed.

"Dat's a good thing, so how much he or she hittin' for?"

"She's hittin' for forty stacks because da nature of his charge," said Scrap.

"Forty thousand! Damn we gotta get on a serious grind."

"We good don't trip. I got it, plus I just came from givin' her a retainer fee," Scrap said.

"Slim where da fuck you goin' get forty stacks from to pay da lawyer off?" Worl asked, taking a sip of the juice he had in his hand.

"Would you believe me if I told you while you were gone I came across eight hundred and forty stacks," Scrap said.

Juice instantly flew out Worl's mouth, "damn, my bad Slim! Are you fuckin' serious?" He hissed, looking in the glove box for napkins.

"Dead azz serious!" He exclaimed.

"How da fuck... I can't believe... tell me you ain't bullshittin'," he countered shockingly.

"I'm definitely not bullshittin', but somethin' terrible came with it," he stated, his demeanor changing. "Not only did Block and I punish Big Lyn's nephew, Elmo, and his two men Zay and Gizz, but China's at da hospital in critical condition," scrap explained.

The information was like a slap in his face. Worl didn't know how to digest the information. "I'm lost! How did all of this come about, and how is China mixed up in all of this?"

"Bruh I can't really explain how she's mixed up in it, but all I know is dat she was at Big Lyn's spot on 14th when I slid past there."

"And?" Worl asked, waiting to hear the full story.

Scrap began to meticulously explain the incident, filling in all the blanks so Worl would have a clear picture. Worl had mixed feelings after hearing what took place, asking himself would he had done the same thing.

"Dat's a messed up situation," said Worl.

"Who you tellin'," agreed Scrap.

"Ra-Ra goin' to be messed up when she finds out 'bout her friend."

"Yeah I'm hip, but don't tell her, she goin' to be wonderin' how you found out," said Scrap.

"I ain't sayin' nothin' to her at all," he countered, "but all I'm sayin' is, she's goin' to be leary about why she hasn't heard from her, I'm pretty sure they talk everyday. Besides dat, what we goin' to do about this Big Lyn situation? From what you told me, dat bread might have to stay put up for a minute," Worl suggested.

"Dat's what I plan on doin' until I figure things out."

"Yeah dat's ya best bet," Worl added. "There's no way dat he could link you to dat house is it?"

"Naw, I doubt it," Scrap answered, just as his cellphone started ringing. He gave Worl a worried look after realizing who the caller was.

"Who's dat?" Asked Worl, picking up on Scrap's glare.

"Big Lyn," he replied, pressing the button.

Chapter 88

Maurice had given Reno a deadline on when to take Bo out. This was the night that Reno was hoping would never come, but it had, and there was no turning back. As Reno was waiting on Bo to pick him up, he realized that he was getting more and more nervous by the minute. *I can't do this,* he thought, *but if I don't my family is in danger.*

The sound of the horn startled him. "Shit! He got here quick," he stated. His nerves were in over drive, making the forty-five-minute wait seem shorter. *Damn! What am I goin' to do?* He was walking slower than usual, and his head hung low as he got in Bo's car.

"Wassup bruh?" Greeted Bo.

"Not too much," replied Reno.

"Ma Dukes said she wants you to come through on Sunday for dinner after she comes from church, 'cause you haven't been by to see her lately," explained Bo.

Reno didn't respond, he just stared out the window.

"You heard me?" Questioned Bo.

"Uh, yeah I heard you."

"What's wrong wit' you? You actin' like you lost ya best friend or somethin'!"

"Only if you knew," Reno mumbled.

"What you say?" Asked Bo, glancing over towards him.

"I said, we know that ain't true," he cleaned up.

"Of course not, cause I wouldn't be here," Bo joked.

Reno gave up a half smile, before asking where they were going.

"I'm bout to swing past Rittenhouse and see if we can bump into these niggas, Ty haven't been answerin' his phone. Them clowns probably was bullshittin' from the jump," he stated.

"You think so."

"Hope not, but why else would Slim not be answerin'."

"Who knows, anything could've happened," suggested Reno.

"True, but you ain't goin' to believe what I found out when I stopped by one of Maurice's traps."

"You stopped by one of his traps," Reno grimaced. "You haven't been stopping by none of his spots! You don't think that was some hot azz shit, especially after you had me tellin' that nigga you was plottin' on 'em! Nigga that shit was stupid from the jump! You could've gotten both of us killed with that dumb shit! You didn't give a fuck that you threw me under the bus, if you did you wouldn't have done it! But you know what, if you don't care neither do I!" He barked, pulling his gun out and pointing it at Bo. "Pull this muthafucka over!"

"This some kind of a joke or somethin'," retorted Bo.

"Do I look like I'm jokin," answered Reno, gravely.

"This has to be a bad dream, cause ain't no way somethin' like this could possibly be happenin'," Bo stated, pulling over on the side of the street.

"Slim I asked if you were sure 'bout pullin' that move on that nigga," said Reno feeling remorseful for what their brotherhood had come to, as a tear dropped from his eye.

"Bruh, what are you talkin' bout! We both agreed to this."

"Maybe so, but I didn't agree to be thrown into the lion's den, that nigga threatened to kill my family if I didn't kill you," Reno hissed.

"Then what am I? I am ya family," he expressed. "You allowed the same nigga that we plotted against, to turn you against me. We're like brothers, my mother changed your diapers, and vice versa. This what it comes down to, after everything we done been through! It's obvious the love I had for you wasn't mutual," he sympathized.

"This isn't as easy for me as you tryin' to make it out to be," he assured him.

"I can't tell, but you know what?"

"What!"

"If you caught the news, and kept ya ears to the street then you would've known that what you 'bout to do is irrelevant. Not only were Blac and Reggie killed earlier, but someone put that bag on Maurice's head.

"Yeah right!" Reno responded, not believing what he just heard. "Then why would you go past the trap houses, or still be lookin' for Ty and them?"

"'Cause as soon as I caught the incident on the news I flew past the traps to make it seem like Maurice needed me to scoop some money up, but the bread was already gone. I'm goin' around Rittenhouse, cause I'm more than sure they most likely responsible for what happened, and I'm still tryin' to find away to get this bread off of Maurice. Especially without his two henchman, before it's to late," he explained.

As Reno sat there taking in what Bo had told him, he started feeling stupid for ever pulling his gun out. He knew that he'd made a terrible mistake by doing so, but it was too late to go back to how things were. The old saying, "never pull your gun out unless you going to use it," had become a reality for him, he had to use it, "I'm sorry bruh."

"Me too," countered Bo.

"For what," Reno frowned.

"This!" He spat, placing three shells into Reno's chest. The look on his face was depressing to watch, but it had to be done. Reno battled to catch his breath but eventually took his last, slumping forward. Depressed from taking his childhood friend's life, he retrieved the gun from Reno's clutch before pulling off. Any resentment he felt was justified by Reno's actions. Now, how was he going to explain to his mother that Reno wouldn't be able to make it to dinner on Sunday?

Chapter 89

It took some debating, but Ms. Cathy eventually convinced Maurice to go home and try to get some rest, the bags under his eyes made it clear that he was in desperate need of some.

After realizing that it had been hours since he'd last seen or heard from either of his henchman, he agreed.

Not only was he unprotected, but the feeling he had in his gut, told him that something had happened. If that was the case, he was sure to be next on the menu. Everything he grinded for and built seemed to be crumbling, but he always kept a back up plan for situations as such. Luckily for him, he had a substantial amount in his stock accounts, cause that eight hundred and forty thousand dollars he lost knocked a serious dent in his cash flow.

Seeing that he didn't have anyone around at the moment, Ms. Cathy offered him a ride, hoping to maybe discuss the connection she'd felt earlier, on the way. She was a single independent woman who knew what she wanted in a man, and he met her standards. She couldn't understand why she was always attracted to street dudes. That was one of the reasons she even agreed to doing side jobs for Maurice. It wasn't about the money, she didn't need any, it was the thrill she got from it.

Her sisters used to always question her about it, and she would respond by jokingly, quoting Tupac Shakur, saying, "She 'needs a Thug in her life'." She used to also say that a square dude wasn't well rounded enough for her liking. Despite her preference, she never got slowed up, or side tracked from reaching her goals in life. Her sisters eventually stopped judging her for her taste in men, and started evaluating her on her work ethics. Not only did she graduate high school top of her class, but she'd done eight years of college. Ms. Cathy was the type of women that could have any man she chose, yet she was choosing Maurice, but was he willing to choose her?

"I just wanna say thanks for everything you've done, and I mean that," Maurice stated genuinely, as they parked in front of his home in Riggs Park. "You have to be one of the most resilient people that I know, cause I know that your job alone has to be overwhelming."

"It can be at times, but that's what I signed up for. Besides, I like being able to help or save people's lives if I can," she replied.

"That's good to know. I'm glad to have someone like you on my side," he smiled.

"Well I'm elated to know that you feel that way," she countered. "So this is where Mr. Maurice resides, huh?" She asked, changing the subject.

"Unfortunately, this is where I used to dwell," he corrected. "I'm in the process of movin'. It's time to put some space between myself and this area for a while. Too much been goin' on lately."

"Sorry to hear that, but that can be a good thing," she replied.

"Yeah maybe," was his response. "Do you care to come in?"

"Sure," she answered, wondering what took him so long to ask.

"Follow me," he directed, exiting her vehicle.

Looking like a true couple, they strolled into the house together.

"This is real nice!" She complimented when she entered.

"Thanks! It's fair for a square," he joked. "Care for somethin' to drink?"

"Don't mind if I do. What do you have to offer?"

After he told her what he had in stock, she agreed to a glass of cranberry juice. They then headed into the den area, where he told her to make herself at home.

"Excuse me while I go check on my dog. It's been almost a day and a half, I know I have some cleanin' and feedin' to do," he stated, handing her the remote for the television.

"Thank you," she replied taking the remote. As Maurice went to tend to his dog's needs, she couldn't help but glance around and admire what she saw. She could immediately tell that the inside had been upgraded. Once she finished briefly surveying the interior, she sat back on the couch, turning the television on. She didn't find anything to her liking at the moment, so she settled for the news.

Shortly after, Maurice emerged from the basement to join her, "Sorry for leaving you up here like that, but I had to make sure my baby girl was straight," he said.

"Well I know she feels special," she replied, showing a set of pretty white teeth. "You treat all your women with such care?"

"Only the ones I got love for," he responded, staring into her eyes passionately.

"So what category do I fit in?" She asked sensing the attraction between them.

"That depends."

"On?" She questioned.

"Where you wanna be," he replied.

"If it's up to me, then I would love to be that woman in your life," she admitted.

"Is that so?" He countered inching closer, now invading her space.

"Pretty much," she assured him, not breaking eye contact.

Truth be told, Maurice was always fond of Ms. Cathy. He just never thought that she would be interested in a street dude. Only a fool would turn down Ms. Cathy's offer. Not only was she the spitting image of Thelma off of Good Times, face and body wise, but she was one of the head physician in the hospital.

"I must admit that the feelin' is mutual, but I must warn you that there's a lot goin' on in my life right now. I seriously doubt you would want to be tangled up with me, especially since it could possibly jeopardize your job," he said.

"All my life I've been picked on about my decision in the men I chose," she smiled, "But not once has that deterred me from accomplishing any of my goals. You wanna know why?"

"Why is that?" He replied.

"Cause I always chose men that had morals and principles, such as yourself," she accentuated, now standing so close to him that she could feel his body heat.

"I admire a woman that knows what she wants in her man," he stated, closing in for a kiss, but just when their lips slightly touched, he noticed something on his television from the corner of his eye that put things to a halt.

"What's wrong?" She asked, instantly seeing the seriousness in his glare. When she followed his stare, she noticed the ten o'clock news had a familiar face plastered on the screen. Maurice grabbed the remote to turn up the volume.

"Twenty-six-year-old Antonio Stewart was found in the middle of 1st Place, northwest Washington D.C. with two gunshots wounds to his face. One witness says the victim was seen entering a new model, dark color, four door Lexus. Shorty after, authorities were called to the scene of a burning vehicle that matched the description of the same automobile used in the Antonio Stewart's shooting. When the fire was put out authorities then found an additional unidentified corpse in the trunk," the news anchor communicated, leaving Maurice speechless.

He immediately felt as if he was living in a house of cards, and with any slight movement the structure would come crashing down without warning. He couldn't believe what he was seeing on TV, and knew more than likely the body found in the trunk was Reggie's.

"Let me grab a few things, we need to get out of here!" He stated sternly, walking off to retrieve a few items, before exiting the house.

Chapter 90

The following morning, Block was in the day room with a few of the other inmates, when he overheard his name being called by one of the correctional officers.

"Davon Weems!" Shouted the female officer.

"Wassup C.O.!" He answered.

"Legal visit," she confirmed.

"Damn already," he stated as he stood from the table. "Imma see y'all when I get back from seeing what this fake azz public pretender talkin' bout'," he belittled, stepping away from the table. He quickly grabbed his hallway pass from the officer then went to go meet his lawyer. When he stepped in the visiting room he noticed a petite, blonde headed, Caucasian female standing there.

"How are you Mr. Weems?" She greeted. "My name is Micki Clocks, and I'll be representing you," she expressed, extending her hand to greet him.

"Nice to meet you," he replied, returning the friendly gesture. "Aren't you a paid lawyer?"

"Yes I am," she assured him.

"So who hired you?"

"Uhm," she hesitated, flipping through some papers. "Your cousin, Shawn Dixon. I normally don't meet with clients so soon, but I had to speak with someone else, and decided to pull you out while I'm here," she said.

"Well I'm glad you decided to pull me out," he smiled.

She gave a slight grin before getting to the matter at hand. "I was reviewing the police report, and it seem as though your prints were found at the scene of a homicide," she explained. "Now, even though these are serious accusation, if these fingerprints are the only evidence they plan to use, with no eye witness, I'll have this case thrown out at the grand jury. But it's too early to assume what evidence they'll try and use to convince the grand jury to get an indictment. I do see that you don't have a criminal background, and that's a plus. My advice to you is to stay out of trouble, and watch what you say over the phones, cause all that does is makes my job harder."

"You have my word on dat Ms. Clocks," he assured her.

"Good," she replied, once again shaking his hand. "I'll keep in touch," she concluded, wrapping things up.

Block left the attorney visit with a sigh of relief, after hearing her speak of his case. Once he made it back to his unit, he immediately got on the phone so he could call Scrap and thank him, but didn't get an answer. After trying again, and having the same results, he tried Ode, who instantly picked up.

"Wassup big boy?" Answered Ode, after accepting the call.

"Ain't too much, just came back from seeing my lawyer," Block replied.

"Oh yeah! What they talkin' bout?"

"She ain't talkin' bad, but it's too early to speculate," Block responded. "Wassup wit you though?"

"Shit! Pullin' up at da hospital, Ty's 'bout to get discharged," Ode confirmed.

"Dat's a good thing!" He said with excitement. "Tell'em I said wassup."

"Dat's a bet," assured Ode.

"You talk to Scrap, cause I been tryin' to call 'em?"

"Nah I haven't heard from him, why what's good?"

"Ain't nothin', just tryin' to thank 'em for gettin' da attorney, dat's all."

"If I talk to'em before you, I'll let'em know," Ode gave his word.

"Yeah you do dat, cause we'll probably be locked down, they got us on this half a day shit," Block uttered.

"I got you. You need anything?"

"I'm straight for now. I'll probably hit you tomorrow. I'm 'bout to finish whippin' these fools in dominoes, before we lock in," stated Block, wrapping up their conversation.

"Aight big boy! Hit me whenever."

"Bet! Luv nigga!" Block concluded.

"Luv!" Ode countered, ending their call.

Chapter 91

Ode parked, then high stepped into the hospital, eager to finally pick up his partner. Once he got off the elevator he walked into Ty's room with a huge grin. "Wassup fool," greeted Ode, dapping his man up.

"What's good nigga," Ty replied.

"I know you ready to get outta here."

"Hell yeah! You already know," Ty responded.

"How you feelin'?"

"Besides being a lil' sore, I'm good," he assured him.

"Can't keep a good man down, huh?" Ode commented.

"Not even wit' cement blocks tied to'em," he smiled, grabbing his things. "I wish this doctor would hurry up with these discharge papers, so a nigga can get outta here," he exclaimed.

"Slim, I got somethin' to tell you!" Ode exclaimed, bringing his right fist and left palm together.

"What?"

"Slim, guess who I ran into yesterday when I was comin' to see you!"

"Who, fool?"

"Blac and Reggie," he blurted out.

"Oh yeah? And what happened?" Ty inquired animated.

"Let's just say old rivalries die hard," he uttered.

"You bullshittin'," he hissed shockingly.

"Ya' boy a workhorse," he boasted, bragging on finally seeking vengeance, before explicating what had occurred, from start to finish.

"So what you do wit' da bamma's car?"

"I burnt dat jo'nt up around Fort Lincoln, before hiking to South Dakota Avenue and Bladensburg Road, then caught a cab back to my car," he explained.

"You went hard as shit, but I respect it," Ty shot back.

"I had to go hard for my niggas, plus witnessing Lil Kent gettin' gunned down," he said, briefly drifting off in deep thought. "Ain't no way I was lettin' them clowns get away," proclaimed Ode.

"You did what you had to do," he remarked. "Now all we have to do is catch up wit' Maurice."

"He gonna get his next, plus he's more vulnerable now dat his two henchmen gone."

"Well since you took dat nigga's arms, I wanna be da one to take his head," Ty announced vehemently, as the doctor strolled in with his paperwork.

"Mr. Dixon how are you feeling?" Asked the doctor.

"Feelin' good, doc."

"Well sign right here for me, and you'll be good to go," said the doctor, handing over the paper.

Ty quickly took the paper, signed it and gave it back to the doctor with a friendly smile, before shaking his hand.

"That'll be all," confirmed the doctor.

"Thanks," countered Ty as him and Ode left the room.

The two were fooling around as they strolled through the hospital. Nearing the exit, Ode noticed the last face he expected to see.

"Slim, today must be our lucky day," Ode uttered, halting Ty as they were walking.

"What you talkin' 'bout?"

"Look over by da vending machines," directed Ode, as Ty glanced over in that direction.

"I know dat ain't Slim," Ty replied, feeling his blood starting to boil.

"Dat's definitely him," confirmed Ode.

"You strapped," asked Ty

"You know it," assured Ode.

"Let me get dat," Ty demanded, as Maurice walked off from the vending machines.

Ode underhandedly passed Ty his gun, as the two went in pursuit. While the doctors and patients roamed about, they were unnoticeably closing the gap between them and their target. Ode was right on Ty's heels the entire time, ready for whatever was to come their way. Maurice turned down a hall that had a smaller portion of people, which was more suitable for the unavoidable situation. Not thinking about the consequences of his actions, Ty slowly started pulling the pistol from his waistband, while picking up pace. As Maurice entered a room, the elevator opened, revealing the same two homicide detectives that recently questioned him about being shot. On cue, Ty spun around, swiftly pushing Ode into the corner, out of sight.

"What da hell is you doin'?" Uttered Ode, caught off guard from Ty's sudden actions.

"Shhhh!" Whispered Ty, hushing Ode from drawing attention.

"You see them two getting off da elevator? Those the same two detectives dat questioned me da other day."

"Slim you ain't goin' believe this!" Ode countered, after zooming in on the two detectives.

"Believe what?" Ty questioned.

"Those da same two dat was followin' me yesterday after I left from talkin' to Shell," confirmed Ode.

"Damn! This nigga Maurice lucky as shit," hissed Ty, realizing that he might've just been exonerated from his death sentence.

"We'll catch dat bamma some other time, cause we most definitely can't let them see us both together. These fools will start tryin' to peace shit together," Ode suggested.

"No bullshit," agreed Ty, as they waited for the detectives to leave out of sight so they could exit the hospital.

"C'mon let's go!" Ode rushed sensing that the coast was clear for them to exit the hospital unseen.

Chapter 92

Maurice's paranoia had gotten the best of him, his instincts were telling him that he was being followed. Unsure, he decided he would take precautionary actions, and put China's room under an unknown name. The first person he saw when he walked into the room was Scrap, "Scrap what's good?" He spoke a bit uneasy.

"I'm coolin'," he replied sensing Maurice's discomfort, "is everything aight?" A concerned Scrap inquired.

"Yeah! Just been a long night that's all," he replied.

Maurice played it cool, as he spoke to Scrap about the sudden changes he planned on making. Due to his lack of knowledge of how she actually made it to the hospital, he felt he probably should've made the change sooner.

"Where Ms. Cathy go?" Maurice asked Scrap.

"Here I am!" She answered before Scrap got a chance to, as she walked into the room.

Maurice didn't waist anytime going about switching rooms, and putting China under an alias, just to be on the safe side. Ms. Cathy quickly agreed without question. Now the next step was for him to make sure that China would be moved undetected, in case he was being followed. Maurice told Scrap to walk and talk with him, while he allowed Ms. Cathy to do the switch. He tried to throw Scrap off by having casual conversation, but his body language and demeanor told Scrap that something else had his attention. Maurice was scanning the area for anyone suspicious, until he received a call from Ms. Cathy confirming the change was made.

After twenty more minutes of waiting, Ms. Cathy texted him with the new room number. Satisfied that the area seemed safe, the pair headed to the alternate room. Scrap sensed that something wasn't right by them shifting rooms but he chose to not intervene, it wasn't his personal concern. Maurice acknowledged the fact that Scrap simply went along with the program without question, and that was a good sign. Maurice made it clear to Scrap that until China healed he was the only person he would need to talk to about her.

Over the course of a few weeks, time had passed without any difficulties. Maurice and Scrap had bonded more, and China's condition had improved, but she was still unable to open her eyes or talk. The pair had stuffed her room with so many balloons, get well cards and teddy bears, it was hard to even set foot in the door. They were standing by her side through it all, which was more beneficial for Maurice. The beef had subsided, due to him always being at the hospital.

In that short period of time, Maurice and Ms. Cathy had also gotten much closer. She was about to move out of her home and into his. He eventually transferred all of his and China's belongings from his house in Riggs Park, into their new home in Accokee. Once the residence was vacant, Maurice contacted his former real estate agent to put the house on the market. The agent was so eager to get back into Maurice's good graces that not only was he highly pleased to help, but he sold the house within three weeks. All he wanted in return was for Maurice to promise to do more business with him in the near future, to which he agreed. Maurice was moving real light now days, especially after discovering that someone had put a price on his head. Even though he was staying under the radar, he still was making minor moves just to keep some form of income generating.

On the other hand, Scrap and his circle were slowly but surely making a huge come up. The product that Worl had gotten from Fito panned out to being the best China on the market. With the money that Scrap had stashed, along with the cash they had pouring in, he and his partner's would soon be on top. With the exception of China being hospitalized, things couldn't have been going any smoother for Scrap. His comrade Block still hadn't been indicted on the charges that he was being accuse of, plus Scrap exonerated himself from Big Lyn's suspicion by denying any knowledge of the incident pertaining to the demise of his nephew, and associates. When questioned about Block's whereabouts around the time, his response was that Block was incarcerated.

Big Lyn, trusting and caring for Scrap like a son, honered his word, for the moment. Other than that, there was one other thing that still concerned Scrap, and that was the beef that had already consumed the lives of several people, including the innocent. Their main target seemed to have vanished, and that worried him to some degree. He knew sooner or later their enemy would be sure to retaliate for what happened to his two trustees. Still, no one other than Ode and Ty knew how Maurice actually looked, so it was impossible for anyone else to do anything without either of their presence. For the time being they were going to play things by ear, and hopefully be prepared when the time came. After weeks without any form of retribution, Scrap and his circle started to believe that Maurice either went into hide out or simply relocated, but what Scrap didn't know was that the enemy had been within arms reach the entire time.

They say what you don't know won't hurt you, but they also say that the unknown could possibly be the cause of one's demise.

Chapter 93

On a nice Wednesday evening, Ode and Ty decided to hit Pentagon city mall in Alexandria, Virginia, and do a little bit of shopping. Ode bought himself an Elie Tahari jacket, a water color plaid shirt, a pair of Barker Black Striped and Lacoste mid-strap sneakers. Ty on the other hand only copped himself a Michael Kors Utility Coat, and a pair of Mark Nason Facility leather sneakers. The two opted to hit the food court, after leaving from out of Bloomingdale's. They were fooling around as they were going down the escalator when Ty spotted a familiar face that he'd been longing to see since the day he got shot.

"Ay Slim, tell me dat ain't who I think it is," Ty uttered, tapping Ode on his shoulder, gesturing to the person he was speaking of.

"Dat's most definitely him," confirmed Ode.

"C'mon before we miss this clown, it looks like he's heading towards da exit," hissed Ty, as the pair rushed down the escalator. "Here take da bags and get da car, while I follow this fool!"

"Bet," countered Ode, rushing off to get the vehicle.

The two branched off in different directions, Ty picked up his pace to close the gap between himself and his mark. Ty wasn't about to let this opportunity pass by, especially after letting Maurice slip away at the hospital several weeks ago. When their target entered the parking garage, Ty began to sprint lightly. Ty's target pulled out his keys, indicating that his vehicle was nearby. Ty eased his pistol out as he approached him.

"Ay, Bo!" Ty called out, figuring he had the upper hand in the matter.

"Damn where you pop up from, and how come you never got back at me?" Bo replied with a smile as Ty walked up on him.

"Get back at you! Nigga you set me up!" Barked Ty, pointing his gun at Bo's stomach.

"Set you up? I don't know what you talkin' 'bout," Bo said, confused.

"Now you wanna play stupid, huh," hissed Ty just as Ode was pulling up with the car. "Get ya absent minded azz in, and let's see if we can help refresh ya memory."

After Ty forced him into the vehicle he immediately searched Bo, stumbling across a weapon on his hip, "You let a nigga get close up on you and you strapped?" Asked Ty.

"Just think about it, you really think I would've let you walk up on me if I knew dat I done somethin' to you," he reasoned. The more Ty thought about it, the more he was convinced that Bo had a point, "I promise dat I had nothin' to do wit' whatever it was dat happened to you. All I know is dat every time I tried callin' you I never got an answer. I just figured y'all reneged on da move," Bo proclaimed.

"So you sayin' dat you had nothin' to do wit' me gettin' shot?" Questioned Ty.

"Shot," he blurted shockingly, "I swear dat's new news to me! I definitely didn't have no part in dat. It was all Maurice, dat nigga even turned my right hand man against me, some how convinced him to try and kill me. Da same nigga I'd known since diapers, and da same one I had in da car wit' me da same day I met up wit' you."

Even though Ty hated to admit it, he was actually believing his story, "you think he had someone followin' you?" Ty asked.

"It's possible! I wouldn't put it past 'em," Bo stated. "You know what?"

"What's dat?" Asked Ty.

"I do remember seeing a curly head, red dude staring at me oddly one day when my partner and I were shopping, but he quickly stepped off after I spotted him."

"You said a curly head, red dude?" Asked Ty.

"Yeah," assured Bo.

"Da dude dat shot me was a curly head, red nigga. He must've been followin' you da whole time."

"He had too," Bo agreed.

"So what happened wit' ya so called partner?"

"Let's just say dat my actions were justified. I'm still here to talk about it, he's not," he said seriously.

After a few moments of thought, Ty believed that Bo was being truthful, and tucked his gun away.

"So wassup wit' Maurice, have you seen'em?"

"I'm glad you asked. I crossed paths wit' em bout three weeks ago, and been on his line ever since," Bo confirmed.

"So you know where to find'em?"

"Not exactly, but I do know where he been goin' da past two Wednesdays," he replied with a devilish grin.

"Today is Wednesday," said Ty.

"My point exactly," he smiled.

Ty matched Bo's mischievous glare, as he quickly caught on to his point. "Ode, change of plans, our lil' host is goin' to take us to Maurice," Ty announced. "I hope you ain't bullshittin' fo' your sake."

"In my position, I wouldn't dare," assured Bo.

"Good! Go 'head and tell 'em where to go, while I figure out what to do when we get there," Ty ordered. Bo unhesitantly began directing Ode, while explaining how he crossed paths with Maurice in the first place.

Chapter 94

Three weeks before...

Even though his actions were justifiable, Bo still felt resentment for having to take the life of the one person that he considered to be like a brother. So he stood there at Reno's grave stone, wondering why he had put him in a compromising situation. Bo had no choice but to defend himself. As Bo opened his eyes, he just so happened to look over to his right and spotted Maurice getting out of a vehicle with a female acquaintance by his side, casually walking up to a pair of burials. Not wanting to be seen, Bo quickly hopped into his car, and watched momentarily before deciding to pull off.

To Bo's surprise, when he revisited the next week, Maurice was already there, alone. Bo thought about trying to tail Maurice, and see where he led him, but Bo wasn't alone. He had a female passenger, who he wouldn't dare break the law around. Instead of hanging around, knowing that Maurice was only a few yards away he quickly made up an excuse to come back some other time. Before leaving though, he glanced at his watch, making a mental note of the time and day of the week.

He made a promise to himself to come back the following Wednesday around the same time. Bo made it his business to arrive early, so that he wouldn't miss Maurice in case he did show up. Sure enough, Maurice showed up the next week. Once he witnessed Maurice pulling into the cemetery, Bo left sure that Maurice's visit was a part of his weekly schedule.

***

Bo had secretly began concocting a plan to get back at Maurice for pressuring Reno to turn on him. So when Bo got snatched up and questioned about Maurice's whereabouts, he was more than pleased to assist Ty and Ode in locating Maurice.

Chapter 95

While Maurice drove to his weekly appointment at the cemetery the fog that been clouding his brain, all of a sudden cleared. When he'd talked to Kita the day before she got killed, she explained to him about the purse she had seen China with the day after the robbery. When he questioned China about the purse, she admitted that she'd received it from a friend. If that was the case, then that led him to believe that friend was Scrap. If the facts were true, then it was a strong possibility that Scrap was somehow connected to Ode and Ty.

"Who you payin' respect to?" Asked Scrap, bringing Maurice back to reality.

"Two close associates of mine, they were killed not too long ago," replied Maurice.

"Sorry to hear dat," Scrap sympathized.

"Yeah, me too, Blac and Reggie were two loyal soldiers," Maurice countered.

Scrap tensed up a bit after hearing the two familiar names. All sorts of hasty thoughts shot through his mind, as Maurice parked. As soon as he got out, Scrap quickly pulled out his cellphone and sent a text to Ode, asking him how Maurice actually looked. A brief description came through followed by Ode telling him not to worry about Maurice anymore and that him and Ty were already on his line as they spoke. The description that Ode gave was identical to the person he'd become close to, but if Ode and Ty were trailing Maurice like Ode said, then danger was lurking. Scrap glanced around, quickly scanning the area, but didn't see anything out of the ordinary. All he noticed was a small portion of people at various grave sights and a couple of landscapers digging holes near a burial plot a few yards away. When Maurice walked back towards the car, Scrap sent a text to Ode, asking him their current location.

Scrap wanted to ask Maurice when his two men got killed, and more importantly, did he know anyone from the Riggs Park area. The only problem was he couldn't do it without causing suspicion from Maurice.

There was an awkward silence when Maurice got back in, each had something they needed to ask and neither knew how to start the conversation. Maurice took the initiative and began to speak first but Scrap had a startling look on his face as he read Ode's text message, telling him they were at the cemetery.

"You alright?" Asked Maurice, noticing Scrap's change of demeanor. Before Scrap could respond he looked up and saw the two landscapers running towards them with automatic weapons.

"It's a hit! Get down!" Shouted Scrap, grabbing Maurice's shoulder, and pulling him down. Scrap tried to take cover behind the darkness of the tinted window but it was no use. The guns delivered a horrible assault, destroying the car.

Chapter 96

Two days later, Block was in the day room reading the Washington Post when he stumbled across an article in the Metro section that immediately caught his attention. The more he read, the more his body tensed from anger. Once he finished, he jumped up, then stormed over to grab the phone dangling from the wall. The first number he dialed was Ode who answered, and accepted his call right away.

"Wassup big boy?" Answered Ode.

"Shid you tell me, cause you don't sound like nothin' wrong, but from what I'm reading in today's Metro, ain't nothin' right!" He hissed.

"What are you talkin' 'bout, I'm lost," Ode countered.

"Where you at now?" Asked Block.

"Me and Ty standing on the avenue in front of Food Barn."

"Well one of y'all run in there and grab the newspaper."

"I'm doin' it now," he assured Block, quickly purchasing a paper, then flipping straight to the Metro section.

Ode searched for the article, as someone was confronting Block about the phone.

"You see it?" Asked Block, ignoring the inmate that was standing before him, grilling him in a threatening manner about using the phone.

"Naw I don't see noth..." he started to say, just when his eyes landed on an article. "Hold up fo' a sec," Ode stated, reading the article that was headlined as, "Graveyard Decimation."

He instantly knew what the article was about. The excitement from feeling as if their feud had finally come to an end, quickly turned into confusion after viewing the names of the victims that were inside the vehicle. He called out to Ty, who quickly trotted over after hearing the severity in his partner's voice.

"Wassup?" Questioned Ty as he approached Ode.
"Slim you ain't goin to believe this!" Ode exclaimed, passing the newspaper to Ty so he could read the article that had him feeling as if the world was coming to an end.

To Be Continued...

A READING GROUP GUIDE
CONCRETE JUNGLE
By DARRELL, BRACEY, JR.

ABOUT THIS GUIDE

The suggested questions are intended to enhance your group's reading of this book.

DISCUSSION QUESTIONS

1. Do you think Ty overreacted by shooting Maurice in his foot over a dice game?

2. Do you fault Ode for Lil' Kent's death?

3. Do you blame Tyshelle for disconnecting herself from Ode after the incident with her little brother?

4. If you were Maurice would you have accepted Big Lyn's partnership even after y'all's strained past?

5. Was Big Lyn wrong for sending his family member to infiltrate Maurice's circle?

6. Did Big Lyn outsmart Maurice or did he play himself?

7. How do you feel about the way Scrap reacted when he saw his lady friend in Big Lyn's spot being abused?

8. What should Scrap do with the money that he took from Big Lyn's spot?

9. Should Worl have told Ra-Ra about her bestie being hospitalized?

10. How do you feel about Scrap Lying to Big Lyn about being at the spot where his nephew and two associates were killed?

About The Author

Hailing from Washington, D.C., Darrell "DB" Bracey, Jr. is an up-and-coming author who aspires to become a household name in the Urban Book Industry. Witnessing firsthand the writing success of his fellow comrade and author Jason Poole, who authored *Larceny*, *Victoria's Secret* and *Prince of the City*, inspired Bracey to pursue a writing career of his own.

From there, he swiftly realized his creative writing skills, and started documenting his experiences by detailing the ensnaring claws of street life using artistical expression as a conduit. A life plagued with hardships and shortcomings further encouraged Bracey to seek out his God-gifted talent. In doing so, he was ambitious and wise enough to utilize his negative situation as a stepping stone to fortify his future as an author and publisher.

During the stages of his adolescent years, he kept in mind a gem that he picked up along the way, 'whether useful or detrimental, if you give a person with a creative mind enough time to think, the end result could be beyond expectations."

That saying, along with a strong will to provide a legacy for his family to build on, moved him in the direction of authoring his debut urban, street tale, *Concrete Jungle*.

For more information, interviews or correspondence with the author Darrell Bracey, Jr., you can contact him via email at: BoutDatLyfe70 @gmail.com

Bloc Extension Publishing   Bout Dat Lyfe Publishing

-Presents-

Coming Soon…

Eyes of Betrayal: Divided Loyalties   by Byron R. Dorsey

A Gain For A Lost   by Darrell Bracey, Jr.

Concrete Jungle 2   by Darrell Bracey, Jr.

BLOC EXTENSION PUBLISHING, LLC
"Your Urban Literary Haven"

MAIL ORDER FORM

Book Title	Qty.	List Price	Total
1. Concrete Jungle		$14.95	$ _____
By Darrell Bacey, Jr.	_____		S/H $ _____

Total $ _____

Shipping/Handling (Via U.S. Media Mail) For U.S. Orders: Include $3.50 S/H for the first book and $1.75 S/H for each additional book. For International Orders: Include $9.00 S/H for the first book and $5.00 S/H for each additional book.

Discount Offer: Buy two books and get 50% discount off the third book. S/H charges apply.

Offers and Prices are subject to change without notice.

Forms of Accepted Payment:
We accept all major credit cards, institutional checks, money orders, and personal checks.
Make all checks and money orders payable to Bloc Extension Publishing, LLC.

 To order online with a debit or credit card, log onto:
www.blocextension.com
You can Fax this order form with payment to: 301.313.0272
Please allow 5-7 buisness days for delivery.

Credit Card Payment: ___Visa_____ Mastercard__ AMEX_ Discover

Card Number:_____ Name on Card:_____ Exp. Date:_

Send this form with payment to: Bloc Extension Publishing, LLC
                    Attn: Order Processing
                    P.O. BOX 457
                    Riverdale, MD 20738

Name:_____
Inmate Reg. Number:_____ (If incarcerated)
Institution:_____ (If incarcerated)
Address:_____ Apt. #_____ (If applicable)
City:_____ State:_____ Zip Code:_____
Email Address:_____ (Required to receive order
confirmation/status)

To check the status of your order, please email: info@blocextension.com

We Help You Self-Publish Your Book

You're The Publisher And We're Your Legs.

We Offer Editing For An Extra Fee, and Highly Suggest It, If Waved, We Print What You Submit!

Crystell Publications is not your publisher, but we will help you self-publish your own novel.

Don't have all your money? …. No Problem!
Ask About our Payment Plans
Crystal Perkins-Stell, MHR
Essence Magazine Bestseller
We Give You Books!
PO BOX 8044 / Edmond – OK 73083
www.crystalstell.com
(405) 414-3991
    Don't have all your money up-front…. No Problem!

Ask About our Awesome Pay What You Can Plans

Plan 1-A 190 - 250 pgs $719.00　　　　**Plan 1-B 150 -180 pgs $674.00**
Plan 1-C 70 - 145pgs $625.00

2 (Publisher/Printer) Proofs, Correspondence, 3 books, Manuscript Scan and Conversion, Typeset, Masters, Custom Cover, ISBN, Promo in Mink, 2 issues of Mink Magazine, Consultation, POD uploads. 1 Week of E-blast to a reading population of over 5000 readers, book clubs, and bookstores, The Authors Guide to Understanding The POD, and writing Tips, and a review snippet along with a professional query letter will be sent to our top 4 distributors in an attempt to have your book shelved in their bookstores or distributed to potential book vendors. After the query is sent, if interested in your book, distributors will contact you or your outside rep to discuss shipment of books, and fees.

Plan 2-A 190 - 250 pgs $645.00　　　　**Plan 2-B 150 -180 pgs $600.00**
Plan 2-C 70 - 145pgs $550.00

1 Printer Proof, Correspondence, 3 books, Manuscript Scan and Conversion, Typeset, Masters, Custom Cover, ISBN, Promo in Mink, 1 issue of Mink Magazine, Consultation, POD upload.

We're Changing The Game.
No more paying Vanity Presses $8 to $10 per book!

Made in the USA
Monee, IL
03 August 2021